ROGUE

For Maxine, being married to Blake Williams had been an amazing adventure. Charismatic Blake made millions and grabbed headlines. His only shortcoming was as a husband—first his work, and then his never-ending quest for fun.

For five years now, Blake and Maxine had worked out an amicable divorce. Then, everything changed...For Maxine, when she fell in love with Dr. Charles West, a man who was everything Blake was not. For Blake, when he saw orphaned children in need of shelter after an earthquake.

Now, Blake wants Maxine in his life again—as a partner in a humanitarian project that could change countless lives. For Maxine, the choice is clear. But Blake's sudden transformation raises questions she's never managed to answer...and some she's afraid to ask. After all, Maxine is on the cusp of a new life and almost certain that Blake Williams, a.k.a. the Rogue, is a man capable of doing anything—except change...Or is he?

ROGUE

Danielle Steel

**WINDSOR
PARAGON**

First published 2008
by Bantam
This Large Print edition published 2008
by BBC Audiobooks Ltd
by arrangement with Transworld Publishers Ltd
A Random House Group Company

Hardcover ISBN: 978 1 408 41369 2
Softcover   ISBN: 978 1 408 41370 8

British Library Cataloguing in Publication Data available

Printed and bound in Great Britain by
Antony Rowe, Chippenham, Wiltshire

To my infinitely precious children,
Beatie, Trevor, Todd, Nick, Sam,
Victoria, Vanessa, Maxx, and Zara,
who provide the love and laughter in my life,
keep me honest, give me hope, and
inspire me to do the very best I can.
All nine of you are my heroes!
I love you so much!
Mom/D.S.

rogue: a mischievous person,
a scamp,
a rascal,
an impish or playful young person.
—*Webster's New Collegiate Dictionary*

CHAPTER 1

The small single-engine Cessna Caravan pitched and rolled alarmingly over the swamps west of Miami. The plane was just high enough for the landscape to have a postcard quality to it, but the wind rushing in through the open hatch distracted the young woman clutching the safety strap so that all she could see was the vast expanse of sky beneath them. The man standing behind her was telling her to jump.

'What if my parachute doesn't open?' she said, glancing over her shoulder at him with a look of terror. She was a tall, beautiful blonde with a gorgeous body and exquisite face. Her eyes were huge with fear.

'Trust me, Belinda, it will open,' Blake Williams promised her with a look of total confidence. Skydiving had been one of his many passions for years. And it was always a joy for him to share the wonders of it with someone else.

Belinda had agreed to it the week before, over drinks in a very prestigious private nightclub in South Beach. The following day, Blake had paid for eight hours of instruction for her and a test jump with the instructors. Belinda was ready for him now. It was only their third date, and Blake had made skydiving sound so enticing that after her second cosmopolitan, she had laughingly said yes to the invitation to skydive with him. She didn't realize what she was getting into, and she still looked nervous now, and wondered how she had let him talk her into it. The first time she'd

1

jumped, with the two instructors he'd arranged, had scared her to death, but it was exciting too. And jumping with Blake would be the ultimate experience. She could hardly wait. He was so charming, so handsome, so outrageous, and so much fun that even though she barely knew him, she was ready to follow him and try almost anything in his company, even stepping out of a plane. But now she was terrified again, as he turned her face toward him and kissed her. The sheer thrill of being in his presence made the jump easier for her. Just as she had been taught in her lesson, she stepped out of the plane.

Blake followed her within seconds. She squeezed her eyes shut and screamed as they free-fell for a minute, and then she opened her eyes and saw him as he gestured to her to pull the ripcord on her parachute, just as the instructors had taught her to do. Suddenly they were drifting slowly to earth as he smiled at her and gave her a proud thumbs-up. She couldn't believe she'd done it twice in one week, but he was that kind of charismatic person. Blake could make people do almost anything.

Belinda was twenty-two years old, a supermodel in Paris, London, and New York. She had met Blake while visiting friends in Miami. He had flown in from his house in St. Bart's to meet up with a pal of his own, and had arrived in his new 737. He had chartered the smaller plane and a pilot for their jump.

Blake Williams appeared to be an expert at everything he did. He was an Olympic Class skier and had been since college, had learned to fly his own jet, with a copilot in attendance, given its size and complexity. And he had been skydiving for years. He had an extraordinary knowledge of art, and one of the most famous collections of contemporary and pre-Columbian art in the world. He was knowledgeable in wines, architecture, sailing, and women. He loved the finest things in life, and enjoyed sharing them with the women he went out with. He had an MBA from Harvard, an undergraduate degree from Princeton; he was forty-six years old, had retired at thirty-five, and his entire life was devoted to self-indulgence and pleasure, and sharing them with those around him. He was generous beyond belief, as Belinda's friends had told her. He was the kind of man every woman wanted to be with—rich, smart, good looking, and devoted to having fun. And in spite of his enormous success before he retired, he didn't have a mean bone in his body. He was the catch of the century, and although most of his relationships in the last five years had been brief and superficial, they never ended badly. Even when their fleeting affairs with him were over, women loved him. And as they floated slowly down to a well-chosen strip of unpopulated beach, Belinda looked at him with eyes filled with admiration. She couldn't believe she had jumped out of a plane with him, but it had been the most exciting thing she'd ever done. She didn't think she'd do it again, but as they held hands in midair with the blue sky all around them, she knew she would remember Blake and this moment for the rest of her life.

'It's fun, isn't it?' he shouted, and she nodded. She was still too overwhelmed to speak. Her jump with Blake had been much more exciting than the one with the two instructors days before. And she

3

couldn't wait to tell everyone she knew what she'd done, especially with whom.

Blake Williams was everything people said he was. He had enough charm to run a country, and the money with which to do it. Despite her initial terror, Belinda was actually smiling when her feet touched the ground a few minutes later, and two waiting instructors unhooked her parachute, just as Blake landed a few feet behind her. As soon as they were free of their parachutes, he had her in his arms and kissed her again. His kisses were as intoxicating as everything else about him.

'You were fantastic!' he said, sweeping her off the ground, as she grinned and laughed in his arms. He was the most exciting man she'd ever met.

'No, *you* are! I never thought I'd do something like that, it was the craziest thing ever.' She'd only known him for a week.

Her friends had already told her not to plan on having a serious relationship with him. Blake Williams went out with beautiful women all over the world. Commitment was not for him, although it had been once upon a time. He had three kids, an ex-wife he said he was crazy about, a plane, a boat, half a dozen fabulous houses. He just wanted to have a good time, and made no pretense of wanting to settle down, since his divorce. For the time being anyway, all he wanted to do was play. His early killing in the high-tech dot-com world had been legendary, as had been the success of the companies he'd invested in since. Blake Williams had everything he wanted, all his dreams had already come true. And as they walked away from the beach where they'd landed, toward a waiting

4

Jeep, Blake put an arm around Belinda, drew her closer to him, and gave her a long, searing kiss. It was a day and a moment that Belinda knew would be engraved in her mind forever. How many women could boast that they had jumped out of a plane with Blake Williams? Possibly more than she knew, although not every woman he went out with was as brave as Belinda.

*   *   *

The rain pelted against the windows of Maxine Williams's office on East 79th Street in New York. It was the highest recorded rainfall in New York in November for more than fifty years, and cold, windy, and bleak outside, but cozy in the office where Maxine spent ten or twelve hours a day. The walls were painted a pale buttery yellow, and she had quiet abstract paintings on the walls in muted tones. The room was cheerful and pleasant, and the big overstuffed easy chairs where she sat talking to her patients were comfortable and inviting, and upholstered in a neutral beige. The desk was modern, stark, and functional, and so impeccably organized it looked as though you could perform surgery on it. Everything about Maxine's office was tidy and meticulous, and she herself was perfectly groomed without a hair out of place. Maxine had her entire world in full control. And her equally efficient, reliable secretary, Felicia, had worked for her for almost nine years. Maxine hated mess, disorder of any kind, and change. Everything about her, and her life, was smooth, orderly, and seamless.

The diploma framed on her wall said that she

5

had gone to Harvard Medical School and graduated magna cum laude. She was a psychiatrist, and one of the foremost experts in trauma in both children and adolescents. She had extensive experience with schizophrenic and bipolar adolescents, and one of her subspecialties was suicidal teenagers. She worked with them and their families, often with excellent results. She had written two highly respected books for laymen, about the effect of trauma on young children. She was frequently invited to other cities and countries to consult after natural disasters, or man-made tragedies. She had been part of the consulting team for the children in Columbine after the school shooting, had written several papers on the effects of 9/11, and had advised the New York public schools. At forty-two, she was an expert in her field, and appropriately admired and acknowledged by her peers. She turned down more speaking engagements than she accepted. Between her patients, the consulting she did with local, national, and international agencies, and her own family, her days and calendar were filled.

She was always incredibly diligent about spending time with her own children—Daphne was thirteen, Jack twelve, and Sam had just turned six. As a single mother, she faced the same dilemma as every working mother, trying to balance her family responsibilities and her work. And she got almost no help from her ex, who usually appeared like a rainbow, unannounced and breathtaking, only to disappear again. All the responsibilities relating to her children fell to her, and her alone.

She sat staring out the window, thinking about them, waiting for her next patient to arrive, when

6

the intercom buzzed on her desk. Maxine expected Felicia to tell her that her patient, a fifteen-year-old boy, was coming through the door. Instead she said that Maxine's husband was on the phone. Maxine frowned at the word.

'My *ex*-husband,' she reminded her. Maxine and the kids had been on their own for five years, and as far as she was concerned, they were doing fine.

'Sorry, he always says he's your husband . . . I forget . . .' He was so likable and charming, and always asked about her boyfriend and her dog. He was one of those people you couldn't help but like.

'Don't worry, he forgets too,' Maxine commented drily, and smiled as she picked up the phone. She wondered where he was now. You never knew with Blake. It had been four months since he'd seen the kids. He had taken them to visit friends in Greece in July, and he always loaned Maxine and the children his boat every summer. The children loved their father, but they also knew that they could count on their mom, and that their dad came and went like the wind. Maxine was well aware that they seemed to have an unlimited capacity for forgiving him his quirks. And so had she, for ten years. But eventually his total self-indulgence and lack of responsibility had worn thin despite his charm. 'Hi, Blake,' she said into the phone, and relaxed in her chair. The professional distance and demeanor she kept always vanished when she talked to him. In spite of the divorce, they were good friends, and had stayed very close. 'Where are you now?'

'Washington, D.C. I just came up from Miami today. I was in St. Bart's for a couple of weeks.' A vision of their house there came instantly into her head. She hadn't seen it in five years. It was one of the many properties she had willingly relinquished to him in the divorce.

'Are you coming to New York to see the kids?' She didn't want to tell him that he should. He knew it as well as she did, but he always seemed to have something else to do. Most of the time anyway. Much as he loved them, and always had, they got short shrift, and they knew it too. And yet they all loved him, and in her own way, she did too. There seemed to be no one on the planet who didn't love him, or at least like him. Blake had no enemies, only friends.

'I wish I could come to see them,' he said apologetically. 'I'm leaving for London tonight. I've got a meeting with an architect there tomorrow. I'm redoing the house.' And then he added, sounding like a mischievous child himself, 'I just bought a fantastic place in Marrakech. I'm flying there next week. It's an absolutely gorgeous, crumbling palace.'

'Just what you need,' she said, shaking her head. He was impossible. He bought houses everywhere he went. He remodeled them with famous architects and designers, turned them into showplaces, and then bought something else. Blake loved the project even more than the end result.

He had a house in London, one in St. Bart's, another in Aspen, the top half of a palazzo in Venice, a penthouse in New York, and now apparently a house in Marrakech. Maxine couldn't help wondering what he was going to do with that. But whatever he did, she knew it would be as amazing as everything else he touched. He had

8

incredible taste, and bold ideas about design. All his homes were exquisite, and he owned one of the largest sailboats in the world, although he only used it a few weeks a year, and lent it to friends whenever he could. The rest of the time he was flying around the world, on safari in Africa, or making art forays in Asia. He'd been to Antarctica twice and came back with stunning photographs of icebergs and penguins. His world had long since outgrown hers. She was content with her predictable, well-regulated life in New York, between her office and the comfortable apartment where she lived with their three children, on Park Avenue and East 84th Street. She walked home from her office every night, even on a day like this. The short walk revived her after the hard things she listened to all day, and the troubled kids she treated. Other psychiatrists often referred their potential suicides to her. Dealing with difficult cases was her way of giving to the world, and she loved her work.

'So Max, how's by you? How are the kids?' Blake asked, sounding relaxed.

'They're fine. Jack's playing soccer again this year, he's gotten pretty good,' she said with pride. It was like telling Blake about someone else's children. He was more like their favorite uncle than their father. The trouble was, he had been that way as a husband too. Irresistible in every way, and never there when there was something hard to do.

First, Blake was building his business, and after his windfall, he was just never around. He was always somewhere else having fun. He had wanted her to give up her practice, and Maxine just couldn't. She had worked too hard to get where she was. She couldn't imagine walking away from it, and didn't want to, no matter how rich her husband suddenly was. She couldn't even conceive of the kind of money he'd made. And eventually, although she loved him, she couldn't do it anymore. They were polar opposites in every way. Her meticulousness was in sharp contrast to the mess he made. Wherever he sat, there was an avalanche of magazines, books, papers, half-eaten food, spilled drinks, peanut shells, banana peels, half-drunk sodas, and bags of fast food he forgot to throw away. He was always dragging the blueprints for his latest house, his pockets were full of notes about phone calls he had to return and never did. And eventually, the notes got lost. People were always calling wondering where he was. He was brilliant in business, but otherwise his life was a mess. He was an adorable, charming, lovable flake. She got tired of being the only grown-up around, particularly once they had kids. As the result of a movie premiere he flew out to attend in L.A., he had missed Sam's birth. And when a babysitter let Sam roll off the changing table eight months later, and he broke a collarbone and an arm, and got a hell of a knock on the head, Blake was nowhere to be found. Without telling anyone, he had flown to Cabo San Lucas to look at a house for sale, built by a famous Mexican architect he admired. He had lost his cell phone on the way, and it took two days to locate him. In the end, Sam was okay, but Maxine had asked Blake for a divorce when he got back to New York.

It had just never worked once Blake made his money. Max needed a man who was more human scale, and who was going to stick around, for some of the time at least. Blake was never there. Maxine had decided she might as well be alone, rather than bitching at him all the time when he called, and spending hours trying to track him down when something went wrong for her or the kids. When she told him she wanted a divorce, he had been stunned. And they had both cried. He tried to talk her out of it, but she had made up her mind. They loved each other, but Maxine insisted that it didn't work for her. Not anymore. They no longer wanted the same things. All he wanted to do was play, and she loved being there for her children, and her work. They were just too different in too many ways. It was fun when they were young, but she grew up, he didn't.

'I'll go to one of Jack's games when I get back,' Blake promised, as Maxine watched the torrential rain beat against the windows of her office. And when would that be? she thought to herself, but she didn't say the words. He answered her unspoken question. He knew her well, better than anyone else on the planet. That had been the hardest part of giving him up. They were so comfortable together, and loved each other so much. In many ways, they still did. Blake was her family, and always would be, and the father of her kids. That was sacred to her. 'I'm coming in for Thanksgiving, in a couple of weeks,' he said, and Maxine sighed.

'Should I tell the children or wait?' She didn't want to disappoint them yet again. He changed plans at the drop of a hat and left them in the lurch, just as he had done to her. He was distracted easily. It was the one thing she hated about him, particularly when it impacted their children. He didn't have to see the look in their eyes when she said Daddy wasn't coming after all.

Sam didn't remember their living together, but he loved his father anyway. He had been one year old when they divorced. He was used to life as it was, relying on his mom for everything. Jack and Daffy knew their father better, although even their memories of the old days had grown dim.

'You can tell them I'll be there, Max. I won't miss it,' he promised in a gentle voice. 'What about you? Are you okay? Has Prince Charming showed up yet?' She smiled at the question he always asked. There were a lot of women in his life, none of them serious, and most of them very young. And there were no men in her life at all.

She didn't have the interest or the time.

'I haven't had a date in a year,' she said honestly. She was always honest with him. He was like a brother to her now. She had no secrets from Blake. And he had no secrets from anyone, since most of what he did wound up in the press. He was always in the gossip columns with models, actresses, rock stars, heiresses, and whoever else was at hand. He'd gone out with a famous princess for a short time, which only confirmed what Max had thought for years. He was way, way out of her league, and living on another planet from the world in which she lived. She was earth. He was fire.

'That's not going to get you anywhere,' he scolded her. 'You work too hard. You always did.'

'I love what I do,' she said simply. That wasn't news to him. She always had. He could hardly get her to take a day off in their early days, and she wasn't much better now, although she spent her weekends with the children and had a call group cover for her. That was an improvement at least. They went to the house in Southampton that she and Blake had had when they were married. He had given it to her in the divorce. It was beautiful, but much too plebeian for him now. And it suited Maxine and the children to perfection. It was a big rambling old family house, right near the beach.

'Can I have the kids for Thanksgiving dinner?' he asked her cautiously. He was always respectful of her plans, he never just showed up and disappeared with the kids. He knew how much effort she put into creating a solid life for them. And Maxine liked to plan ahead.

'That'll work. I'm taking them to my parents' for lunch.' Maxine's father was a physician too, an orthopedic surgeon, and as precise and meticulous as she was. She came by it honestly, and he was a wonderful example to her, and was very proud of her work. Maxine was an only child, and her mother had never worked. Her childhood had been very different from Blake's. His life had been a series of lucky breaks from the first.

Blake had been adopted at birth by an older couple. His biological mother, he had learned later after some research, had been a fifteen-year-old girl from Iowa. She was married to a policeman when he went to meet her, and had had four other children. She had been more than a little startled when she met Blake. They had nothing in common, and he felt sorry for her. She had led a hard life, with no money, and a husband who drank. She told him his biological father had been a handsome, charming, wild young man, who was

seventeen when Blake was born. She said his
father died in a car crash two months after
graduation, but he hadn't intended to marry her
anyway. Blake's very Catholic grandparents had
forced his mother to put the baby up for adoption
after she waited out her pregnancy in another
town. His adoptive parents had been solid and
kind. His father was a Wall Street tax lawyer in
New York who had taught Blake the principles of
sound investment. He made sure Blake went to
Princeton and later Harvard for his MBA. His
mother had done volunteer work, and taught him
the importance of 'giving back' to the world. He
had learned both lessons well, and his foundation
supported many charities. Blake wrote the checks,
although he didn't know the names of most of
them.

Both his parents had been solidly behind him
but had died when he was first married to Maxine.
Blake was sorry they had never known his children.
They had been wonderful people, and had been
loving, devoted parents. They hadn't lived to see
his meteoric rise to success either. He sometimes
wondered how they would have reacted to the way
he was living his life now, and occasionally, late at
night, he worried that they might not approve. He
was well aware of how fortunate he had been, how
he indulged himself, but he enjoyed himself so
much with everything he did, it would have been
difficult to roll the film backward now. He had
established a way of life that gave him immense
pleasure and enjoyment, and he wasn't doing
anyone any harm. He wanted to see more of his
children, but somehow there never seemed to be
enough time. And he made up for it when he saw

14

them. In his own way, he was their dream dad come to life. They got to do everything they wanted, and he was able to indulge their every whim and spoil them as no one else could. Maxine was the solidity and order they relied on, and he was the magic and the fun. In some ways, he had been that to Maxine too, when they were young. Everything changed when they grew up. Or rather, she did, and he didn't.

He asked Max then how her parents were. He had always been fond of her father. He was a hardworking, serious man with good values and solid morals, even if he lacked imagination. In some ways, he was a sterner, even more serious version of Maxine. And despite their very different styles and philosophies about life, he and Blake had gotten along. Her father had always teasingly called Blake a 'rogue.' Blake loved it when he called him that. To him it sounded sexy and exciting. Max's father was disappointed in recent years that Blake didn't see more of the children, although he was well aware that his daughter more than made up for it wherever Blake fell short. And he was sorry she was shouldering everything alone.

'I'll see you Thanksgiving night then,' Blake said as he ended the call. 'I'll call you that morning and let you know what time I'll be in. I'll get a caterer to come in and do dinner. You're welcome to join us,' he said generously, and hoped she would. He still enjoyed her company. Nothing had changed, he thought she was a fantastic woman. He just wished she'd relax and have more fun. He thought she had taken the Puritan work ethic to an extreme.

Her intercom buzzer rang as she was saying

goodbye to Blake. Her four o'clock patient, the fifteen-year-old boy, had arrived. She hung up, and opened the door to her office, as her patient wandered in. He sat down in one of the two big easy chairs before he looked at her directly and said hello.

'Hi, Ted,' she said comfortably. 'How's it going?' He shrugged, as she closed the door and their session began. He had tried to hang himself twice. She had hospitalized him for three months, and he was doing better after two weeks at home. He had begun showing signs of being bipolar when he was thirteen. She was seeing him three times a week, and once a week he went to a group for previously suicidal teens. He was doing well, and Maxine had a good relationship with him. Her patients liked her a lot. She had a great way with them. And she cared about them deeply. She was a good doctor and good person.

The session lasted fifty minutes, after which she had a ten-minute break, managed to return two phone calls, and started her last session of the day with a sixteen-year-old anorexic girl. As usual, it was a long, hard, interesting day, that required a lot of concentration. Afterward, she managed to return the rest of her calls, and by six-thirty she was walking home in the rain, thinking about Blake. She was glad that he'd be coming for Thanksgiving, and she knew their children would be thrilled. She wondered if that meant he wouldn't be coming to see them for Christmas. If anything, he'd probably want them to meet him in Aspen. He usually ended the year there. With all his interesting options and houses, it was hard to know where he'd be at any given time. And now, with Morocco added to the list, it would be even harder to track or pin him down. She didn't hold it against him, it was just the way he was, even if it was frustrating for her at times. There was no malice in him, but no sense of responsibility either. In many ways, Blake refused to grow up. It made him delightful to be with, as long as you never expected too much. Once in a while he'd surprise them, and do something really thoughtful and wonderful, and then he'd fly off again. She wondered if things would have been different, if he hadn't made the fortune he did at thirty-two. It had changed his life and theirs forever. She almost wished he hadn't made all that money on his dot-com windfall. Their life had been sweet at times before that. But with the money, everything had changed.

Maxine met Blake while she was doing her residency at Stanford Hospital. He had been working in Silicon Valley, in the world of high-tech investments. He had been making plans for his fledgling company then, she'd never fully understood it, but was fascinated by his incredible energy and passion for the ideas he was developing. They had met at a party she didn't want to go to, but a friend had dragged her along. She'd been working in the trauma unit for two days straight and was half asleep the night they met. Blake had woken her up with a bang. The next day he had taken her for a helicopter ride, and they had flown over the bay, and under the Golden Gate Bridge. Being with him had been thrilling, and their relationship had taken off like a forest fire in a strong wind after that. They were married in less than a year. She was twenty-seven when they

17

got married, and it had been a whirlwind year. Ten months after their wedding, Blake sold his company for a fortune. The rest was history. He turned the money into even more, seemingly without effort. He was willing to risk it all and was truly a genius at what he did. Maxine had been dazzled by his foresight, skill, and brilliant mind.

By the time Daphne was born, two years after their wedding, Blake had made an unheard-of amount of money, and wanted Max to give up her career. Instead, she became chief resident in adolescent psychiatry, gave birth to Daphne, and found herself married to one of the richest men in the world. It was a lot to adjust to and digest. And as a result of either denial or overconfidence in the ability of nursing her baby to keep her from getting pregnant, she got pregnant with Jack six weeks after Daphne was born. By the time the second baby came, Blake had bought the house in London and the one in Aspen, had ordered the boat, and they moved back to New York. He retired soon after that. And even after Jack was born, Maxine didn't give up her career. Her maternity leave was shorter than one of Blake's trips, and he was all over the map by then. They hired a live-in nanny, and Maxine went back to work.

It was a handicap working while Blake wasn't, but the life he was leading frightened her. It was too freewheeling, opulent, and jet set for her. While Maxine opened her own practice, and signed up for an important research project on childhood trauma, Blake hired the most important decorator in London to do their house, and a different one to do Aspen, and bought the house in St. Bart's as a Christmas gift for her, and a plane

18

for himself. For Maxine, it was happening much too fast, and after that, it never slowed down. They had houses, babies, and an unbelievable fortune, and Blake was on the covers of both *Newsweek* and *Time*. He went on making investments, which continued to double and triple his money, but he never went back to work in any formal sense. Whatever he did, he managed to accomplish on the computer and phone. And eventually, their marriage seemed to be happening on the phone as well. Blake was as loving as ever when they were together, but most of the time, he just wasn't around.

At one point, Maxine even thought about giving up work, and talked to her father about it. But in the end, her conclusion was that there wasn't much point. What would she do then? Fly around with him from one house to another, hotels in other cities where they didn't have houses, or on the fabulous vacations he took, on safari in Africa, climbing mountains in the Himalayas, financing archaeological digs, or racing boats? There was nothing Blake couldn't accomplish, and even less that he was afraid to attempt. He had to do, try, taste, and have it all. She couldn't imagine dragging two toddlers along to most of the places he went, so much of the time she stayed home with the kids in New York, and she could never quite bring herself to let go and give up her work. Every suicidal kid she saw, every traumatized child, convinced her that there was a need for what she did. She had won two prestigious awards for her research projects, and at times she felt almost schizophrenic, trying to meet up with her husband on his jet-set life in Venice, Sardinia, or St. Moritz, going to the nursery school to pick up their children in New York, or working on psychiatric research projects, and giving lectures. She was leading three lives all at once. Eventually, Blake stopped begging her to come with him, and resigned himself to traveling alone. He was no longer able to sit still, the world was at his feet, and never big enough for him. He became an absentee husband and father almost overnight, while Maxine tried to make a contribution to bettering the lives of suicidal and traumatized adolescents and young children, and their own. Her life and Blake's couldn't have been further apart. No matter how much they loved each other, eventually the only bridge they had left between them was their kids.

For the next five years, they led separate lives, meeting briefly all over the world, when and where it suited Blake, and then she got pregnant with Sam. He was an accident that happened when they met for a weekend in Hong Kong, right after Blake had been trekking with friends in Nepal. Maxine had just won a new research grant on anorexia in young girls. She discovered she was pregnant, and unlike the other pregnancies, this time she wasn't thrilled. It was one more thing for her to juggle, one more child for her to parent by herself, one more piece of the puzzle that was already too complicated and too big. But Blake was overjoyed. He said he wanted half a dozen kids, which made no sense to Maxine. He hardly saw the ones they had. Jack was six and Daphne seven when Sam was born. Having missed the birth, Blake flew in the day after, with a box from Harry Winston in his hand. He gave Maxine a thirty-carat emerald ring, which was spectacular, but not what she wanted from him. She would much rather have had time together. She missed their early days in California, when they were both working and happy, before he won the dot-com lottery that radically changed their lives.

And when Sam rolled off the changing table eight months later, broke his arm, and hit his head, she couldn't even find his father for two days. When she finally caught up with him, after Cabo, he was on his way to Venice, looking at palazzos, trying to buy one as a surprise. By then, she was tired of surprises, houses, decorators, and more homes than they could ever visit. Blake always had new people to meet, new places to go to, new businesses he wanted to acquire or invest in, new houses he had to build or have, new adventures to embark on. Their lives had become completely disconnected by then, so much so that when Blake flew back after she told him about Sam's accident, she burst into tears when she saw him and said she wanted a divorce. It was all too much. She had sobbed in his arms and said she just couldn't do it anymore.

'Why don't you quit?' he had suggested calmly. 'You work too hard. Just concentrate on me and the kids. Why don't we get more help, and you can fly around with me.' He hadn't taken her request for a divorce seriously at first. They loved each other. Why would they want a divorce?

'If I did that,' she said miserably, burrowed into his chest, 'I'd never see my kids, just like you don't anymore. When was the last time you were home for more than two weeks?' He thought about it and looked blank. She had a point, although he was

21

embarrassed to admit it.

'Gosh, Max, I don't know. I never think about it like that.'

'I know you don't.' She cried harder and blew her nose. 'I don't even know where you are anymore. I couldn't find you for days when Sam got hurt. What if he died? Or I did? You wouldn't even know.'

'I'm sorry, baby, I'll try to stay in better touch. I just figure you have everything in control.' He was happy to leave her in charge while he played.

'I do. But I'm tired of doing it alone. Instead of telling me to quit, why don't you stop traveling so much and stay home?' She had little hope of it, but she tried.

'We have so many great houses, and there's so much I want to do.' He had just provided the backing for a London play, written by a young playwright he had been sponsoring for two years. He loved being a patron of the arts, far more than he liked staying home. He loved his wife and adored his children, but he was bored just hanging around New York. Maxine had made it through eight years of the changes in their circumstances, but she couldn't do it anymore. She wanted stability, sameness, and the kind of settled life that Blake now abhorred. He loved pushing the outer limits of the envelope until there was no envelope at all. He defined the term 'free spirit' in ways Maxine could never have predicted. And since he was never around anyway, out of touch most of the time, she figured she might as well do it alone. It had gotten harder and harder to kid herself that she had a husband, and that she could count on him at all. She had finally realized that she couldn't. Blake loved her, but ninety-five percent of the time he was gone. He had his own life, interests, and pursuits, which hardly included her at all anymore.

So with tears and regrets, but the utmost civility, she and Blake had divorced five years before. He gave her the apartment in New York and the house in Southampton, would have given her more houses if she'd wanted, but she didn't, and he had offered her a settlement that would have stunned anyone. He felt guilty about what an absentee husband and father he had been in recent years, but he had to confess that it suited him very well. He hated to admit it but he felt as though he were in a straitjacket in a matchbox, confined to the life Maxine lived in New York.

She refused the settlement, and took only child support for their children. Maxine made more than enough in her practice to support herself, she wanted nothing from him. And as far as she was concerned, it was Blake's windfall, not hers. None of his friends could believe that in her position she had been so fair. They didn't have a prenuptial agreement to protect his assets, since he'd had none when they met. She didn't want to take anything from him, she loved him, wanted the best for him, and wished him well. All of that had combined to make him love her even more in the end, and they had remained close friends. Maxine always said he was like her wild wayward brother, and after her initial shock over the girls he went out with, most of them half his age, or hers, she had gotten philosophical about it. Her only concern was that they be nice to her kids.

Maxine herself had had no serious relationships

23

since him. Most of the physicians and psychiatrists she met were married, and her social life was limited to her kids. For the past five years, she had had her hands full with her family and her work. Occasionally she dated men she met, but she hadn't had sparks with anyone since Blake. He was a tough act to follow. He was irresponsible, unreliable, disorganized, an inadequate father despite all his good intentions, and a lousy husband in the end, but there wasn't a man on the planet, in her opinion, who was kinder, more decent, more good-hearted, or more fun. She often wished that she had the courage to be as wild and free as he. But she needed structure, a firm foundation, an orderly life, and she didn't have the same inclination as Blake, or the guts, to follow her wildest dreams. Sometimes she envied him that.

There was nothing in business or life that was too high-risk for Blake, which was why he had been such a huge success. You had to have balls for that, and Blake Williams had them in spades. Maxine felt like a mouse compared to him. Although she was a remarkably accomplished woman herself, she was far more human scale. It was just too bad their marriage hadn't worked out. And Maxine was infinitely glad they had their kids. They were the joy and hub of her life, and all she needed for now. At forty-two, she wasn't desperate to find another man. She had rewarding work, patients she cared about deeply, and terrific kids. It was enough for now, more than enough sometimes.

The doorman tipped his hat as Maxine walked into the building on Park Avenue, five blocks from her office. It was an old building with large rooms, built before World War II, and had a dignified air.

She was soaking wet from the rain. The wind had whipped her umbrella inside out and torn it ten steps out of her office, and she had thrown it away. Her raincoat was soaked through, and her long blond hair, pulled back in a neat ponytail when she worked, was plastered to her head. She hadn't worn makeup that day so her face looked fresh and young and clean. She was tall and thin, appeared younger than her age, and Blake had often pointed out that she had spectacular legs, although she rarely showed them off with short skirts. She usually wore slacks to work and jeans on the weekends. She wasn't the kind of woman who took advantage of sex to sell herself. She was discreet and demure, and Blake had often teasingly said she reminded him of Lois Lane. He would take off her reading glasses that she wore for the computer, and loosen her luxuriant long wheat-colored hair, and she looked instantly sexy in spite of herself. Maxine was a beautiful woman, and she and Blake had had three very handsome kids. Blake's hair was as dark as hers was fair, and his eyes the same color blue as hers, and although she was tall, at six feet four he stood a full head taller than she. They had been a striking pair. Daphne and Jack both had Blake's almost jet-black hair and their parents' bright blue eyes, Sam's hair was blond like his mother's, and he had his grandfather's green eyes. He was a beautiful child, and still young enough to be cuddly with his mom.

Maxine rode up in the elevator, dripping pools of water at her feet. She let herself into the apartment, one of only two apartments on the floor. The other tenants had retired and moved to Florida years before, and were never there, so

Maxine and the children didn't have to worry too much about noise, which was a good thing, with three children under one roof, and two of them boys.

She could hear loud music playing as she took her coat off in the front hall and draped it over the umbrella stand. She took her shoes off there too, her feet were soaked, and she laughed when she saw her reflection in the mirror. She looked like a drowned rat, with pink cheeks from the cold.

'What did you do? Swim home?' Zelda, their nanny, inquired as she saw her in the hall. She had a stack of clean laundry in her arms. She had been with them since Jack was born and was a godsend for them all. 'Why didn't you take a cab?'

'I needed the air,' Maxine said, smiling at her. Zelda was plump and round faced, wore her hair in a thick braid, and was the same age as Maxine. She had never married, and had been a nanny since she was eighteen. Maxine followed her into the kitchen, where Sam was working on a drawing at the kitchen table, already in clean pajamas after a bath. Zelda quickly handed her employer a cup of tea. It was always comforting coming home to her, and knowing that everything was in control. Like Max, she was obsessively neat, and spent her life cleaning up after the kids, cooking for them, and chauffeuring them everywhere when their mother was at work. Maxine took over on the weekends. Officially, Zelda was off then, and she loved going to the theater whenever she could, but she usually stayed in her room behind the kitchen relaxing and reading. Her full loyalty was to the children and their mother. She had been their nanny for twelve years and was part of the family. She didn't think much of Blake, whom she considered handsome and spoiled, and a lousy father to the kids. She had always felt they deserved better than they got from him, and Maxine couldn't tell her she was wrong. She loved him. Zelda didn't.

The kitchen was decorated in bleached woods, with beige granite counters and a light hardwood floor. It was a cozy room they all congregated in, and there was a couch and a TV, where Zelda watched her soaps and talk shows. She quoted from them liberally, whenever the opportunity arose.

'Hi, Mom,' Sam said, hard at work with a purple crayon, looking up as his mother walked in.

'Hi, sweetheart. How was your day?' She kissed the top of his head and ruffled his hair.

'Good. Stevie threw up in school,' he said matter-of-factly, switching the purple crayon for green. He was drawing a house, a cowboy, and a rainbow. Maxine didn't read anything into it, he was a normal, happy kid. He missed his father less than the others, since he had never lived with him. His two older siblings were slightly more aware of their loss.

'That's too bad,' Maxine commented on the unfortunate Stevie. She hoped it was something he ate, not a new flu going around school. 'You feel okay?'

'Yup.' Sam nodded, as Zelda looked into the oven and checked on dinner, and Daphne walked into the room. At thirteen, her body was developing new curves, and she had just started eighth grade. All three of them went to Dalton, and Maxine loved the school.

'Can I borrow your black sweater?' Daphne

27

asked, helping herself to a slice of an apple Sam had been eating.

'Which one?' Maxine eyed her with caution.

'The one with the white fur on it? Emma's giving a party tonight,' Daphne said nonchalantly, trying to look like she didn't care, but it was obvious to her mother that she did. It was Friday, and lately there were parties almost every weekend.

'That's a pretty jazzy sweater for a party at Emma's. What kind of party? Boys?'

'Mmm . . . yeah . . . maybe . . .' Daphne said, and Maxine smiled. 'Maybe,' my eye, she thought. She knew perfectly well that Daphne would know all the details. And in Maxine's new Valentino sweater, she was trying to impress someone, for sure an eighth-grade boy.

'Don't you think that sweater's too old for you? What about something else?' She hadn't even worn it yet herself. She was making suggestions, when Jack walked in, still wearing cleats. Zelda screamed the minute she saw them and pointed to his feet.

'Get those things off my floor! Take them off *right now*!' she ordered, as he sat down on the floor, and took them off with a grin. Zelda kept them all in good order, there was no worry about that.

'You didn't play today, did you?' Maxine inquired, as she stooped to kiss her son. He was either playing sports or glued to his computer. He was the family computer expert, and always helped Maxine and his sister with theirs. No problem daunted him, and he could solve them all with ease.

'They canceled because of the rain.'

'I figured they would.' Since she had all of them present, she told them about Blake's Thanksgiving plans. 'He wants you all for dinner Thanksgiving night. I think he'll be here for the weekend. You can stay there if you want,' she said casually. Blake had done fabulous rooms for them in his fiftieth-floor penthouse, full of terrific contemporary art, and state-of-the-art video and stereo equipment. They had an incredible view of the city from their rooms, a theater where they could watch movies, and a game room with a pool table and every electronic game made. They loved staying with him.

'Are you coming too?' Sam asked, looking up at her from his drawing. He liked it better when she was there. In many ways, his father was a stranger to him, and he was happier with his mother near at hand. He seldom spent the night, although Jack and Daphne did.

'I might come for dinner, if you want me to. We're going to Grandma and Grampa's for lunch, so I'll be turkeyed out. You'll have a good time with your dad.'

'Is he bringing a friend?' Sam asked, and Maxine realized she had no idea. Blake often had women with him when he saw the kids. They were always young, and sometimes the children had fun with them, although most of the time, she knew, they found his carousel of women an intrusion, particularly Daphne, who liked being the primary female in her father's life. She thought he was really cool. And she was finding her mother a lot less so these days, which was appropriate for her age. Maxine saw teenage girls who hated their

29

mothers all the time. It passed with time, and she wasn't worried about it yet.

'I don't know if he's bringing someone or not,' Maxine said, as Zelda made a snorting sound of disapproval from the stove.

'The last one was a real dud,' Daphne commented, and then left the kitchen to check out her mother's closet. Their bedrooms were all in close proximity to one another down a long hall, and Maxine liked it that way. She was happy being near them, and Sam often slipped into her bed at night, claiming he had bad dreams. Most of the time, he just enjoyed cuddling up to her, whatever the excuse.

Aside from that, they had a proper living room, a dining room just big enough for them, and a small den where Maxine often worked, writing articles or preparing lectures, or research papers. Their apartment was nothing compared to the opulent luxury of Blake's, which was like a space ship perched on top of the world. Maxine's apartment was cozy and warm, and felt like a real home.

When she went to her bedroom to dry her hair, she found Daphne energetically going through her closet. She had emerged with a white cashmere sweater and a pair of towering high heels, black leather Manolo Blahniks, with pointed toes and stiletto heels, which her mother seldom wore. Maxine was tall enough as it was, and she had only been able to wear heels that high when she was married to Blake.

'Those are too high for you,' Maxine cautioned her. 'I nearly killed myself the last time I wore them. What about some others?'

'Mommmmm . . .' Daphne groaned, 'I'll be fine in these.' To Maxine, they looked too sophisticated for a thirteen-year-old, but Daphne looked more like fifteen or sixteen, so she could get away with it. She was a beautiful girl, with her mother's features and creamy skin, and her father's jet-black hair.

'Must be quite a night at Emma's tonight.' Maxine grinned. 'Hot boys, huh?' Daphne rolled her eyes and walked out of the room, which was further confirmation of what her mother had said. Maxine was a little nervous about what life would be like once boys entered the scene. So far the kids had been easy, but she knew better than anyone that that couldn't last forever. And if it got tough, she'd have to handle it alone. She always had.

Maxine took a hot shower and put on a terrycloth robe. Half an hour later she and her children were at the kitchen table, while Zelda served them a dinner of roast chicken, baked potatoes, and salad. She cooked good, solid wholesome meals, and they all agreed she made the best brownies, snickerdoodles, and pancakes in the world. Maxine often thought sadly that Zelda would have made a great mom, but there was no man in her life, and hadn't been in years. At forty-two, more than likely, that chance had passed her by. She had Maxine's kids to love instead.

At dinner, Jack announced that he was going to a movie with a friend. There was a new horror movie he wanted to see, which promised to be particularly gory. He needed his mother to drop him off and pick him up. Sam was going to a friend's for a sleepover the next day, and planned to watch a DVD that night, in her room, with popcorn, in her bed. Maxine was going to take

Daphne to Emma's house on the way to Jack's movie. The following day she had errands to run, and the weekend would take shape, as it always did, haphazardly, according to the kids' plans and needs.

She was thumbing through *People* magazine later that night, while waiting for a call from Daphne to pick her up, and came across a picture of Blake at a party the Rolling Stones had given in London. He had a well-known rock star on his arm, a staggeringly beautiful girl who practically had no clothes on, as Blake stood next to her and beamed. Maxine stared at his photograph for a minute, trying to decide if it bothered her, and confirmed to herself that it didn't, as Sam snored softly next to her, his head on her pillow, the empty popcorn bowl beside him, and his love-worn teddy bear in his arms.

As she looked at the photograph in the magazine, she tried to remember what it had been like being married to him. There had been the wonderful days in the beginning, and the lonely, angry, frustrating days in the end. None of it mattered anymore. She decided that seeing him with starlets and models and rock stars and princesses didn't bother her at all. He was a face from her distant past, and in the end, no matter how lovable he was, her father had been right. He wasn't a husband, he was a rogue. And kissing Sam softly on his silky cheek, she thought again that she liked her life just the way it was.

CHAPTER 2

During the night, the heavy rain turned to snow.
The temperature dropped considerably, and
everything was blanketed white when they woke
up. It was the first real snow of the year. Sam took
one look at it and clapped his hands in delight.

'Can we go to the park, Mom? We can take out
the disks.' The snow was still falling, and the scene
outside looked like a Christmas card, but Maxine
knew that by the next day it would be a mess.

'Sure, sweetheart.' As she thought about it, she
realized, as she always did, that Blake was missing
the best part. He had traded all of this for jet-set
parties and people all over the world. But in
Maxine's eyes, the best of life was right here.

Daphne came in for breakfast with her cell
phone glued to her ear. She left the table several
times, whispering to a friend, as Jack rolled his
eyes and helped himself to the French toast
Maxine had made. It was one of the few things she
could cook well, and often did. He poured on a
huge amount of maple syrup and commented on
how dumb Daphne and her friends were these days
about boys.

'What about you?' his mother inquired with
interest. 'No girlfriends yet?' He went to a dancing
class, and a coed school, and had plenty of
opportunities to meet girls, but he had no interest
in them yet. His primary interest so far was in
sports. He liked soccer best of all, surfing the
Internet, and video games.

'Yerghk' was his response, as he devoured

another piece of French toast. Sam was lying on the couch, watching cartoons on TV. He had eaten breakfast an hour before when he got up. Everyone came and went at leisure on Saturday mornings, and Maxine cooked for them as they came in. She loved the domestic side of life that she didn't have time for during the week, when she was in a hurry to see patients at the hospital before she went to her office. She was usually out of the house well before eight o'clock, when the kids left for school. But with rare exceptions, she managed to have dinner with them every night.

She reminded Sam then that he had a sleepover at a friend's that night, and Jack chimed in that he did too. Daphne said three of her friends were coming over to watch a movie, and a couple of boys might drop by too.

'Now there's a new chapter,' Maxine commented with a look of interest. 'Anyone I know?' Daphne just shook her head with a look of irritation and walked out of the room. Clearly, to her, the question didn't deserve an answer.

Maxine rinsed the dishes and put them in the dishwasher, and an hour later, she and all three of her children were headed to the park. At the last minute, the two older ones had decided to come along too. She had plastic disks for two of them, and she and Daphne wrapped garbage bags around their bottoms, and slid down the hills with the boys, and other children, with squeals of glee. It was still snowing, and her children were still young enough to act like little kids once in a while, instead of grown up, as they wanted to be. They stayed out till three o'clock and then walked home through the park. It had been fun, and she made

34

them hot chocolate with whipped cream and s'mores when they got home. It was nice to think they weren't so old after all, and still enjoyed the same childhood pastimes they always had.

She dropped Sam off for his sleepover at five o'clock, on East 89th Street, Jack in the Village at six o'clock, and was back at the apartment in time for Daphne's friends to show up with a stack of rented movies. In the end, two additional girls had turned up. She ordered pizza for them at eight o'clock, and Sam called at nine 'to see how she was,' which she knew from experience meant he might not spend the night at his friend's. Sometimes he couldn't pull it off, and came home to sleep with her or in his own bed. She told him she was fine, and he said he was too. She was smiling when she hung up, and could hear squeals of laughter coming from Daphne's room. Something told her they were talking about boys, and she wasn't wrong.

Two extremely uncomfortable-looking thirteen-year-old boys dropped by at ten o'clock. They were shorter than the girls by several inches, showed no signs of puberty, and devoured what was left of the pizza. And only minutes later, with mumbled excuses, they left. They had never made it as far as Daphne's room from the kitchen, and said they had to get home. They had been outnumbered by the girls three to one, but would have left early anyway. The scene was too much for them. The girls looked far more mature, and rushed back to Daphne's room to discuss it as soon as the boys had left. Maxine was smiling to herself, listening to them squeal and giggle, when the phone rang at eleven. She figured it was Sam wanting to come

35

home, and she was still smiling when she answered, expecting to hear her youngest son's voice.

Instead, it was a nurse at Lenox Hill Hospital's emergency room, calling about one of her patients. Maxine frowned and instantly sat up in rapt attention, asking pertinent questions. Jason Wexler was sixteen, his father had died suddenly of a heart attack six months earlier, and his older sister had died in a car accident ten years before. He had taken a handful of his mother's sleeping pills. He suffered from depression, and had tried it before, though not since right after his father's death. He and his father had had a terrible argument the night he died, and Jason was convinced his father's heart attack and death were his fault.

The nurse said his mother was hysterical in the waiting room, Jason was conscious, and they were already pumping his stomach. They thought he was going to be okay, but it was close. His mother had found him and called 911, he had taken a lot of sleeping pills, and if she'd found him any later, he would have been dead. Maxine listened carefully. The hospital was only eight blocks away, and she could walk it at a good clip, in spite of the six inches of snow on the ground that had turned to slush late in the afternoon, and then frozen solid in brown icy patches by nightfall. It was treacherous when that happened.

'I'll be there in ten minutes,' she told the nurse efficiently. 'Thank you for calling.' Maxine had given Jason's mother her home number and cell phone months before. Even when the call group covered for her most weekends, she wanted to be there herself for Jason and his mother if they ever needed her. She had been hoping they never would, and wasn't pleased to learn of his second suicide attempt. And she knew that his mother would be desperately upset. After losing her husband and her daughter, Jason was all she had left.

Maxine knocked on Zelda's door and saw that she was asleep. She wanted to let her know that she was going out to see a patient, and to listen for the girls, just in case. But she hated to wake her, so she closed the door softly without making a sound. It was her day off, after all. And then Maxine walked into Daphne's room as she pulled a heavy sweater over her head. She was already wearing jeans.

'I have to go out to see a patient,' she explained. Daphne knew, as they all did, that her mother went out to see special patients, even on the weekends, and she looked up and nodded. They were still watching DVDs and had gotten quieter as the night wore on. 'Zelda's here, so if you need something, you can get her, but don't make too much noise in the kitchen, please, she's asleep.' Daphne nodded again, her eyes riveted to the screen. Two of her friends had fallen asleep on her bed, and one was doing her nails. The others were avidly watching the film. 'I'll be back in a while.' Daphne knew it was probably an attempted suicide. Her mother never said much about it, but that was the reason she usually went out late at night. Her other patients could wait till the next day.

Maxine put on boots with rubber soles and a ski parka, picked up her purse, and hurried out the door. She was on the street minutes later, walking against a bitter-cold wind, moving south at a good clip down Park Avenue, toward Lenox Hill Hospital. Her face was stinging and raw and her eyes watering by the time she got there, and walked into the emergency room. She checked in at the desk, and they told her what cubicle Jason was in. They had decided he didn't need to go to the ICU. He was groggy but out of danger, and they were waiting for her to admit him for the night, and decide the rest. Helen Wexler pounced on her the minute she walked into the room, clung to her, and began to sob.

'He almost died . . .' she said, hysterical in Maxine's arms, as Maxine led her gently from the room, with a glance at the nurse. Jason was dozing in the bed and hadn't stirred. He was still heavily sedated from the residue of what he'd taken, but he no longer had enough on board to risk his life. Just enough to help him sleep for a long time. His mother kept repeating that he had almost died. Maxine led her a fair distance down the hall, just in case her son woke up.

'But he didn't, Helen. He's going to be all right,' Maxine said calmly. 'You were lucky you found him, and he's going to be fine.' Until the next time. That was Maxine's job to deal with, so that there wouldn't be a third time. Although once suicide was attempted, by any patient, the statistical risk of their trying again was infinitely higher, and the chance of success likelier each time. Maxine wasn't happy that he had tried it a second time.

Maxine got Jason's mother to sit in a chair, and take some deep breaths. And finally, she managed to speak calmly about it. Maxine said she thought Jason should be hospitalized for longer this time. She suggested a month, after which they could see

38

how he was doing, and she recommended a facility she worked with frequently on Long Island. She assured Helen Wexler that they were very good with adolescents. Helen looked horrified.

'A *month*? That means he won't be home for Thanksgiving. You can't do that,' she said, crying again. 'I can't put him away over the holidays. His father just died, this will be our first Thanksgiving wit-out him,' she insisted, as though that made a difference now, with her son at risk for a third suicide attempt. It was amazing what denial did to the mind, and what one clung to, in order not to face the realities of the situation. If Jason succeeded at a third attempt, he would never have another Thanksgiving. It was well worth sacrificing this one. But his mother didn't want to hear that, and Maxine was trying to be firm but compassionate and gentle, she always was.

'I think that right now he needs the protection and the support. I don't want to bring him home too soon, and the holidays are going to be hard for him without his dad too. I seriously think he'll do better at Silver Pines. You can have Thanksgiving with him there.' Helen just cried harder.

Maxine was anxious to see her patient. She told Helen they would talk about it later, but they both agreed that he should spend the night at Lenox Hill. There was no other choice, he was in no shape to go home. Helen was in full agreement with that, just not the rest. She hated the idea of Silver Pines. She said it sounded like a cemetery to her.

Maxine checked Jason quietly while he was sleeping, read the chart, and was alarmed to see how much of the drug he'd taken. He had taken far more than a lethal dose, unlike last time when he had barely taken enough to kill himself. This time had been a far more serious attempt, and she wondered what had brought it on. She was going to spend time with Jason the next morning when he woke up. There was no hope of talking to him now.

She made some notes on Jason's chart of what she wanted. They were going to move him to a private room later that night, and her orders included a nurse with him, on suicide watch. There had to be someone there to observe him even before he woke up. She told the nurse she'd be back the next morning at nine o'clock, and if they needed her sooner, they should call. She left them her home and cell phone numbers, and then sat down again with Jason's mother outside. Helen seemed even more devastated than before, as reality began to hit her. She could easily have lost her son that night, and been alone in the world. The very thought of it nearly drove her over the edge. Maxine offered to call her physician, in case she wanted sleeping pills, or some mild sedation, which Maxine didn't want to prescribe herself. Helen wasn't her patient and Maxine didn't know her history or what other medications she might be on.

Helen said she had already called her doctor. He was supposed to call her back, but he was out. She said Jason had used all her sleeping pills, so she had no more at home. She started crying harder again as she said it, and she clearly didn't want to go home alone.

'I can ask them to put a cot in Jason's room for you if you like,' Maxine said gently, 'unless that would be too upsetting for you.' If so, she'd have to go home.

'I'd like that,' Helen said softly, her eyes wide as she looked at Maxine. 'Is he going to die?' she whispered then, terrified of knowing but trying to brace herself for the worst.

'This time? No,' Maxine said, shaking her head solemnly, 'but we have to be as sure as we can be that there won't be a next time. This is serious business. He took a lot of pills. That's why I want him to stay at Silver Pines for a while.'

Maxine didn't want to tell the boy's mother now that she wanted him there for a lot longer than a month. She was thinking more like two or three months, and maybe an interim support facility after that, if she thought he needed it. Fortunately, they could afford it, but that wasn't the issue. She could see in Helen's eyes that she wanted Jason to come home, and she was going to fight Maxine on a longer hospital stay. It was a very foolish position for her to take, but Maxine had dealt with that before. If Jason was sent to a psychiatric hospital, they'd have to face that this wasn't just a 'little mishap,' he was truly sick. Maxine had no doubt in her mind that he was suicidal and severely clinically depressed. He had been ever since his father's death. It was more than his mother wanted to face, but at this point she had no choice. If she took him home with her the next day, it would be against doctor's orders, and she would have to sign a release. Maxine hoped it wouldn't come to that. Hopefully, she'd calm down by the next day, and do the safest possible thing for her son. Maxine didn't like admitting him either, but she had no doubt about how important it was for him. His life was at stake.

Maxine asked the nurses to set up a cot for Helen in her son's room, once they moved him out of the ER. She left her with a warm touch on her shoulder, and checked Jason again before she left. He was doing fine. For now. There was a nurse with him, who would go to his room with him. He would not be left alone again. There was no locked ward at Lenox Hill, but Maxine thought he would be fine with a nurse close at hand, and his mother there too. And it would be many hours before he woke up.

She walked back to the apartment in the icy cold. It was after one A.M. when she got home. She glanced into Daphne's room, and everything seemed peaceful there. All the girls had fallen asleep, two in sleeping bags, the rest on Daphne's bed. The movie was droning on, and they were still dressed, and then as she looked at them, she noticed an odd smell. It wasn't a smell she had ever noticed in Daphne's room before. She had no idea why, but she walked to her closet and opened the door, and was startled to see two empty six-packs of beer. She looked at the girls again, and realized they weren't just asleep, they were drunk. They seemed a little young to her to be sneaking beer, but in fact it wasn't unknown at that age. She wasn't sure whether to cry or to laugh. She didn't know when it had started, but they had taken full advantage of her going to the hospital. She hated to do it, but she would have to ground Daphne the next day. She lined up the empty bottles on her dresser, neatly, for them to see when they woke up. They had managed to consume two bottles of beer each, which was plenty for kids that age. So, she whispered to herself, adolescence has begun. She

42

lay in bed afterward, thinking about it, and for a minute she missed Blake. It would have been nice to share the moment with someone. Instead, as usual, she would have to play the heavy the next day, wearing a kabuki mask of disappointment as she read the riot act to her daughter, and talked to her about the deeper meaning of trust. When in fact, Maxine well understood she was a teenager and that there would be many, many nights in their future when someone did something stupid, her own kids or others took advantage of a situation, or experimented with alcohol or drugs. And it surely wasn't the last time that one of her children would get drunk. Maxine knew she would be lucky if it didn't get much worse than this. And she also knew that she had to take a firm stand about it the next day. She was still thinking about it when she fell asleep. And when she got up in the morning, the girls were still sleeping.

The hospital called her while she was getting dressed. Jason was awake and talking. The nurse said his mother was with him, and she was very upset. Helen Wexler had called her own physician, and according to the nurse, instead of reassuring her, he had unnerved her more. Maxine said she'd be in shortly, and hung up. She heard Zelda in the kitchen then, and went in to pour herself a cup of coffee. Zelda was sitting at the kitchen table, with a mug of steaming coffee, and the Sunday *Times*. She looked up when she saw Maxine walk in and smiled.

'Peaceful night?' Zelda asked, as Maxine sat down at the table with a sigh. Sometimes she felt as though Zelda was her only support system in bringing up the kids. Her parents never offered much advice, although they meant well. And Blake had been a no-show all their lives. Zelda was it.

'Not exactly,' Maxine said with a rueful grin. 'I think we hit some kind of milestone last night.'

'Most pizza eaten in the history of the world by six teenage girls?'

'No,' Maxine said in measured tones, with laughter in her eyes. 'First time one of my kids got drunk on beer.' She smiled, and Zelda looked at her with wide eyes.

'Are you kidding?'

'No. I found two empty six-packs in Daffy's closet when I checked. It wasn't pretty. Fully dressed bodies sprawled everywhere, when I walked in, and everyone sound asleep, or I guess 'passed out' would be the correct term.'

'Where were you when they did it?' Zelda was surprised that Daphne had had the guts to drink while her mother was in the next room. And she was faintly amused too, although neither woman was pleased. It was the beginning of a whole new scene that they weren't looking forward to. Boys, drugs, sex, and booze. Welcome to the teenage years. The worst was yet to come.

'I had to go see a patient last night. I was out from eleven to one. One of them must have brought the beer in her backpack. I've never thought about that before.'

'I guess from now on we check,' Zelda said matter-of-factly, not in the least embarrassed to challenge Daphne and her friends. She was not about to let any of them get drunk on her watch, and she knew Maxine wouldn't either. And before you knew it, Jack would be in the midst of it too, and one day Sam. What a thought. Zelda wasn't looking forward to any of it, but she had every intention of sticking around. She loved the family, and her job.

The two women chatted for a few minutes, and then Maxine said she had to go back to Lenox Hill to see her patient. Zelda was off, but she wasn't going anywhere. She said she'd keep an ear out for the girls, and hoped they felt like shit when they woke up. Maxine laughed in response.

'I left the empty bottles on her dresser, just so they know I'm not as dumb as I look.'

'They're going to freak when they see that,' Zelda said, amused.

'They should. It was a pretty sneaky thing to do, and an abuse of my trust and hospitality . . .' She looked at Zelda with a grin. 'I'm warming up for my speech to her. How do I sound?'

'Good. Grounding her and cutting off her allowance might be a nice touch too.' Maxine nodded. She and Zelda always shared pretty much the same point of view. Zelda was firm but reasonable, kind but sensible, and not too strict. She wasn't a tyrant, but she wasn't a pushover either. Maxine had full confidence in her, and her sound judgment, whenever she herself wasn't around. 'What did you go out for last night? A suicide?' Zelda asked. Maxine nodded, serious again. 'How old?' Zelda respected her enormously for what she did.

'Sixteen.' Maxine offered no other details. She never did. Zelda nodded. Worse than that, she could always see it in Maxine's eyes when one of them died. Zelda's heart went out to the parents as much as to the kid. Teenage suicide was a terrible thing. And judging how busy Maxine's practice

45

was, there was a lot of it in New York, and everywhere else. Compared to that, two six-packs of beer shared among six thirteen-year-old girls didn't seem like such a tragedy. What Maxine dealt with every day was.

Maxine left a few minutes later and walked the short distance to Lenox Hill, as she always did. It was windy and cold, but the sun was out, and it was a beautiful day. She was still thinking of her daughter and her caper the night before. It was definitely the beginning of a new era for them, and she was grateful again for Zelda's help. They were going to have to keep a close watch on Daphne and her friends. She was going to mention it to Blake when he was in town too, just so he was aware. They couldn't fully trust her anymore, and probably wouldn't be able to for years. It was a little daunting thinking about it. It was all so easy when they were the age of Sam. And how quickly time sped by. Soon they would all be teenagers, up to mischief of all kinds. But at least, for the moment anyway, it was pretty normal stuff.

When she got to Jason's room at the hospital, he was sitting up in bed. He looked groggy, worn out, and pale. His mother was sitting in a chair, talking to him, crying and blowing her nose. It didn't look like a happy scene. And the nurse on suicide watch was sitting quietly on the other side of the bed, trying not to intrude and be discreet. All three of them looked up when Maxine walked in.

'How are you feeling today, Jason?' Maxine glanced at the nurse and nodded, and the woman quietly left the room.

'Okay, I guess.' He looked and sounded depressed, a normal reaction to the overdose of

46

drugs he'd taken, and he'd obviously been depressed before that anyway. His mother looked almost as bad, as though she hadn't slept, with dark circles under her eyes. She had been extorting a promise from him not to do it again, when Maxine walked in, and Jason had reluctantly agreed.

'He says he won't do it again,' Helen explained, as Maxine looked him in the eye. What she saw there troubled her.

'I hope that's true,' Maxine said, quietly unconvinced.

'Can I go home today?' Jason asked, sounding flat. He didn't like having a nurse in the room with him, and she had explained that she couldn't leave the room, unless she was replaced by someone else. He felt like he was in jail.

'I think we need to talk about that,' Maxine said, standing at the end of the bed. She was wearing a pink sweater and jeans and looked almost like a kid herself. 'I don't think that's a good idea,' she said honestly. She never lied to her patients. It was important that she told them the truth as she saw it. They trusted her because of it. 'You took a lot of pills last night, Jason. I mean really a lot. You weren't kidding around this time.' She looked at him, he nodded, and then looked away. He was embarrassed now in the cold light of day.

'I was kind of drunk. I didn't know what I was doing,' he said, trying to brush it off.

'I think you did,' Maxine said quietly. 'You took a lot more than last time. I think you need to take some time off now and think about it, work on it, do some groups. I think it's important that we deal with this, and I'm sure it's tough now with the

47

holidays coming up, having lost your dad this year.' She had hit the nail on the head, and his mother stared at her with a look of panic. She looked as though she was about to jump out of her skin. Her own anxiety was sky high, and she was suffering the same things as her son, without the guilt. Jason being convinced he had killed his dad tipped the scale for him. Dangerously so. 'I'd like you to go someplace where I've worked with kids before. It's pretty nice. The kids there are from fourteen to eighteen. Your mom can visit you every day. But I think we need to get a handle on what's happening now. I don't feel comfortable sending you home just yet.'

'How long?' he asked, sounding noncommittal and trying to be cool, but she could see the fear in his eyes. It was a scary thought for him. But his succeeding at his next suicide attempt frightened her even more. She had a lifetime commitment not to let that happen, if she could do anything about it. And often, she could. She wanted this to be one of those times, and to avert tragedy before it happened to them again. They'd had enough.

'Let's try it for a month. Then we'll talk, and see what you think and how you feel about it. I don't think you'll love it, but I think you might like it there.' And then she added, smiling, 'It's coed.' He didn't smile in response. He was too depressed to care about girls right now.

'What if I hate it and don't want to stay?' He looked her in the eye.

'Then we'll talk.' If they had to, they could ask to have him committed by the courts, since he had just proven he was a danger to himself, but that would be traumatic for him and his mother.

48

Maxine much preferred voluntary commitment, whenever possible. Jason's mother spoke up then.

'Doctor, do you really think . . . I was talking to my doctor this morning, and he was saying that we should give Jason another chance . . . he says he was drunk and didn't know what he was doing, and he just promised me that he won't do it again.' Maxine knew better than anyone that his promise wasn't worth a damn. And Jason knew it too. His mother wanted it to be something she could rely on, but she couldn't. Without question, her son's life was at risk.

'I don't think we can count on that,' Maxine said simply. 'I'd like you to trust me on this,' she added quietly. She noticed that Jason wasn't arguing with her, his mother was. 'I think your mom is upset that you won't be at home for Thanksgiving, Jason. I told her she can have Thanksgiving with you there. Visits are encouraged.'

'Thanksgiving's going to suck this year anyway, without my dad. I don't care.' He closed his eyes and laid his head back on his pillow, shutting them out. Maxine gestured to his mother to follow her outside, and as soon as they left the room, the private duty nurse went back in to sit with him. He would be closely watched at Silver Pines too. And at Silver Pines, the wards were locked, which was what Maxine knew Jason needed. Right now anyway, and maybe for a while.

'I think this is the right thing to do,' Maxine explained to her, as tears rolled down Helen's cheeks. 'It's my strong recommendation. It's up to you, but I don't think you can protect him properly at home. You can't stop him from doing it again.'

'Do you really think he'll try?' His mother

looked terrified.

'Yes, I do,' Maxine said clearly. 'I'm almost certain of it. He's still convinced he killed his father. It's going to take time to get him past that idea. And in the meantime, he needs to be in a facility where he'll be safe. You won't get a moment's sleep if he's at home,' she added, and his mother nodded.

'My own doctor thought we could give him another chance. He said boys his age often do this for attention.' She was repeating herself, as though hoping to convince Maxine, who understood the situation far better than she.

'He meant it, Helen. He knew what he was doing. He took three times the fatal dose of your medication. Do you want to risk that again, or have him jump out the window? He could run past you and do it in a flash. You can't give him what he needs right now at home.' She wasn't pulling any punches, and slowly his mother nodded, and started crying harder. She couldn't bear the thought of losing her son.

'All right,' she said softly. 'When does he have to go?'

'I'll see if they have a bed for him today or tomorrow. I'd like to get him out of here as soon as possible. They can't protect him properly here either. This isn't a psychiatric hospital. He needs to be at a place like Silver Pines. It's not as bad as you think, and it's the right place for him right now, at least until he's no longer in crisis, maybe after the holidays.'

'You mean Christmas too?' Helen Wexler looked panicked.

'We'll see. We'll discuss that later, when we see

how he's doing. He needs some time to get his bearings.' His mother nodded and then went back into his room, while Maxine went to call Silver Pines. Five minutes later, everything was all set. Luckily, they had room for him. And Maxine arranged to have him transferred by ambulance at five o'clock that afternoon. His mother could go with him to help settle him in, but she couldn't spend the night.

Maxine explained everything to both of them, and said she would go to visit Jason there the next day. She would have to move some patients to do it, but it was a good day for that. She knew she had nothing crucial on her calendar in the afternoon, and her only two crisis cases were scheduled for the morning. He seemed peaceful about going there, and Maxine was still talking to them when a nurse came in and said there was a Dr. West on the phone for her.

'Dr. West?' Maxine looked blank. 'Is he asking me to admit a patient for him?' Physicians did that all the time, but she didn't recognize his name. And then suddenly Jason's mother looked embarrassed.

'He's my doctor. I asked him to talk to you because he thought Jason should come home. But I understand . . . I guess . . . I'm sorry . . . do you mind talking to him anyway? I don't want him to feel I asked him to call for nothing. We'll send Jason to Silver Pines, maybe you could just tell Dr. West it's all arranged.' Helen looked awkward, and Maxine told her not to worry about it. She spoke to other physicians all the time. She asked if he was a psychiatrist, and Helen said he was her internist. Maxine left the room to take the call at

51

the nurses' station. She didn't want to have the conversation within earshot of Jason. It was purely a formality now anyway. She picked up the line with a smile, expecting to talk to some friendly, naïve doctor, who wasn't used to dealing with adolescent suicides on a daily basis, as she was.

'Dr. West?' Maxine said, sounding young, efficient, and pleasant. 'I'm Dr. Williams, Jason's psychiatrist,' she explained.

'I know,' he said, sounding condescending with just those two words. 'His mother asked me to call you.'

'So I understand. We've just finished making arrangements for him to be admitted to Silver Pines this afternoon. I think it's the right placement for him right now. He took a lethal dose of his mom's sleeping pills last night.'

'It's amazing what kids will do for attention, isn't it?' Maxine listened to him in disbelief. He was not only patronizing to her, he sounded like a total jerk.

'This is his second attempt. And I don't think three times the fatal dose is a ploy for attention. He's telling us loud and clear he wants out. We need to address that in a very serious way.'

'I really think the boy would do better at home with his mother,' Dr. West said as though talking to a child, or a very, very young nurse.

'I'm his psychiatrist,' Maxine said firmly, 'and my professional opinion is that if he goes home with his mother, he'll be dead within a week, possibly twenty-four hours.' It was as blunt as she could get, and she wouldn't have said it to Jason's mother. But she wasn't going to pull any punches with the condescending, very arrogant Dr. West.

52

'That seems a little hysterical to me,' he said, sounding annoyed this time.

'His mother has agreed to admit him. I don't think we have any other choice. He needs to be in a locked ward, under careful watch. There's no way to set that up in a foolproof way at home.'

'Do you lock up all your patients, Dr. Williams?' He was downright insulting, and Maxine was starting to get mad. Who the hell did he think he was?

'Only the ones in danger of killing themselves, Dr. West, and I don't think your patient is going to be in great shape if she loses her son. What would your assessment be of that?'

'I think you need to leave the assessment of my patients to me,' he said, sounding huffy.

'Precisely. Good point. And I suggest you leave mine to me. Jason Wexler is my patient, I've been seeing him since his first suicide attempt, and I'm not liking what I see at all, or what I'm hearing from you, as a matter of fact. If you'd like to look up my credentials on the Internet, Dr. West, be my guest. Now, if you'll excuse me, I need to go back to my patient. Thanks for the call.' He was still blustering when she hung up, and she had to hide the fact that she was livid when she walked back into Jason's room. It wasn't their problem that she and Helen's physician had hated each other on the phone. He was the kind of pompous jerk who cost lives, as far as Maxine was concerned, and a real menace, dismissing the seriousness of the crisis Jason was in. He needed to be in a locked psychiatric facility just like Silver Pines. Screw Dr. West.

'Did everything go all right?' Helen looked at

her anxiously, and Maxine hoped that she couldn't see how angry she was. She covered her anger with a smile.

'It was fine.' Maxine examined Jason then, and stayed with him for another half hour, telling him what Silver Pines would be like. He pretended not to care or be scared, but Maxine knew he was. He had to be. This was a frightening time for him. First he had almost died, and now he was stuck having to face life again. As far as he was concerned, it was the worst of both worlds.

She left them, and assured Helen that she would be available all day and that night and the next day for calls. And then after signing his discharge papers, she left the hospital and walked home. She was fuming about that idiot doctor, Charles West, on her brief walk up Park Avenue. And Daphne and her friends were still asleep when she got home. It was almost noon by then.

This time, Maxine strode into her daughter's room and raised the shades. The bright morning sunlight poured into the room, and she called out loudly, telling them to rise and shine. None of them looked well as they groaned and got up. And then, as she climbed out of bed, Daphne spotted the lineup of empty beer bottles on her dresser and saw the look in her mother's eyes.

'Oh shit,' she said softly, glancing swiftly at her friends. They all looked scared.

'You might say that,' Maxine said coolly, glancing at the others, then, 'Thanks for dropping by, girls. Get dressed and get your stuff. The party's over. And as for you'—she turned to Daphne again—'you're grounded for the month. And whoever brings any kind of alcohol here again

54

won't be allowed to come back. You all violated my hospitality and my trust. I'll speak to you later,' she said to Daphne, who looked panicked. The girls began to whisper frantically as soon as Maxine left the room. They dressed hurriedly, and all they wanted to do now was leave. Daphne had tears in her eyes.

'I told you it was a dumb idea,' one of the other girls said.

'I thought you hid the bottles in the closet,' Daphne complained.

'I did.' They were all near tears. It was the first time they had done anything like it, but surely not the last. Maxine knew that better than they did.

'She must have checked.'

The girls were dressed and gone in under ten minutes, and Daphne went looking for her mother. She found her in the kitchen, talking quietly to Zelda, who looked at Daphne with stern disapproval and didn't say a word. It was up to Maxine how she chose to handle this.

'I'm sorry, Mom,' Daphne said, bursting into tears.

'So am I. I trusted you, Daff. I always have. I don't want anything to screw that up. What we have is precious.'

'I know . . . I didn't mean to . . . we just thought . . . I . . .'

'You're on a month's restriction. No phone calls for the first week. No social life for the month. You go nowhere alone. And no allowance. That's it. And don't let it happen again,' she said sternly. Daphne nodded silently and slunk back to her room. They both heard the door close softly behind her. Maxine was sure she was crying, but

55

she wanted to leave her alone for now.

'And this is only the beginning,' Zelda said glumly, and then both women laughed. It didn't seem like the end of the world to either of them, but Maxine wanted to make a big impression on her daughter so it didn't happen again anytime soon. Thirteen was too young for them to be having beer parties on the sly in her bedroom, so she had made her point.

Daphne stayed in her room for the rest of the afternoon, after turning her cell phone in to her mother. The phone was her lifeline, and giving it up was a major sacrifice.

Maxine picked up both boys by five o'clock, and when he got home, Daphne told Jack what had happened. He was startled but impressed, and told her what she already knew, that it was a really dumb thing to do, and that their mother had been bound to find out. According to Jack, their mother knew everything and had radar of some kind and X-ray vision implanted in her head. It was part of the options package that came with moms.

The four of them had a quiet dinner in the kitchen that night, and all of them went to bed early, since the next day was a school day. Maxine was sound asleep at twelve o'clock when the nurse at Silver Pines called her. Jason Wexler had made another suicide attempt that night. He was in good condition and stable. He had taken off his pajamas and tried to hang himself with them, but the nurse assigned to him had found him and revived him. Maxine realized they had moved him out of Lenox Hill in the nick of time, and thank God his mother hadn't listened to the pompous, idiotic Dr. West. She told the nurse she'd be out to see Jason the following afternoon, and she could only imagine how his mother would take the news. Maxine was grateful he was alive.

As she lay in bed afterward, she realized that it had been a busy weekend after all. Her daughter had gotten drunk on beer for the first time, and one of her patients had attempted suicide twice. All things considered, matters could have been a lot worse. Jason Wexler could have been dead. She was relieved he wasn't, although she would have liked to give Charles West a piece of her mind. He was an utter fool. Maxine was happy that Jason's mother hadn't listened to him, and had trusted her. All that mattered was that Jason was alive. She just hoped he would stay that way. With each attempt he was at greater risk. Compared to that, Daphne's little beer party on Saturday night was child's play, which was all it was anyway. She was still thinking about it when Sam padded into her room in the dark and came to stand next to her bed.

'Can I sleep with you, Mom?' he asked solemnly. 'I think there's a gorilla in my closet.'

'Sure, sweetheart.' She slid over and made room for him, as he cuddled up next to her. She was wondering if she should explain to him that there wasn't a gorilla in his closet, or just let it go.

'Mom?' he was whispering next to her, cozy beside her.

'Yeah?'

'About the gorilla . . . I made it up.'

'I know.' She smiled at him in the dark, kissed his cheek, and a moment later, they were both asleep.

CHAPTER 3

Maxine was in her office at eight o'clock the next morning. She saw patients back to back until noon, then drove to Long Island to see Jason Wexler at Silver Pines, and was there at one-thirty. The only thing she'd eaten was half a banana while driving, and she returned calls from the speakerphone in her car. She was pretty well caught up and on schedule when she got there.

She spent an hour alone with Jason, met with the attending psychiatrist about the events of the night before, and talked to Jason's mother for half an hour. They were all grateful he was at Silver Pines, and that his third suicide attempt had been foiled. Helen was quick to give Maxine credit, and say that she'd been right. She shuddered to think what would have happened if she'd insisted on taking him home. More than likely, this time, he would have succeeded. Unlike what Helen's internist had suggested, these were not bids for attention. Jason wanted out. He was profoundly convinced he had killed his father. He had had conflicting feelings about him all his life, and given that and the argument they'd had the night before, Jason remained convinced that the combination of those facts had killed him. It would take months, or even years, to show him otherwise, and assuage his guilt. Both Helen and Maxine knew now that it was going to be a long haul for Jason. And contrary to his mother's initial hopes, he would not be home in time for Christmas. Maxine was now hoping that they would keep him there for six months to a year, although it was still too soon to say that to his mother. She was badly shaken by his near success at hanging himself the night before. And he had told his mother that morning that if he wanted to kill himself, he would. Nothing could stop him. And much to her chagrin, Maxine knew from experience, he was right. What they had to do now was heal his wounded soul and spirit, and that was going to take time.

Maxine was back on the freeway at four o'clock, and in her office, after some traffic on the bridge, just after five. She had a patient scheduled at five-thirty, and was checking her stack of messages when she got a call from Helen's internist, Dr. West. She thought about not taking the call, assuming she was in for more of the same pompous crap she'd heard from him the day before, and she wasn't in the mood. Although she always remained professional about her patients, and had good boundaries, she was profoundly sad about Jason, and for his mother. He was a lovely boy, and they'd had enough heartache for a lifetime. Reluctantly, she took the call, and braced herself for the arrogance in his voice.

'Yes? Dr. Williams speaking.'

'This is Charles West.' Unlike her, he did not preface it with his title, and she thought he sounded chagrined, which wasn't what she had expected. The voice was smooth and cool, but nearly human as he went on. 'I had a call from Helen Wexler this morning, about Jason. How is he?'

Maxine remained aloof and distant. She didn't trust him. He was probably going to find fault with something she'd done, and insist she send Jason home, as insane as that sounded, but she thought him capable of it, after his comments the previous day. 'About what you'd expect. He was sedated when I saw him, but coherent. He remembers what he did, and why. I was fairly certain he'd try it again, although he promised his mother he wouldn't. He has a lot of guilt about his father.' It was about as much as she was willing to say to him, and more than enough to explain her actions. 'That's not unusual, but he needs some more constructive ways to deal with it, suicide not being one.'

'I know. I'm sorry. I called you to say that I'm really sorry I was such a jerk yesterday. Helen's very close to him, and always has been. Only son, surviving child. I don't think their marriage was great.' Maxine knew that but didn't comment. What she knew was none of his business. 'I just figured he wanted attention, you know how kids are.'

'Yes, I do,' Maxine said coldly. 'Most of them don't commit suicide to get attention. They usually have compelling reasons, and I think Jason believes he does. It's going to take a lot of work to convince him otherwise.'

'I have every faith that you can do that,' he said kindly. Much to her amazement, he sounded almost humble, which was a far cry from how he'd sounded the day before. 'I'm embarrassed to admit it, but I looked you up on the Internet. That's some list of credentials you've got behind you, doctor.' He had been enormously impressed, and embarrassed at having dismissed her as some garden-variety Park Avenue shrink who was taking advantage of the Wexlers, and blowing their problems out of proportion. He had read her CV, schools, degrees, noted her books, lectures, committees she had served on, and knew now that she had advised schools all over the country on trauma in younger children, and that the book she had written on suicide in teens was considered the definitive work written on the subject. She was a major force and authority in her field. It was he who looked like nobody compared to her, and although he had a fair amount of self-confidence, he couldn't help but be impressed by her. Anyone would be.

'Thank you, Dr. West,' Maxine said coolly. 'I knew Jason was serious about his second attempt. This is what I do.'

'To say the least. I just wanted to apologize to you today for being such a fool yesterday. I know how wound up Helen can get, and she's on the edge these days. I've been her physician for fifteen years, and I've known Jason since he was born. Her husband was a patient of mine too. I never realized that Jason was so troubled.'

'I think it precedes his father's death. His sister's death shook them all up, understandably, and he's at a tough age. Sixteen-year-old boys are very vulnerable, and there are a lot of expectations in that family, academically and otherwise. Surviving only child, all of that. It's not easy for him. And his father's death blew him right off the map.'

'I get that now. I'm really sorry.' He sounded sincerely contrite, which impressed her.

'Don't worry about it. We all misjudge things. It's not your field. I wouldn't want to be making diagnoses about meningitis or diabetes. That's why we have specialties, doctor. It was nice of you to call.' He had eaten humble pie, and he was the last person she would have guessed would do that. 'You should probably keep an eye on Helen. She's pretty shaken up. I referred her to a psychiatrist who does very good grief work, but having Jason in the hospital for the next several months, particularly over the holidays, won't be easy for her. And you know how it is with things like that, sometimes that kind of stress hits the immune system.' Helen had already commented to Maxine that she'd had three bad colds and several migraines since her husband's death. Jason's three attempted suicides and hospitalization were not likely to improve her health, and Charles West knew that too.

'I'll keep an eye on her. You're right, of course. I always worry about my patients after the death of a spouse or a child. Some of them come down like a house of cards, although Helen's pretty tough. I'll give her a call and see how she's doing.'

'I think she's in shock after last night,' Maxine said honestly.

'Who wouldn't be? I don't have kids myself, but I can't imagine anything worse, and she's already lost one, and now almost lost another, after being widowed. It doesn't get much worse than that.'

'Yes, it does,' Maxine said sadly. 'She could have lost him too. Thank God she didn't. And we're going to do everything we can to see that that doesn't happen. That's my job.'

'I don't envy you. You must deal with some pretty tough stuff.'

'I do,' she said calmly, glancing at her watch. Her next patient was due in five minutes. 'It was nice of you to call,' she said again, trying to wrap things up, and she meant it. A lot of physicians wouldn't have bothered.

'Now I'll know to whom to refer my patients with troubled kids.'

'A lot of what I do is in trauma, with younger kids. As a therapist, it's less depressing than just working with suicidal teens. I deal with long-term effects of major situational traumas, like nine-eleven.'

'I saw your interview in *The New York Times* on the Internet. It must be fascinating.'

'It was.' Her second book had been on national and public events that had traumatized large groups of children. She was involved in several studies and research projects, and had testified numerous times in front of Congress.

'If you think there's anything I need to know in terms of Helen, or about Jason, let me know. People don't always tell me what's going on. Helen is pretty good about that, but she's also very private. So if you pick up anything important, give me a call.'

'I will.' Her buzzer sounded. Her five-thirty patient was there, on the dot. A fourteen-year-old anorexic who was doing better than she had the year before, after a six-month hospitalization at Yale. 'Thanks again for your call. It was nice of you to do that,' Maxine said pleasantly. He wasn't such a bad guy after all. Calling her to acknowledge his mistake had been a decent thing to do.

'Not at all,' he said, and they hung up. Maxine got up from her desk and let a pretty young girl into her office. She was still extremely thin and looked far younger than she was. She looked ten or eleven, although she was about to turn fifteen. But

63

she had nearly died of her anorexia the year before, so things were looking up. Her hair was still thin, she had lost several teeth during her hospitalization, and there would be some question for years to come about her ability to have children. It was a serious disease.

'Hi, Josephine, come on in,' Maxine said warmly, motioning to the familiar chair, which the pretty teenager curled up in like a kitten, with huge eyes that sought out Maxine's.

Within minutes, she had confessed, of her own volition, to stealing some of her mother's laxatives that week, but after careful consideration, she hadn't used them. Maxine nodded and they talked about it after that, among other things. Josephine had also met a boy she liked, now that she was back in school, and was feeling better about herself. It was a long, slow road back from the terrifying place she had been, when she weighed barely more than sixty pounds at thirteen. She was up to eighty-five now, still light for her height, but no longer as disastrously emaciated. Their current goal was a hundred. And for the moment, she was still gaining a pound a week, and hadn't slipped.

Maxine had one more patient after that, a sixteen-year-old girl who cut herself, had scars up and down her arms, which she covered, and had attempted suicide once at fifteen. Maxine had been called in by her family physician, and they were making slow but steady progress.

Maxine called Silver Pines before leaving her office, and was told that Jason had put jeans on and joined the other residents for dinner. He hadn't said much, and had gone back to his room right afterward, but it was a beginning. He was still

64

on close suicide watch, and would be for a while, until the attending physician and Maxine felt more comfortable about him. He was still very depressed, and very much at risk, but at least he was safe at Silver Pines, which was why she had sent him there.

Maxine was in the elevator of her apartment building at seven-thirty, exhausted. As she walked into the apartment, Sam flew by her at full speed, dressed as a turkey and gobbling loudly, and she grinned. It was good to be home. It had been a long day, and she was still sad about Jason herself. She cared a lot about her patients.

'Halloween is over!' she called out to him, as he stopped, grinned, and ran back her way to throw his arms around her waist and hug her. He nearly knocked her down when he did. He was a solid little kid.

'I know. I'm the turkey in the school play,' he said proudly.

'They got that part right,' Jack commented as he sauntered by in soccer shorts and cleats, making marks and leaving clumps of dirt on the carpet, which didn't concern him in the least. He was carrying a stack of video games he had borrowed from a friend.

'Zelda's going to have a fit,' his mother warned him, glancing at the carpet, and as soon as she said it, the nanny appeared scowling at them all.

'I'm going to throw those shoes out the window, if you don't park them at the door, Jack Williams. You're going to wreck all our rugs and floors! How many times do I have to tell you?' She hmphed loudly and stomped back into the kitchen, as he sat down on the floor and took his shoes off.

65

'Sorry,' he mumbled, and then grinned up at his mother. 'We won against Collegiate today. They're wimps. Two of them cried when they lost the game.' Maxine had seen boys on Jack's team cry too. Boys took their sports seriously, and were rarely gracious winners or losers, as she knew.

'That's nice that you won. I'm coming to the game on Thursday.' She had cleared her calendar to do it. And then she turned to Sam, gazing up at her adoringly in his turkey costume. 'When's your play?'

'The day before Thanksgiving,' he said, looking delighted.

'Do you have any lines to learn?' He gobbled loudly for her in answer, as Jack covered his ears and walked away, and Zelda shouted from the kitchen, 'Dinner in five minutes!'

She walked out again to see Maxine and lowered her voice. 'We waited for you.' She tried to hold dinner on the evenings that Maxine worked late, except when it was just too much for the children. But she was good about making it possible for Maxine to share dinner with her children. Zelda knew how important that was to her. It was one of the many things Maxine appreciated about her. She was never sneaky or passive/aggressive about keeping Maxine from her kids, or screwing things up for her, as some of her friends' nannies did. Zelda was devoted to them in every way, and had been for twelve years. And she had no desire whatsoever to usurp Maxine's motherly role with the kids.

'Thanks, Zellie,' Maxine said, and then glanced around. She hadn't seen her daughter yet, just the boys. 'Where's Daff? In her room?' Sulking

66

probably, she assumed, after being put on restriction the day before.

'She took her cell phone back, and was calling on it,' Sam volunteered before Zelda could answer, and the nanny frowned at him. She was going to tell Maxine herself at the right time. She always did, and Maxine knew she could trust her.

'It's not nice to tattle on your sister,' Zelda scolded, and Maxine raised an eyebrow, and headed for Daphne's room. As Sam had suggested, she found her on her bed, happily chatting on her cell phone. Daphne jumped when she saw her mother. Maxine advanced toward her with her hand held out for the phone. Looking nervous, Daphne put the cell phone in it, after rapidly disconnecting her friend without saying goodbye.

'Do we still have an honor system around here, or do I have to lock it up?' Things were definitely changing with Daphne at a rapid rate. There was a time, not long before, when she would have respected the punishment and not snatched back her phone. Thirteen was changing everything, and Maxine didn't love it.

'Sorry, Mom.' She didn't look directly at her mother, and then Zelda was calling them to dinner, and they all headed for the kitchen, Jack in bare feet and his soccer shorts, Daphne in the clothes she'd worn to school, and Sam still proudly wearing his turkey costume. Maxine took off the jacket to her suit, and changed into flat shoes. She had worn high heels all day. She always looked professional for work, and relaxed when she got home. If she'd had time, she would have changed into jeans, but dinner had waited long enough, and she was starved, as were the kids.

It was an easy, comfortable dinner, and Zelda sat down with them, as she always did. It seemed mean to Maxine to make her eat alone, and with no father at the table, Maxine had always invited her to join them. The children talked about what they'd done that day, except for Daphne, who said little, and knew she was still in disgrace. And she was embarrassed about the incident with the phone. She had figured out that Sam had squealed on her, so she glared at him, and whispered under her breath that she would get him later. And Jack talked about his game and promised to help his mother set up a new computer program. Everyone was in good spirits, and went back to their respective rooms after dinner, including Maxine, who was beat, after a long day. Zelda stayed in the kitchen to clean up. And Maxine wandered into Daphne's room to chat.

'Hi, can I come in?' she asked her daughter from the doorway. She usually asked permission, particularly right now.

'Whatever,' Daphne answered, which Maxine knew was as good as she would get, given the restriction, and the incident with the phone.

Maxine walked into the room, and sat down on the bed where Daphne was lying watching TV. She had done her homework before her mother got home. She was a good student, and got good grades. Jack was a little more erratic, given the temptation of his video games, and Sam didn't get homework yet. 'I know you're mad at me about the restriction, Daff. But I didn't love the beer party. I want to be able to trust you and your friends, particularly if I have to go out.' Daphne didn't answer, she just looked away, and then she finally turned toward her mother with resentment in her eyes.

'It wasn't my idea. And someone else brought the beer.'

'You still let it happen. And I assume you drank some too. Our home is sacred, Daffy. So is my trust in you. I don't want anything to screw that up.' She knew without question that something would. It was to be expected at Daphne's age, and Maxine understood that, but she still had her parental role to play. She couldn't just pretend it hadn't happened, and not react. And Daphne knew that too. She was just sorry they got caught.

'Yeah, I know.'

'Your friends have to respect us when they come here. And I don't think beer parties are such a hot idea.'

'Other kids do worse,' her daughter said, sticking her chin out. And Maxine knew that. Much worse. They smoked pot, or even used hard drugs, or drank hard liquor, and these days a lot of girls had already had sex at Daphne's age. Maxine heard about it regularly in her practice. One of her patients had been giving random blow jobs since sixth grade. 'So why is it such a big deal if we had some beer?' Daphne pressed.

'Because it's against our rules. And if you start breaking some rules, where is it going to stop? We have certain agreements with each other, spoken or otherwise, and we have to respect them, or renegotiate them at some point, but not right now. But rules are rules. I don't bring guys home and have wild sex parties here. You expect me to behave a certain way, and I do. And I don't sit around my room getting drunk on beer and passing out at night. How would you feel if I did that?' Daphne smiled in spite of herself at the unlikely vision of her mother.

'You never go out with anyone anyway. Lots of my friends' moms bring boyfriends home. You just don't have one.' The words were designed to hurt, and they did, a little.

'Even if I did, I wouldn't be getting drunk in my room. When you're a little older, you can have a drink with me, or in front of me. But you're not of legal drinking age, and neither are your friends, and I don't want that going on here. And surely not at thirteen.'

'Yeah, I know.' And then she added, 'Daddy let us have wine last summer in Greece. He even gave some to Sam. And he didn't get crazy about it.'

'That's different. You were with him. He gave it to you, and you weren't drinking behind his back, although I'll admit I'm not crazy about that either. You're all too young to drink. You don't need to start that now.' But that was Blake, and his ideas were a lot different from hers, and his rules for himself and his children nonexistent. And he did bring women along, if you could call them that. Most of them were barely more than girls, and one of these days as the kids got older, the women he went out with would be the same age as his children. Maxine thought he was far too easy and freewheeling in front of them, but he never listened to what she said. She had mentioned it to him many times, and all he did was laugh, and do it again.

'When I'm older, will you let me drink here?' Daphne was checking things out.

'Maybe. If I'm around. But I won't let your

friends drink here if they're under age. I could get in a lot of trouble for that, particularly if something went wrong, or someone got hurt. It's just not a good idea.' Maxine was a person who believed in rules, and followed them to the letter. Her children knew that about her, and so did everyone else, including Blake.

Daphne didn't comment. She'd heard the speech before, when they discussed it. She knew that other parents had much looser rules, some had none at all, and some were like her mom. It was the luck of the draw. Sam appeared in the doorway then in his turkey costume, looking for his mother.

'Do I have to have a bath tonight, Mom? I was real careful. I didn't get dirty at all today.' Maxine smiled in answer, and Daphne turned up the TV, which was the signal to her mother that she'd heard enough and didn't want to hear more. Maxine bent to kiss her and left the room with her youngest son.

'I don't care how careful you were today. Yes, you have to take a bath.'

'That sucks.' Zelda was waiting with an ominous look, and Maxine left Sam to her, stopped in to see Jack, who swore he had done his homework, and went back to her own room, and turned on the TV. It was a nice, quiet, easy night at home, the kind she loved best.

She thought about what Daphne had said to her, that she never went out. It wasn't entirely true. She went to dinner parties occasionally, given by old friends, or couples from their married days. She went to the opera, theater, and ballet, though not as much as she should have, she knew. It seemed like such an effort, and she loved staying home after a long day. She went to movies with her children, and medical dinners she couldn't get out of. But she knew what Daphne meant and she was right. Maxine hadn't had a date in a year. It bothered her sometimes, particularly when she was aware of the passage of time. She was forty-two years old, after all, and hadn't had a serious man in her life since Blake. She dated once in a while, but she hadn't met anyone who set her bells and sirens off in years, and she didn't have much opportunity to meet them. She was either at work or with her kids, and most of the other physicians she met were married, or looking to cheat on their wives, which wasn't what she wanted, or would do. Eligible, appealing men in their forties and fifties were few and far between. All the good ones were married, or appeared to be, and what was left floating around were guys who had 'issues' or intimacy problems, who were gay or commitment phobic, or wanted to date women half her age. Finding a man to have a relationship with was not as easy as it looked, and she wasn't losing sleep over it. She figured that if it was meant to happen one day, it would. And in the meantime, she was fine like this.

When she and Blake first broke up, she had always assumed she'd find someone else, maybe even get married again, but now that seemed less and less likely every year. Blake was the one swinging from the chandeliers, enjoying an active dating life, with gorgeous young girls. Maxine was sitting home night after night, with her children and their nanny, and she wasn't sure she wanted it any other way. She certainly wouldn't have traded time with her children for a hot date. And in the end, what was so bad about this? For an instant, she allowed herself to think of nights in her husband's arms, dancing with him, laughing with him, walking on the beach with him, and making love. It was a little scary thinking that she might never have sex again, or even be kissed. But if that was the way things shook out for her, then she was fine like this. She had her kids. What else did she need? She always told herself that was enough.

She was still thinking about it, when Sam walked in fresh from his bath, in clean pajamas and bare feet, with damp hair smelling of shampoo, and hopped onto her bed. 'Whatcha thinking about, Mom? You look sad.' What he said startled her out of her reverie as she smiled at him.

'I'm not sad, sweetheart. I was just thinking about stuff.'

'Grown-up stuff?' he asked with interest, as he turned up the volume of the TV with the remote.

'Yeah, kind of.'

'Can I sleep with you tonight?' At least he didn't invent a gorilla this time, and she smiled at him.

'Sure. Sounds good to me.' She loved it when he slept with her. He cuddled up next to her, and it gave them both the comfort they needed. With small, yummy Sam in her bed at night, tucked in next to her, what else could she possibly want? No date or passing romance or relationship could ever be as sweet.

CHAPTER 4

On Thanksgiving morning Maxine checked on the children in each of their rooms. Daphne was lying on her bed talking to a friend on the cell phone, which had officially been returned to her. She was still on restriction and had no social life, but at least she had her phone life back. Jack was in front of his computer, wearing a blue shirt, gray slacks, and a blazer, and Maxine helped him tie his tie. And Sam was still in his pajamas, glued to the TV, watching the Macy's Thanksgiving Day parade. Zelda had left earlier to spend the day with a friend who worked for a family in Westchester, and was doing Thanksgiving lunch for a bunch of nannies she knew. They were a special breed, who gave their lives to the children they cared for and loved, and had none of their own.

Maxine got Sam's clothes out for him and reminded Daphne to get off the phone and get dressed. Her daughter walked into her bathroom with her cell phone still glued to her ear and slammed the door. And Maxine walked back into her own room to get ready. She was planning to wear a beige pantsuit with a matching cashmere turtleneck sweater and high heels. She pulled the sweater over her head, and started brushing her hair.

Ten minutes later Sam came in, with his shirt buttoned wrong, his fly open, and his hair sticking up all over the place, and she grinned.

'Do I look okay?' he asked confidently, as she brushed his hair down, and told him to zip up his fly.

'Oh,' he said with a grin, as she buttoned his shirt for him, and told him to get his tie. He made a face. 'Do I have to wear that too? It strangles me.'

'Then we won't tie it so tight. Grampa always wears a tie, and Jack is wearing one today.'

'Daddy never wears a tie,' Sam countered with a look of pain.

'Yes, he does.' Maxine held firm. Blake looked great in a suit. 'He does when he goes out.'

'Not anymore.'

'Well, you have to on Thanksgiving. And don't forget to get your loafers out.' She knew that otherwise, he would want to wear his running shoes to lunch at his grandparents'. As he went back to his own room to get his tie and shoes, Daphne appeared in the doorway in a short black miniskirt, black stockings, and high heels. She had come to her mother's room to borrow another sweater, her favorite pink one, and tiny diamonds sparkled in her pierced ears. Maxine had given them to her for her thirteenth birthday and allowed her to have her ears pierced. Now she wanted a second set of holes in her ears. 'Everyone' had two pierces at least at school. So far Maxine hadn't given in, and her daughter looked lovely with her dark hair brushed softly around her face. Maxine handed over the pink sweater, just as Sam walked in with his shoes and a mystified expression.

'I can't find my tie,' he said, looking pleased.

'Yes, you can. Go back and look again,' Maxine said firmly.

'I hate you,' he said, the expected response, as

75

Maxine got into her suit, slipped into high heels, and put pearl earrings on.

Half an hour later, they were all dressed, both boys had their ties on, with ski parkas over their blazers, and Daphne was wearing a short black coat with a little fur collar that Blake had given her for her birthday. They looked neat, respectable, and well dressed, and walked the short distance down Park Avenue to their grandparents' apartment. Daphne wanted to take a cab, but Maxine said the walk would do them good. It was a beautiful sunny November day, and the children were all looking forward to their father's arrival that afternoon. He was flying in from Paris, and they were due at his apartment in time for dinner. Maxine had agreed to go along. It would be nice to see Blake.

The doorman at her parents' apartment building wished them all a happy Thanksgiving as they got into the elevator. Maxine's mother was waiting for them at the door when they got out. She looked strikingly like Maxine, in an older, slightly heavier version, and Maxine's father was standing just behind her with a broad smile.

'My, my,' he said kindly, 'what a good-looking group you are.' He kissed his daughter first, shook hands with the boys, while Daphne kissed her grandmother, and then smiled at her grandfather, while he gave her a hug.

'Hi, Grampa,' she said softly, and they followed their grandparents into the living room. Their grandmother had done several beautiful arrangements of fall flowers, and the apartment looked as neat and elegant as ever. Everything was impeccable and in good order, and the children sat down politely on the couch and chairs. They knew that at their grandparents' house they had to behave. Their grandparents were kind and loving, but they weren't used to having that many children around at once, particularly boys. Sam sneaked a deck of cards out of his pocket, and he and his grandfather started a game of Go Fish! while Maxine and her mother went out to the kitchen to check on the turkey. Everything had been meticulously set out and prepared—gleaming silver, immaculately pressed linens, the turkey was all cooked, and the vegetables were cooking. Sharing Thanksgiving was a tradition they all loved. Maxine always enjoyed visiting with her parents. They had been supportive of her all her life, and particularly so since her divorce from Blake. They had liked him, but thought he had been over the top ever since his big win in the dot-com boom. The way he lived now was entirely beyond their understanding. They worried about his influence on the children, but had been relieved to see that Maxine's solid values and constant attention had continued to ground them. They were crazy about their grandchildren and loved having them come to visit and sharing holidays with them.

Maxine's father was still busy with his practice, teaching and still attending surgeries of special cases, and he was extremely proud of his daughter with her own medical career. When she had decided to go to medical school and follow in his footsteps, it had pleased him no end. He was a little startled by her decision to specialize in psychiatry, a world he knew little about, but he was impressed by the career and reputation she had forged for herself in her field. He had proudly given away many copies of both of her books.

Her mother checked on the sweet potatoes in the oven, poked the turkey again to make sure it wasn't drying out, and turned to Maxine with a warm smile. She was a quiet, reserved woman who had been satisfied all her life to be in the background, be supportive of her husband, and she was proud to be a physician's wife. She had never felt the need for a career of her own. She was of a generation that was happy to stand behind their men, bring up their children, and as long as there was no pressing financial need, stay home instead of work. She had done extensive charity work for the Junior League, was a volunteer at the hospital where her husband was on staff, and she enjoyed reading for the blind. She was satisfied, happy, and her life was full, but she worried that her daughter had too much responsibility on her shoulders, and worked too hard. It bothered her more than it did her husband that Blake was an absentee father, although her own husband hadn't been directly involved with his own daughter either. But the reasons for it, and his demanding practice, seemed far more comprehensible and respectable to Marguerite Connors than Blake's obsessive and totally irresponsible pursuit of fun. She had never been able to understand what he was doing or how he behaved, and she thought it remarkable that Maxine was so patient about it, and so tolerant of his complete lack of responsibility toward their children. In fact, she felt downright sorry for them for what they were missing, and for Maxine. And it worried her that there wasn't a serious man in her life.

'How are you, dear? As busy as ever?' Marguerite asked. She and Maxine talked a few times a week, but rarely said anything substantive. Had Maxine felt the need, she would have been more inclined to discuss things with her father, who had a more realistic view of the world. Her mother had been so sheltered through nearly fifty years of marriage that she was far less able to be helpful in any practical way. And Maxine hated to worry her. 'Are you working on a new book?'

'Not yet. And my practice always gets a little crazy before the holidays. There's always some lunatic doing something to put kids in jeopardy or traumatize them, and my adolescent patients get upset about the holidays, like everyone else. Holidays always seem to drive everyone a little nuts,' Maxine said, helping her mother put the rolls in the bread basket after they'd been warmed. Their dinner looked beautiful and smelled great. Although she had help during the week, her mother was a terrific cook, and took great pride in cooking holiday meals herself. She always prepared Christmas dinner too, which was a huge relief for Maxine, who had never been as domestic, and was more like her father in many ways. She also had his realistic, practical view of the world. She was more scientific than artistic, and as the breadwinner in her own family, she was more down to earth. To this day, her father still wrote the checks and paid the bills. Maxine was well aware that if anything ever happened to him, her mother would be completely lost in the real world.

'Holidays are always busy for us too,' Marguerite said as she took the turkey out of the oven. It looked like it was ready to be photographed for a magazine. 'Everyone seems to break something during ski season, and as soon as it gets cold, people start falling on the ice and breaking hips.' She had done it herself three years before, and had had a hip replacement. She had come out of it very well. 'You know how busy your father gets this time of year.'

Maxine smiled in answer, helping her get the sweet potatoes out of the oven, and setting them down on the island in the center of the kitchen. The crust of marshmallows covering them was a perfect golden brown. 'Dad's always busy, Mom.'

'So are you,' her mother said proudly, and went to get her husband to carve the turkey. When Maxine followed her back into the living room, he was still playing cards with Sam, and the other two children were watching football on TV. Her father was a huge fan, and had been the orthopedic surgeon for the New York Jets for years. He still saw them as patients in his practice.

'Turkey time,' her mother announced, as her father got up to go and carve the turkey. He apologized to Sam and looked at his daughter with a grin. He'd been having a good time.

'I think he cheats,' her father commented about his grandson.

'Definitely,' Maxine agreed, as her father disappeared into the kitchen to do his job.

Ten minutes later the turkey was carved, and he brought it to the dining table, as his wife called out to all of them to come and sit down. Maxine found great pleasure in the family ritual, and was grateful that they were all there together and her parents were in good health. Her mother was seventy-eight, and her father seventy-nine, although both were in great shape. It was hard to believe that her parents were now that old.

Her mother said grace, as she did every year, and then her father passed the turkey platter around. There was stuffing, cranberry jelly, sweet potatoes, wild rice, peas, spinach, chestnut puree, and rolls her mother made from scratch. It was a veritable feast.

'Yumm!' Sam said as he piled the sweet potatoes with the marshmallow topping onto his plate. He took gobs of cranberry jelly, a healthy portion of stuffing, a slice of white turkey meat, and no vegetables at all. Maxine said nothing to him, and let him enjoy the meal.

As always, the conversation was lively whenever they got together. Their grandfather asked them respectively how they were doing in school, and was particularly interested in Jack's soccer games. And by the time lunch was over, they were so full they could hardly move. The meal had been finished off with apple, pumpkin, and mince pies, with a choice of vanilla ice cream or perfectly whipped cream. Sam's shirttail was hanging out when he left the table, the neck of his shirt was open, and his tie was askew. Jack looked more respectable, but had taken his tie off too. Only Daphne looked like a perfect lady, the way she had when she arrived. All three children went back to the living room to watch football, as Maxine sat and relaxed over coffee with her parents.

'It was a fantastic meal, Mom,' Maxine said honestly. She loved the way her mother cooked, and wished she could have learned it from her. But she didn't have the interest or the skill. 'It always is fantastic when you cook,' she added, and her mother beamed.

'Your mother is an amazing woman,' her father said, and Maxine smiled at the look they exchanged. They were cute. After all these years, they were still in love. Their fiftieth anniversary was coming up the following year. Maxine was already thinking about giving a party for them. As their only child, the responsibility fell to her. 'The kids are looking great,' her father commented, as Maxine helped herself to a chocolate mint from a silver tray her mother had set down in front of them as Maxine groaned. It was hard to believe she could swallow anything else after the enormous meal, but somehow she did.

'Thanks, Dad. They're fine.'

'It's a shame their father doesn't see more of them.' It was a comment he always made. As much as he had enjoyed Blake's company at times, as a father he thought he was a disgrace.

'He's coming in tonight,' Maxine commented noncommittally. She knew what her father thought, and she didn't entirely disagree.

'For how long?' her mother asked. She shared her husband's point of view, that Blake had turned out to be a big disappointment as a husband and father, although she liked him.

'Probably for the weekend,' if he stayed that long. With Blake, that was never a sure thing. But at least he was coming, and seeing them on Thanksgiving. That wasn't automatically a given with him, and the kids were happy with whatever time they got, however brief.

'When did he see them last?' her father asked with obvious disapproval.

'July. In Greece, on the boat. They had a great

82

time.'

'That's not the point,' her father said sternly. 'Children need a father. He's never around.'

'He never was,' Maxine said honestly. She didn't have to defend him anymore, although she didn't like being unkind, or to upset the kids by making negative comments about him, which she never did. 'That's why we got divorced. He loves them, he just forgets to show up. As Sam says, it sucks. But they seem very well adjusted about it. They may get upset about it later, but for now, they seem to be okay. They accept him for what he is, a lovable, unreliable guy who loves them, and is a lot of fun to be with.' It was a perfect assessment of Blake. Her father frowned and shook his head.

'What about you?' he asked, always concerned about his daughter. Like her mother, he thought she worked too hard, but he was enormously proud of her, and just very sorry she was alone. It didn't seem fair to him, and he resented Blake for how things had turned out, far more than Maxine did herself. She had made her peace with it long since. Her parents never had.

'I'm fine,' Maxine said blandly, in answer to her father's question. She knew what he meant. They always asked.

'Any nice young man on the horizon?' He looked hopeful.

'Nope,' she said with a smile. 'I'm still sleeping with Sam.' Both her parents smiled.

'I hope that changes one of these days,' Arthur Connors said, with a look of concern. 'Eventually, those kids are going to grow up, before you know it, and you're going to find yourself alone.'

'I think I've got a few years left before I need to

panic about it.'

'It goes mighty fast,' he said, thinking about her. 'I blinked and you were in medical school. And now look at you. You're an authority in your field on childhood trauma and adolescent suicide. When I think about you, Max, I still think you're fifteen.' He smiled warmly at her, and her mother nodded.

'Yeah, me too, Dad. Sometimes I look at Daphne, wearing my clothes and high heels, and I wonder how that happened. Last time I looked, she was three. Jack's suddenly as tall as I am, overnight, and five minutes ago, Sam was two months old. It's weird, isn't it?'

'It's even weirder when your "children" are the age you are. You'll always be a kid to me.' She liked that about their relationship. There had to be somewhere in the world, and people in it, where you could still be a kid. It was too hard to be a grown-up all the time. That was the nice thing about still having parents, there was a feeling of safety not having to be the oldest member of the family yet.

She wondered sometimes if Blake's crazy wild behaviors stemmed from a fear of getting old. She couldn't totally blame him if that was the case. In many ways, responsibility was what he feared most, and yet he had been so extraordinary in business. But that was different. He had wanted to be a 'wunderkind' or golden boy forever, and now he was all grown up and middle-aged. She knew it scared him more than anything else, and he couldn't run fast enough to get away from facing himself. It was sad in a way, and he had missed so much. While he was running faster than the speed of sound, his kids were growing up, and he had lost her. It seemed like a high price to pay to be Peter Pan.

'Well, don't talk yourself into being old yet,' her father said then. 'You're still a young woman, and any man would be lucky to have you. At forty-two, you're still a kid. Don't lock yourself up, and forget to go out and have some fun.' They all knew that she didn't go out much. He was afraid sometimes that she was still in love with Blake and pining for him, but her mother insisted that wasn't the case. She just hadn't met anyone yet. And they both wanted her to find the right man this time. Her father had tried to fix her up with a few physicians initially, but it had never worked out, and Maxine had said she preferred to find her own dates.

She helped her mother clear the table and make order in the kitchen, but Marguerite told her the housekeeper would be back the next day, so they joined the others in the living room, avidly watching the game on TV. And reluctantly, at five o'clock, Maxine pried the children away. She hated to do it, but she didn't want them to be late for Blake. Every moment they shared with him was precious. Her parents were sorry to see them leave. They hugged and kissed, and she and the children thanked them for the terrific meal. It was what everyone's Thanksgiving should be, and Maxine was grateful for the family she had. She knew just how lucky she was.

She and the children walked slowly back up Park Avenue to their own building. It was five-thirty by then. The kids changed out of their good clothes, and unusually promptly for him, Blake called at six. He had just gotten in. He was on his way in from the airport, and told them to be at his place at seven. He said everything was set and waiting for them. He was having dinner catered by a restaurant, and knowing they would have had turkey at their grandparents', he said he had ordered something different. Dinner would be ready by nine, and they could hang out till then. Just hearing about it, the children were thrilled.

'Are you sure you still want me to come?' Maxine asked cautiously. She hated to intrude on their time with him, although she knew Sam would be more comfortable with her around. But he had to get used to being with Blake at some point. He never spent enough time with him to get over that hump. Blake didn't mind. He loved having Maxine around, and always made her feel welcome. Even five years after the divorce, they still enjoyed each other's company, as friends.

'I'd love it,' Blake said in answer to her question. 'We can catch up while the kids run around.' The children always had a ball at his place, playing video games, and watching movies. They loved his projection room and the enormous, comfortable seats. He had every modern high-tech gadget there was, since he was a kid himself. Blake always reminded her of Tom Hanks in the movie *Big*, an enchanting boy masquerading as a man. 'See you at seven,' Blake promised as Maxine hung up and reported to the kids. They had an hour to relax and pack their things to stay with him. Sam looked a little uncertain about it, and she reassured him that he'd be fine.

'You can sleep with Daffy if you need to,' she reminded him, and he looked pleased with that. She mentioned it to Daphne a few minutes later and told her to take care of Sam, and suggested that Sam sleep with her. Daphne didn't mind.

All four of them were in a cab together an hour later, on their way to Blake's apartment. Just going up in the elevator reminded them of being in a rocket ship. You needed a special code to get to his penthouse apartment. He had two entire floors, and from the moment he opened the door to them, it was pure Blake and the magical world he lived in. The music on the extraordinary sound system was blaring, the art and lighting were amazing, the view was beyond spectacular with glass exterior walls, picture windows, and enormous skylights. The inner walls were mirrored to reflect the view, the ceilings were nearly thirty feet tall. He had taken over two floors and turned them into one apartment with a circular staircase in the middle, and he had every possible game, toy, stereo, TV, gimmick, and gadget. He had a movie playing on a screen that covered an entire wall, and handed Jack the headphones to watch it. He kissed and hugged all of them, and gave Daphne a new cell phone in pink enamel with her initials engraved in it, and he showed Sam how to work the new video game chair and paddles he'd had installed in his absence. They were all busy playing with toys, and getting acclimated to their rooms again, when Blake finally had a peaceful moment to smile at his ex-wife and put a friendly arm around her.

'Hi, Max,' he said calmly. 'How are you? Sorry about all the chaos.' He was as dazzling as ever. He had a deep tan, which made his electric blue eyes even more startling. He was wearing jeans, a black turtleneck sweater, and black alligator cowboy boots that had been made for him in Milan. There was no question, Maxine reminded herself, he was a knockout. Everything about him was appealing, and incredibly handsome, for about ten minutes. And then you realized you couldn't count on him, he never showed up, and no matter how charming he was, he was never going to grow up. He was the best-looking, smartest, most adorable Peter Pan in the world. It was great if you wanted to play Wendy, but if not, he just wasn't the right man. She had to remind herself of that at times. Being in his aura was a heady experience. But she knew better than anyone that he wasn't a responsible adult. Sometimes she felt like he was her fourth child.

'They love the chaos,' she reassured him. Being with him was a three-ring circus. And who didn't love that at their age? It was a lot harder to take at hers. 'You look great, Blake. How was Morocco, or Paris, or wherever you were?'

'The house in Marrakech is going to be terrific. I've been there all week. I was in Paris yesterday.' She laughed at the contrast between their lives. She had been at Silver Pines, seeing Jason, on Long Island. It was a far cry from the glamor of her ex-husband's life, but she wouldn't have traded places with him for the world. She couldn't have lived that way anymore. 'You look great too, Max. Still too busy? Seeing a million patients? I don't know how you do it.' Particularly knowing what heavy things she dealt with. He admired the work she did, and the kind of mother she was. She had been a great wife too. He always said so.

'I like it that way,' Maxine said, smiling. 'Someone has to do it, and I'm glad it's me. I love working with kids.' He nodded, knowing how true that was.

88

'How was Thanksgiving with your parents?' He used to feel stifled at those Thanksgivings, and yet in a funny way he loved them too. They were what every family should be, and so few were. He hadn't had a holiday like that in five years.

'It was nice. They love the kids, and they're so sweet. They're both in remarkably good shape for their age. My father is still operating, though not as much, and teaching and practicing full time, at seventy-nine.'

'You will be too,' Blake said, as he poured champagne into two glasses and handed her one. He always drank Cristal. She took it and sipped it, admiring the view from his apartment. It was like flying over the city. Everything he owned or touched had that magical quality to it. He was what people dreamed of being if they hit it big, but very few people had Blake's style and ability to pull it off.

She was surprised he didn't have a woman with him this time, and a few minutes later, he explained it with a rueful smile. 'I just got dumped,' he said, by a twenty-four-year-old supermodel, who had run off with a major rock star, who Blake said had a bigger plane. Maxine couldn't help laughing at the way he said it. He didn't seem upset, and she knew he wasn't. The girls he went out with were just playmates for him. He had no desire whatsoever to settle down, and didn't want more kids, so eventually the young women he went out with had to marry someone else. Marriage with him was never an option, and the farthest thing from his mind. As they sat in his living room and chatted, Sam wandered in, and hopped up on his mother's lap. He sat watching

89

Blake with interest, as though he were a family friend and not his father, and then inquired about the girlfriend he'd had with him the previous summer. Blake looked at him and laughed.

'You've missed two since then, champ. I was just telling your mom. I got dumped last week. So it's just me this time.' Sam nodded at the explanation, and glanced at his mother.

'Mom doesn't have a boyfriend either. She never goes out. She has us.'

'She should go out,' Blake said, smiling at both of them. 'She's a very beautiful woman, and one of these days you guys are going to grow up.' It was exactly what Maxine's father had said that day after lunch. She had another twelve years until Sam left for college. She was in no hurry, despite everyone else's concerns. He asked Sam about school then, not knowing what else to say, and Sam told his father he had been the turkey in the school play. Maxine had emailed Blake the pictures of it, as she always did of important events. She had sent a slew of them to him of Jack at his soccer games.

The children wandered in and out, chatting easily with their parents, and getting used to Blake again. Daphne looked at him with open adoration, and when she left the room, Maxine told him about the incident with the beer, just so he was aware of it, and didn't let it happen when Daphne was with him.

'Come on, Max,' he chided her gently, 'don't be so uptight. She's just a kid. Don't you think restriction for a month is a little over the top? She's not going to turn into an alcoholic from two beers.' It was the kind of reaction she expected from him, and not one she liked. But she wasn't surprised. It was one of the many differences between them. Blake didn't believe in rules, for anyone, and least of all himself.

'No, she isn't,' Maxine said quietly. 'But if I let them have beer parties now, at thirteen, where are we going to be at sixteen or seventeen? Crack parties when I'm out seeing patients, or heroin? She's got to have limits, and respect for boundaries, or we're going to be in deep shit in a few years. I'd rather put the brakes on now.'

'I know,' he sighed, the blue eyes looking brighter than ever as he glanced at her sheepishly. He looked like a boy who had just been scolded by his mother or teacher. It was a role Maxine didn't like, but had had with him for years. She was used to it by now. 'You're probably right. It just doesn't seem like such a big deal to me. I did a lot worse at her age. I was stealing scotch out of my father's bar at twelve, and selling it in school for a hell of a profit.' He laughed and so did Max.

'That's different. That's business. You were an entrepreneur at that age, not a drunk. I'll bet you weren't drinking it.' He was not an excessive drinker as a rule, and had never done drugs. He was just wild in every other way. Blake was allergic to boundaries of any kind.

'You're right.' Blake laughed harder at the memory. 'I didn't do that till I was fourteen. I was more interested in staying sober and getting the girls drunk that I went out with. That seemed like a much better plan to me.'

Max shook her head, laughing at him. 'Why is it I think that hasn't changed?'

'I don't need to get them drunk anymore,' he confessed with a shameless grin. They had the strangest relationship, like great friends, more than people who had been married for ten years and had three children. He was like the crazy pal she saw two or three times a year, while she was the responsible one, bringing up children and going to work every day. They were night and day.

Dinner arrived promptly at nine o'clock, and everyone was hungry by then. He had ordered it from the best Japanese restaurant in the city, and it was prepared in front of them, with all kinds of flourishes and exotic touches, and a chef who flamed everything, chopped up the shrimp and flipped it in the air and caught it in his pocket. The kids loved it. Everything Blake did or organized was spectacular and different. Even Sam was looking relaxed and happy by the time she left. It was nearly midnight by then, and the kids were watching a movie in the projection room. She knew they'd be up till two or three A.M. It wouldn't do them any harm, she didn't begrudge them a minute of their time with him. They could sleep when they came home to her.

'When are you leaving?' she asked him as she put her coat on, afraid that he would say 'tomorrow,' which she knew would upset the kids. They wanted at least a few days with him, particularly not knowing when they would see him again, although Christmas was coming, and he usually managed to spend some time with them during the holidays.

'Not till Sunday,' he said, and noticed the look of relief on her face.

'That's good,' she said softly. 'They hate it when you leave.'

'Me too,' he said almost sadly. 'If it's okay with

you, I want to take them to Aspen after Christmas. I don't have any firm plans yet, but it's a nice time to be there, over New Year's.'

'They'll love it.' She smiled at him. She always missed them when they went away with him, but she wanted them to have a father, and it wasn't easy to manage with him. You had to catch him when he was willing, and able to make plans with them.

'Do you want to have dinner with us tomorrow night?' he offered, as he walked her to the elevator. He still enjoyed spending time with her, he always had. He would have stayed married to her forever. It was Maxine who had wanted out, and he didn't blame her. And he'd had a good time since then. But he loved still having her in his life, and was glad she had never shut him out. He wondered if that would change when she found a serious man, and he never doubted that she would one day. He was surprised it had taken this long.

'I might,' she said, looking relaxed. 'See how it goes with the kids. I don't want to intrude.' They needed time alone with their father, and she didn't want to interfere with them.

'We love having you along,' he assured her, and then hugged her goodbye.

'Thanks for dinner,' she said as she got on the elevator, and waved at him as the doors closed. The elevator shot down fifty floors, and her ears popped as she stood there thinking about him. It was strange. Nothing had changed. She still loved him. She always had. She had never stopped loving him. She just didn't want to be with him anymore. It didn't even bother her that he went out with girls in their twenties. It was hard to define their relationship. But whatever it was, and however strange, it worked for both of them.

The doorman hailed her a cab as she came out of the building. As she rode uptown to her own apartment, she thought about what a nice day it had been. It was strange to find it silent and dark when she walked in. She turned on the lights, walked into her bedroom, and thought of Blake and her children in his insanely luxurious apartment. The one she lived in looked better to her than ever. There was no part of his life that she still wanted. She had no need for that kind of excess and self-indulgence. She was happy for him, but what she had was all she wanted.

For the thousandth time since she left him, she knew she had made the right decision. Blake Williams was every woman's dream, but no longer hers.

CHAPTER 5

Maxine was sound asleep at four A.M. when the phone rang at her bedside. It took longer than usual to wake her up, as she had been sleeping deeply. She often fell into a deeper sleep when her children weren't around. As she glanced at the clock, she hoped that nothing had gone wrong at Blake's apartment. She wondered if Sam had had a nightmare and wanted to come home. She answered the phone automatically, before fully waking up and without thinking.

'Dr. Williams,' she said briskly, to mask the fact that she'd been sound asleep, although who would have expected her to be otherwise at four A.M.?

'Maxine, I'm sorry to call you at this hour.' It was Thelma Washington, the doctor on call for her over the Thanksgiving holiday and weekend. 'I'm at New York Hospital with the Andersons. I thought you'd want me to call. Hilary overdosed last night. They found her at two A.M.' She was a bipolar fifteen-year-old with a heroin problem, who had attempted suicide four times in the past two years. Maxine was instantly awake. 'We got her in as fast as we could. The paramedics administered naloxone, but it's not looking good.'

'Shit. I'll be right in.' Maxine was already standing up as she said the words.

'She hasn't regained consciousness, and the attending doesn't think she will. It's hard to say,' Thelma filled her in.

'She made a miraculous recovery last time. She's a pretty tough little kid,' Maxine commented.

'She'll have to be. It seems like she took one hell of a cocktail. Heroin, cocaine, speed, and the blood workup shows rat poison. They've apparently been cutting street heroin with some pretty nasty stuff these days. They had two kids die of it here last week. Maxine . . . don't get your hopes up. I don't mean to sound negative about it, but if she makes it through this, I'm not sure how much of her there'll be left.'

'Yeah, I know. Thanks for calling me. I'll get dressed and be right in. Where is she?'

'Trauma ICU. I'll be waiting for you here. Her parents are pretty upset.'

'I'll bet.' The poor people had been through it four times with a child who had been difficult since she was two. She was a nice kid, but between her bipolar disease and her heroin addiction, she had been on the fast track to disaster since she was twelve. Maxine had been seeing her for two years. She was the only child of extremely dedicated, loving parents who had done everything they could. There were some kids that, no matter how hard you tried, you just couldn't help.

Maxine had hospitalized her four times in the last two years, with very little effect. The minute she was discharged from the hospital, she was off and running again with the same disastrous friends. She had told Maxine repeatedly that she couldn't help herself. She just couldn't stay clean, and she claimed that the medications Maxine prescribed for her never took the edge off like what she bought on the street. Maxine had been afraid of this outcome for the last two years.

She was dressed in less than five minutes in loafers, a heavy sweater, and jeans. She grabbed a warm coat out of the closet, picked up her purse, and rang for the elevator. She found a cab immediately, and was at the hospital fifteen minutes after Thelma Washington, her relief doc, had called. Thelma had gone to Harvard with her, was African-American and one of the best psychiatrists she knew. And after school, and over the years of covering each other's practices, they had become friends. Privately or professionally, she knew she could always count on Thelma. They were very similar in many ways, and equally dedicated to their work. Maxine felt completely at ease leaving her patients in her hands. Maxine saw Thelma before she saw the Andersons, and Thelma quickly brought her up to speed. Hilary was in a deep coma, and so far nothing they had administered to her had brought her around. She had done it alone at home, while her parents were out. She hadn't left a note, but Maxine knew she didn't need to. She had often told Maxine that she didn't care if she lived or died. For her, and for others like her, being bipolar was just too hard.

Maxine looked upset as she read the chart, and Thelma stood by. 'Jesus, she took everything but the kitchen sink,' Maxine said, looking grim, and Thelma nodded.

'Her mother said her boyfriend dumped her last night, on Thanksgiving. I'm sure that didn't help.' Maxine nodded and closed the chart. All the right things had been done. All they could do now was wait to see what happened. It was no secret to either of them, or to Hilary's parents, that if she didn't regain consciousness soon, there was a good chance she would be brain damaged forever, if she lived, which was still doubtful. Maxine was surprised she had survived what she'd taken.

'Any idea when she did it?' Maxine asked, as the two women walked down the hall together. Thelma looked tired and worried. She hated cases like this. Her own practice was far more mellow than Maxine's, but she liked covering for Maxine. Working with her patients was always a challenge.

'Probably a few hours before they found her, which is the problem. The stuff had plenty of time to work through her system. It's why the naloxone didn't help, according to the paramedics who brought her in.' Naloxone was a drug that reversed the effects of powerful narcotics, if administered soon enough. It made the difference between life and death in overdoses, and had saved Hilary four times before. It had made no difference this time,

97

which was a very bad sign to both physicians.

Maxine went in to see Hilary before she saw her parents. She was on a respirator, with a trauma ICU unit still working on her. She was naked on the table, covered by a thin drape. The machine was breathing for her, she was immobile, and her face was gray. Maxine stood looking at her for a long moment, spoke to the team that had been with her since she got there, and had a word with the attending. Her heart was holding up, although the monitor had reported arrhythmia several times. There was no sign of life in the fifteen-year-old girl, who looked more like a child lying there. Her hair was dyed black, and she had tattoos up and down both arms. Hilary had marched to her own drummer, despite her parents' efforts to convince her otherwise.

Maxine nodded at Thelma, and together they went to see the parents in the waiting room. They had been with Hilary initially until the team asked them to leave. It was too upsetting to her parents to watch what was happening, and the residents and nurses needed room to move.

Angela Anderson was crying when Maxine walked in to see them, and Phil had his arms around her, and had obviously been crying too. They had been through this before, but it didn't get easier, only harder, and they were acutely aware that Hilary might have gone too far this time.

'How is she?' they both asked in unison, as Maxine sat down with them and Thelma left the room.

'About the same as when she came in. I just saw her. She's putting up a good fight. She always

98

does.' Maxine smiled sadly at them, it made her heart ache to see the agony in their eyes, and she was sad too. Hilary was such a nice girl. So troubled, but so sweet. 'There were some poisons in the drugs she took,' Maxine explained. 'That happens on the streets. Mostly, I think our problem is that it all had time to work through her system before she was found. And there's only so much a heart can take. She took a very heavy dose of some very powerful drugs.' It wasn't news to them, but she had to give them some kind of warning that this might not have a happy ending. There was nothing else she could do. The trauma team was doing everything they could.

Thelma brought them all coffee a few minutes later, and then Maxine went back to see Hilary again. Thelma followed her out, and Maxine told her to go home. There was no point in both of them being up all night. Maxine was going to stay. She thanked Thelma before she left, and stuck around to see how Hilary's heart was doing. Its beating was becoming more irregular, and the resident said her blood pressure was coming down, none of it good signs.

For the next four hours, Maxine went back and forth between the Andersons and their daughter, and at eight-thirty, Maxine decided to let them come in to the unit to see her. She was well aware by then that it might be the last time they'd see their daughter alive. Hilary's mother sobbed openly as she touched her, and bent to kiss her, and her father stayed to be with his wife, but he could hardly bear to look at their child. The respirator was still breathing for her, but it was barely keeping her alive.

And as soon as they settled in the waiting room again, the attending physician came in and motioned to Maxine, who followed him back out into the hall. 'It's not looking good.'

'Yeah,' Maxine said, 'I know.' She followed him back to Hilary's area of the ICU again, and almost as soon as they walked in, the monitor set off an alarm. Hilary's heart had stopped. Her parents wanted everything possible done, and the cardiac team did all they could to jolt her heart back to life. Electric shock was administered as Maxine watched, looking grim. They massaged her heart, and administered the paddles several times, to no avail. They worked on Hilary's lifeless form for half an hour, until the resident finally signaled to the rest of the team. It was over. Hilary was gone. They all stood looking at each other for a long, painful moment, and then the resident turned to Maxine, as they turned off the respirator and took it out of Hilary's mouth.

'I'm sorry,' he said softly, and left the room. There was nothing left for him to do.

'Me too,' she said, and then went to find the Andersons. They knew the moment she walked in, and Hilary's mother began to scream. Maxine sat with them for a long time, and held her in her arms as she cried. She hugged Phil too. They asked to see Hilary again, and Maxine led them into the room. They had put her in a room by herself, for them, before taking her to the morgue. Maxine left them alone with her for nearly an hour. And then finally, heartbroken and devastated, they went home.

Maxine signed the death certificate, and all the appropriate forms. It was after ten o'clock in the morning when she finally left, and went downstairs. She was coming out of the elevator when a nurse she knew called her name. Maxine turned and her eyes were grim.

'I'm sorry . . . I just heard . . .' the nurse said kindly. She had been there the last time Hilary came in, and helped to save her life. The team had been just as good this time, but Hilary's chances of survival had been considerably worse. As they spoke, Maxine noticed a tall man in a white doctor's coat standing nearby, watching them, and she had no idea who he was.

He waited until Maxine finished talking to the nurse, who went upstairs for her shift in ICU, and then he approached.

'Dr. Williams?' he asked cautiously. He could see that she was busy, and looked somewhat disheveled and tired.

'Yes?'

'I'm Charles West. The idiot who gave you a hard time about Jason Wexler a few weeks ago. I just thought I'd say hello.' She wasn't in the mood to talk to anyone, but she didn't want to be rude. He'd been nice enough to call and apologize, though, so she made an effort now.

'Sorry, it's been a long night. I just lost a patient in the ICU. A fifteen-year-old who overdosed. You never get used to it. It breaks your heart every time.' It reminded them both of what could have happened to Jason if she'd listened to him, and they were both glad she knew better and hadn't.

'I'm sorry. It doesn't seem fair, does it? I'm here to see a ninety-two-year-old patient with a broken hip and pneumonia, and she's doing fine. And you lose a fifteen-year-old. Can I buy you a cup of coffee?'

Maxine didn't even hesitate. 'Maybe some other time.' He nodded, she thanked him again, and left. He watched her walk across the lobby. He was startled by how she looked. Somehow he had assumed that she was older than she appeared. He had expected a battle-ax of sorts. He had read about her on the Internet, but there was no photograph. She had never put one up. It didn't seem important to her. Her credentials and CV were enough.

Charles West got into the elevator thinking about her, and the kind of night she must have had. The look in her eyes said it all. He had been startled when he'd heard the nurse call out to her, and something had compelled him to wait and talk to her. And all he could think about as he got off the elevator was that he hoped that somehow destiny would cross their paths again.

Charles West was the last thing on Maxine's mind as she hailed a cab and rode home. She was thinking of Hilary and the Andersons, and the terrible loss they'd sustained, the unthinkable agony of losing a child. Maxine hated moments like this, and as a tragedy such as this always did, it made her that much more determined to save all the others from themselves.

CHAPTER 6

Max wasn't in the mood to go out with Blake and the children on Friday night. He called her in the afternoon, and she told him what had happened

102

the night before. He was sympathetic, and praised her again for what she did. She didn't feel deserving of it at the moment. He said he was taking the children shopping that afternoon, and invited her to come. He insisted they'd have a ball, but she resisted, and he could hear that she was down. In fact, he had been planning to take the children Christmas shopping for her, and Tiffany and Cartier were on their list, but he didn't mention it to her. Instead, he invited her to meet them for dinner, and she declined that too. He felt sorry for how upset she was about the death of her patient, and whispered to the children to be extra nice to her, when he passed the phone to them so they could speak to her too.

She spoke with Sam, and he was happy and doing fine. When Sam begged her to join them, she promised to go to dinner with them the following night. They were having a ball with Blake. He had taken them to 21 for brunch, which they always loved, and for a helicopter ride that morning, a favorite pastime with him. She promised to meet up with them the next day, and felt a little better when she hung up.

She called Thelma Washington then and told her how things had turned out, and her friend wasn't surprised. Maxine thanked her for her help, and then called the Andersons. Predictably, they were in bad shape, and still in a state of shock. They had funeral arrangements to make, friends and grandparents to call, all the nightmarish things one had to attend to when one lost a child. Maxine told them again how very sorry she was, and they thanked her for all her help. But even knowing she had done everything possible, Maxine still had an overwhelming sense of defeat and loss.

Blake called her again, as she was dressing to go out for a walk. He was checking up on her to make sure she was okay. He didn't tell her, but he and the children had just bought her a beautiful sapphire bracelet.

She assured him she was fine, and was touched by the call. Even if unreliable, he was always compassionate and thoughtful, just as he was now.

'Christ, I don't know how you do it. I'd be in a psych ward if I did what you do every day.' He knew she always took it hard when one of her patients died, which given the nature of her work, they sometimes did.

'It gets to me,' she admitted, 'but it happens sometimes. I feel so sorry for the parents, she's an only child. I think it would kill me if anything ever happened to ours.' She had seen that special kind of grief too often, the loss of a child. It was what she feared most in life, the one thing she prayed would never happen to them.

'That's awful.' He worried about her. In spite of how well she handled it, he knew she didn't have an easy life, in part thanks to him. And he wanted to do whatever he could for her now. But there was nothing much he could do. And Hilary was her patient, not her child.

'I think I need a day off,' she said with a sigh. 'I'll enjoy seeing you and the kids more tomorrow.' He was taking them to the opening of a play that night, and they were all going out to dinner the next night. 'Besides, you should have time alone with them, without me tagging along.' She was always considerate about that.

'I like it when you tag along,' he said, smiling,

although he loved being alone with his children too. He always came up with fun things for them to do. He was planning to take them skating the next day, and she said she might do that with them. But today, since the children were busy and in good hands, she wanted to be alone. Blake said to call if she changed her mind, and she promised she would. It was nice having him in town, to give her a breather for a change.

She went for a walk in the park and then hung around the house for the rest of the afternoon, and made herself some soup for dinner.

Sam called her before they went to the play, and he was excited about seeing it with his father.

'Have fun with Daddy tonight, and I'll come skating with you tomorrow,' she promised. She was actually looking forward to it, and felt better, although every time she thought of the Andersons and their overwhelming loss, her heart ached for them. She was thinking of them, as she ate her soup in the kitchen, and Zelda walked in.

'Is everything okay?' Zelda looked at her with worried eyes. She knew her well.

'Yeah, fine. Thanks, Zellie.'

'You look like someone died.'

'Actually, one of my patients did. A fifteen-year-old. It was very sad.'

'I hate what you do,' Zelda said fiercely. 'It depresses me. I don't know how you do it. Why can't you do something cheerful like deliver babies?' Maxine smiled at what she said.

'I like being a shrink, and I actually manage to keep them alive sometimes.'

'That's a good thing,' Zelda said, and sat down next to her at the kitchen table. Maxine looked as though she needed company, and Zelda wasn't entirely wrong. She had good instincts about when to talk to her, and when to leave her alone. 'How are the kids doing with their dad?'

'Fine. He took them on a helicopter ride, shopping, out to lunch and dinner, and the opening of a play tonight.'

'He's more like Santa Claus than a dad,' Zelda said accurately, and Maxine nodded as she finished her soup.

'He has to be, to make up for all the times he's not around,' she said matter-of-factly. It wasn't a criticism, it was a fact.

'You can't make up for that with a helicopter ride,' Zelda said wisely.

'It's the best he can do. He doesn't have it in him to stick around, for anyone. He was like that even before he made all that money. He just got worse once he had the means to indulge it. There have always been men like him in the world. In the old days, they became sea captains, adventurers, explorers. Christopher Columbus probably left a bunch of kids at home too. Some guys just aren't made to hang around and be normal husbands and dads.'

'My father was kind of like that,' Zelda admitted. 'He walked out on my mom when I was three. He joined the merchant marine and disappeared. Years later she found out he had another wife and four kids in San Francisco. He had never bothered to divorce her, or even write to her. He just took off, and walked out on her, my brother and me.'

'Did you ever see him, later, I mean?' Maxine asked with interest. Zelda had never previously

106

shared this part of her history. She was fairly private about her own life, and respectful of theirs.

'No, he died before I could. I meant to go out to California and meet him. My brother did. He wasn't too impressed. Our mom died of a broken heart. She drank herself to death when I was fifteen. I went to live with my aunt, and she died when I was eighteen. I've been a nanny ever since.' It explained why she had found her place working in families. They offered the stability and love she had never had as a child growing up. Maxine knew that her brother had died in a motorcycle accident years before. Zelda was essentially alone, except for the family she worked for, and the other nannies she had befriended over the years.

'Did you ever meet your half-brothers and -sisters?' Maxine inquired gently.

'No, I kind of figured they were why my mother died. I never wanted to meet them.' Maxine knew she had worked for the previous family for nine years, until the kids left for college. It made her wonder if Zelda regretted not having children of her own, but she didn't want to ask.

They sat at the kitchen table and chatted while Maxine ate dinner, and then they each went back to their own rooms. Zelda very seldom went out in the evening, even on her days off. And Maxine was kind of a homebody too. She went to bed early that night, still thinking about the patient she had lost that morning, and the agony her parents must have been in. It was a relief to try and put it out of her mind and go to sleep.

She felt better when she woke up the next morning, although still somewhat subdued. She met Blake and the children at Rockefeller Center, and went skating with them. They had hot chocolate afterward at the restaurant at the skating rink, and then went back to his apartment. The children headed straight for the projection room to watch a movie before dinner, and seemed perfectly at home being there with him. They always readjusted quickly when he appeared. Daphne had called two of her friends to come by. She loved showing off his glamorous penthouse, and her handsome father.

Maxine and Blake chatted easily for a few minutes, and then joined the children watching the movie. It was a film that hadn't even been released yet. Blake knew people everywhere and had privileges few others had. He took it as the norm now, and told Maxine he was going to London after New York. He was meeting friends to go to a rock concert there. He knew the stars who would be performing too. Sometimes it seemed, even to Maxine, as though he knew everyone in the world. Several times, he had introduced his children to well-known actors and rock stars, and he was invited backstage everywhere he went.

When the movie ended, Blake rounded them all up for dinner. He had made reservations at a new sushi restaurant that had opened a few weeks before, and was the hot, new trendy place in town. Maxine had never heard of it, but Daphne knew all about it. And they were given the VIP treatment when they arrived. They walked through the main restaurant, and were given a private dining room. It was an excellent dinner, and they all had a good time. They dropped Maxine off afterward, and then Blake and the kids went back to his apartment.

He was bringing them back to Maxine at five the next day before he left. And as usual, when left to her own devices, she spent the day working. She was at her computer, working on an article, when they got home. Blake hadn't come up, as he was late leaving for the airport, and the kids were overflowing with excitement when they walked in. And Sam was particularly happy to see her.

'He's taking us to Aspen for New Year,' Sam announced, 'and he said we could each bring a friend. Can I take you instead, Mom?' Maxine smiled at the offer.

'I don't think so, sweetheart. Daddy might like to bring a lady along, and that would be a little awkward.'

'He says he doesn't have one right now,' Sam said practically, disappointed that his mother had declined the offer.

'But he might by then.' It never took Blake long to find a new one. Women fell into his hands like fruit off a tree.

'What if he doesn't?' Sam persisted.

'We'll talk about it then.' She enjoyed having dinner with Blake when he was in town, and going skating with him and the children. Going on vacation with her ex-husband was a little more of him than she wanted, and undoubtedly more than he wanted of her. When he loaned her his yacht every year, for their summer vacations, he wasn't there. Besides, this was his time to be with the kids. But it was sweet of Sam to ask her.

They told her about all the things they'd done and seen with him in the past three days, and all three of them were in high spirits. They weren't as sad as they often were when he left town, because this time they knew they'd be seeing him a month later in Aspen. She was glad he had made the plan, and hoped he didn't disappoint them if something better came along, or he got distracted elsewhere. The kids loved going to Aspen with him, and anywhere else. He made everything they did an adventure and fun for them.

At dinner, Daphne said her father had told her she could use his apartment any time, even when he wasn't around, and her mother looked surprised by the offer. He had never said that before, and Maxine wondered if Daphne had misunderstood him.

'He said I could take friends over to watch movies in the projection room,' she said proudly.

'Maybe for a birthday party, or something special,' Maxine said cautiously, 'but I don't think you should just hang out there.' She didn't like that idea at all, a bunch of thirteen-year-olds hanging out at his apartment, and she didn't feel comfortable going there herself if he wasn't in town. The subject had never come up before. And Daphne looked annoyed by her answer.

'He's my father, and he said I could, and it's his apartment,' Daphne said, looking angrily at her mother.

'That's true. But I don't think you should go there when he's not around.' A lot could happen in that apartment. And it worried her that Blake was being so free and easy about it. It suddenly made her realize that having teenagers with a father like Blake could turn out to be a major challenge. She wasn't looking forward to it. So far, it hadn't been a problem, but it could be. And Daphne looked as though she was willing to battle for the privilege he

110

had offered. 'I'll talk to him about it,' Maxine said simply, as Daphne stomped off to her bedroom. What Maxine was planning to say to Blake was to warn him not to be manipulated by his children, nor to set them up for disaster by giving them too much freedom as they headed into their teens. She just hoped that he was willing to cooperate with her. If not, the next several years were going to be a nightmare. All she needed was for Blake to give Daphne keys to his apartment. The thought of it and the kind of things that could go on there made her shudder. She was definitely going to say something to him about it. And for sure, Daphne wouldn't like it. As usual, Maxine had to be the heavy.

Maxine finished her article that night, and the children watched television in their bedrooms. They were tired after three days of non-stop excitement with their father. Being with him was like traveling with the flying Wallendas, with all of them on the high wire at the same time. It always took them a while to calm down.

The next morning at breakfast was chaos. Everyone had woken up late. Jack spilled cereal all over the table, Daphne couldn't find her cell phone and refused to leave for school until she did, Sam burst into tears when he discovered he'd left his favorite shoes at his father's apartment, and Zelda had a toothache. Daphne managed to find her phone in the nick of time, Maxine promised Sam that she would buy him the exact same shoes at lunchtime, and prayed that she could find them, and she left for her office to see patients as Zelda was calling her dentist. It was one of those mornings that made you want to rip your hair out

111

and got the day off to a rough start. Zelda took Sam to school on her way to the dentist, and it started raining, as Maxine walked to work. She was soaked by the time she got there, and her first patient was already waiting, something that almost never happened to her.

She managed to make up the time, see all her morning patients, and find the right shoes for Sam at Niketown, which meant skipping lunch. Zelda called to say she had to have a root canal that day, and Maxine was trying to return her calls when her secretary told her Charles West was on the phone. Maxine wondered why he was calling, and if he was referring a patient. She took the call sounding mildly harassed and exasperated. It had been one of those days from beginning to end.

'Dr. Williams,' she said briskly.

'Hi there.' It was not the greeting she expected from him, and she was in no mood for a chatty call. Her last patient was due in, and she had fifteen minutes to finish returning her calls.

'Hello. What can I do for you?' she asked bluntly, realizing as she did that she sounded a little rough around the edges.

'I just wanted to tell you how sorry I was about your patient when I saw you on Friday.'

'Oh,' she said, sounding startled, 'that's very nice of you. It was very upsetting. You do everything you can to avoid it, and sometimes you lose them anyway. I felt awful for her parents. How's your ninety-two-year-old with the hip?' He was impressed that she remembered. He wasn't sure he would have.

'She's going home tomorrow. Thanks for asking. She's amazing. She has a ninety-three-year-old boyfriend.'

'She's doing better than I am,' Maxine said, laughing, which gave him just the opening he wanted.

'Yeah, me too. She has a new boyfriend every year. They drop like flies, and I swear, within weeks she finds a new one. Everyone should be lucky enough to get old like that. I was a little worried when she got pneumonia, but she rallied. I love her. I wish all my patients were like her.' Maxine was smiling at his description of her, and she was still wondering why he had called her.

'Is there anything I can do for you, doctor?' she asked, sounding slightly daunting and formal, but she was busy.

'Actually,' he said, sounding awkward, 'I was wondering if you'd have lunch with me sometime. I still feel like I owe you an apology for the Wexlers.' It was the only excuse he could think of.

'Don't be silly,' she said, glancing at her watch. Of all days for him to call her. She had been playing beat the clock since that morning. 'It was an honest mistake. Adolescent suicidality isn't your specialty. Believe me, I wouldn't know what to do with a ninety-two-year-old with a hip, pneumonia, and a boyfriend.'

'That's generous of you. How about lunch?' he persisted.

'You don't have to do that.'

'I know that, but I'd like to. What are you doing tomorrow?' Her mind went blank at the question. What was this man doing asking her to lunch, and why? She felt silly. She never took time out of her schedule for professional lunches with other physicians.

113

'I don't know . . . I . . . I might have a patient,' she said, groping for a reason to decline the invitation.

'Then what about the next day? You have to eat lunch sometime.'

'Well, yes, I do . . . when I have time,' which wasn't often. She felt foolish when she blurted out that she was free on Thursday. She glanced at her appointment book as she said it. 'But you really don't have to.'

'I'll keep that in mind,' he said, laughing at her. He suggested a restaurant that was near her office, to make it convenient for her. It was small and pleasant and she occasionally had lunch there with her mother. It had been years since she took time out to lunch with girlfriends. She preferred to see patients, and at night she stayed home with the kids. Most of the women she knew were just as busy as she was. She hadn't had much of a social life in years.

They made a date for noon on Thursday, and Maxine looked startled as she hung up the phone. She wasn't sure if it was a date, or a professional courtesy, but either way, she felt slightly silly. She hardly remembered what he looked like. She had been so upset about Hilary Anderson on Friday morning that all she remembered was that he was tall, and had graying blond hair. The rest of his appearance was a blur, not that it mattered. She made a note in her book, returned two more calls as quickly as she could, and saw her last patient.

She had to cook dinner for the children that night, since Zelda was in bed on painkillers. The day ended as it began, harried and stressful. And she managed to burn dinner, so they ordered pizza.

114

The next two days were equally stressful, and it was Thursday morning when she suddenly remembered the lunch date she had made with Charles West. She sat at her desk looking at her appointment book bleakly. She couldn't imagine what had made her do it. She didn't even know him, nor want to. The last thing she needed was lunch with a total stranger. She glanced at her watch and realized that she was already five minutes late, grabbed her coat, and hurried out of the office. She didn't even have time to put on lipstick or comb her hair, not that she cared.

When Maxine reached the restaurant, Charles West was already waiting at a table. He stood up when he saw her walk in, and she recognized him. He was tall, as she had remembered, and nice looking, and appeared as though he was in his late forties. He smiled and stood up as she approached the table.

'I'm sorry I'm late,' she said, slightly flustered, as he noticed the look of caution in her eyes. He knew enough about women to know that, unlike his ninety-two-year-old patient, this was not a woman looking for a boyfriend. Maxine Williams looked distant and guarded. 'I've had a crazy week in the office,' she added.

'So have I,' he said pleasantly. 'I think holidays drive people nuts. My patients all get pneumonia between Thanksgiving and Christmas, and I'm sure yours don't fare well over the holidays either.' He looked very easygoing and relaxed, as the waiter asked if they wanted to order drinks. She declined, and Charles ordered a glass of wine.

'My father is an orthopedic surgeon, and he always says everyone breaks their hip between

115

Thanksgiving and New Year.' Charles looked intrigued when she said it, wondering who her father was.

'Arthur Connors,' she added, and Charles instantly recognized the name.

'I know him. He's a terrific guy. I've referred patients to him.' Charles actually looked like the sort of man her father would have approved of.

'Everyone in New York refers their hardest cases to him. He's got the busiest practice in town.'

'So what made you pick psychiatry instead of going into practice with him?' Charles looked at her with interest as he sipped his wine.

'I've been fascinated by psychiatry since I was a kid. What my dad does always seems like carpentry to me. Sorry, that's an awful thing to say. I just like what I do better. And I love working with adolescents. It seems like you have a better shot at making a difference. By the time they're older, everything's pretty well set. I could never imagine myself with a Park Avenue psychiatric practice listening to a bunch of bored, neurotic housewives, or alcoholic stockbrokers who cheat on their wives.' It was the kind of thing she could only say to another physician. 'I'm sorry.' She looked embarrassed suddenly, as he laughed. 'I know that sounds awful. But kids are so much more honest, and seem much more worth saving.'

'I agree with you. But I'm not sure stockbrokers who cheat on their wives go to shrinks.'

'That's probably true,' she admitted, 'but their wives do. That kind of practice would depress me.'

'Oh, and teen suicides don't?' he challenged her, and she hesitated before she answered.

'They make me sad, but they don't depress me.

116

Most of the time, I feel useful. I don't think I'd make much difference in the lives of normal adults who just want someone to listen to them. The kids I see really need help.'

'It's a good point.' He asked her about her trauma work then, and had actually bought her most recent book, which impressed her, and halfway through lunch he told her he was divorced. He said that he and his wife had been married for twenty-one years, and two years earlier she had left him for someone else. Maxine was startled that he sounded so matter-of-fact about it. He told her it hadn't come as a complete surprise, as their marriage had been difficult for years.

'That's too bad,' Maxine said sympathetically. 'Do you have children?' He shook his head and said his wife hadn't wanted any.

'It's my only regret actually. She had a difficult childhood, and eventually decided she just wasn't up to having kids. And it's a little late for me to start now.' He didn't sound heartbroken about it, but as though it was something he was sorry he'd missed, like an interesting trip. 'Do you have children?' he asked, as their lunch arrived.

'I have three,' she said with a smile. She couldn't imagine a life without them.

'That must keep you busy. Do you have shared custody?' As far as he knew, most people did. Maxine laughed at the question.

'No. Their father travels a lot. He only sees them a few times a year. I have them full time, which works better for me.'

'How old are they?' he asked with an interested look. He had seen how her face lit up when she talked about her kids.

'Thirteen, twelve, and six. My oldest is a girl, the two others are boys.'

'That must be a handful all by yourself,' he said with admiration. 'How long have you been divorced?'

'Five years. We're on very good terms. He's a terrific person, he's just not much of a husband or father. He's too much of a kid himself. I got tired of being the only grown-up. He's more like a wild and crazy uncle for the kids. He never grew up, and I don't think he ever will.' She said it with a smile, and Charles watched her, intrigued. She was intelligent and nice, and he was impressed by the work she did. He was enjoying reading her book.

'Where does he live?'

'All over the place. London, New York, Aspen, St. Bart's. He just bought a house in Marrakech. He leads a sort of fairy-tale life.' Charles nodded, wondering whom she'd been married to, but he didn't want to ask. He was interested in her, not her ex-husband.

They chatted easily all through lunch, and she said she had to get back to see patients, and so did he. He told her how much he'd enjoyed her company, and said he'd like to see her again. She still couldn't figure out if it had been a date, or a professional courtesy, of one physician meeting another. And then he clarified it for her by asking her to dinner. She looked startled when he asked.

'I . . . oh . . . uh . . .' Maxine said, blushing. 'I thought this was just lunch . . . you know . . . because of the Wexlers.' He smiled at her. She looked so surprised that he wondered if she was involved with someone and had expected him to know it, or sense it.

'Are you seeing someone?' he asked discreetly, and she looked even more embarrassed. She was blushing.

'You mean as in dating?'

'Well, yes, as in dating.' He was laughing.

'No.' She hadn't had a real date in over a year, and hadn't slept with anyone in two. Thinking about it that way was actually depressing, and most of the time she tried not to. She just hadn't met anyone she liked in a long time, and sometimes she wondered if she didn't want to. She had gone out with a number of people after she and Blake split up, and had gotten tired of being disappointed. It seemed simpler to just forget it. The blind dates she'd gone on, courtesy of friends, had been particularly awful, and the others, with people she'd met randomly, weren't much better. 'I don't think I date,' she said awkwardly. 'Not in a while anyway. It just seemed kind of pointless.' She knew a number of people who had met through the Internet, and she couldn't imagine doing that, so she had just stopped trying and gave up dating. She hadn't planned it that way, it just happened, and she was busy.

'Would you like to have dinner?' he asked gently. It seemed hard to believe that a woman with her looks, at her age, wasn't dating. He wondered if she'd been traumatized by her marriage, or maybe by some relationship since.

'That would be fine,' she said, as though he had suggested a meeting, and he looked at her with disbelief and amusement.

'Maxine, let's get something clear here. I have the feeling you think I'm inviting you to an interdisciplinary meeting of some kind. I think it's

119

great that we're both physicians. But to be honest, I don't care if you're a go-go dancer or a hairdresser. I like you. I think you're a beautiful woman. You're fun to talk to, you have a nice sense of humor, and you don't appear to hate men, which is rare these days. Your CV would put most people to shame, man or woman. I think you're attractive and sexy. I invited you to lunch because I wanted to get to know you, as a woman. I'm inviting you to dinner, because I want to get to know you better. That's a date. We eat dinner and talk and learn about each other. Dating. Something tells me that is not on your agenda. I can't figure out why, and if there's some serious reason for it, you should probably tell me. But if not, then I would like to ask you out for a date, for dinner. Is that okay with you?' She was smiling at him, and still blushing, as he explained it.

'Yes. Okay. I think I'm a little out of practice.'

'I can't even imagine why that would be, unless you've been wearing a burka.' He thought she was gorgeous, and most men would have agreed with him. She just somehow had managed to take herself off the dating market, and had been hiding her light under a bushel. 'So when would you like to do dinner?'

'I don't know. I'm pretty free. I have a national psychiatric association dinner next week on Wednesday, otherwise I have no plans.'

'How about Tuesday? Why don't I pick you up at seven, and we'll go someplace nice?' He liked good restaurants and fine wines. It was the kind of evening she hadn't had in years, except with Blake and the kids, and those were less adult evenings. When she saw her old married friends, they didn't

120

go to restaurants, and she went to their homes for dinner. And she was even doing that less often. She had let her social life dwindle from lack of attention and interest. Charles had reminded her, without meaning to, of what a slug she had been about going out. She was still startled by his invitation, but agreed to Tuesday. She didn't make a note of their dinner plans, she knew she'd remember, and she thanked him as they got up and left. 'Where do you live, by the way?' She gave him the address, and said that he would meet her children when he picked her up, and he said he'd like that. He walked her back to her office, and she liked striding along beside him. He had been good company over lunch. And then she thanked him for lunch again, and walked back into her office, feeling dazed. She had a date. An honest-to-God dinner date, with a fairly attractive forty-nine-year-old internist. He had told her his age over lunch. She didn't know what to make of it, although she realized with a smile to herself that, if nothing else, her father would be pleased. She'd have to tell him about it the next time they talked. Or maybe after the date.

And then, all thoughts of Charles West went out of her head. Josephine was waiting in her office. Maxine took off her coat and hurried in to begin their session.

CHAPTER 7

Maxine's weekend was insanely busy. Jack had a soccer game, and she had to provide the snacks for their team. Sam went to two birthday parties, and she carpooled for both of them, and Daphne had ten friends in for pizza. It was the first time she had had friends over since the fateful beer party, so Maxine kept a close eye on them, but nothing untoward happened. Zelda was back on her feet again, but had the weekend off. She was going to an art exhibit and planning to see friends.

Maxine worked on another article in her spare time late at night. And two of her patients were hospitalized over the weekend, one for an overdose, and the other for observation as a suicide risk.

She had six kids to visit in two different hospitals on Monday, and a slew of patients in her office. And when she got home, Zelda was sick as a dog with flu and a fever. And she was worse on Tuesday morning. Maxine told her not to worry about it and to stay in bed. Daphne could bring Sam home from school, since Jack had soccer practice and was being carpooled. They could manage. And they would have, if the gods hadn't conspired against her.

Maxine had patients back to back all day. Tuesday was her day to see new patients, she had histories to take, and first meetings with adolescents were crucial, so she needed her wits about her. At noon, Sam's school called her. He had thrown up twice in the last half hour, and

122

Zelda was in no condition to go and get him. Maxine had to do it. She had a twenty-minute break between patients, got a cab, and picked Sam up at school. He looked miserable, and threw up all over her in the taxi. The driver was furious, she had nothing to clean it up with, and she tipped him twenty dollars. She got Sam upstairs, tucked him into bed, and asked Zelda to keep an eye on him, in spite of her fever. It was like leaving the wounded with the maimed, but she had no other choice. She showered, changed, and had to get back to the office. She was ten minutes late for her next patient, which made a poor impression, and the girl's mother complained about it. Maxine explained that her son was sick and apologized profusely.

Two hours later, Zelda called to say Sam had thrown up again, and had a hundred and one fever. Maxine asked her to give him Tylenol, reminded her to take some herself, and at five o'clock, it started raining. Her last patient came in late, and admitted that she'd smoked weed that afternoon, so Maxine stayed past their hour to discuss it with her. The girl had been going to Marijuana Anonymous, and this was a major slip for her, and a particularly bad idea since she was on medication.

Maxine's patient had just left when Jack called her in a panic. He had missed his car pool, and was standing alone on a street corner, in a bad area on the Upper West Side. She wanted to kill the mother who had left him. Her car was downtown in a garage, and it took her half an hour to find a taxi. It was after six when she finally got to Jack, standing shivering in the rain at a bus stop, and it was a quarter to seven when they got home in heavy traffic. They were both wet and cold, and Sam looked awful, and was crying when Maxine walked into her bedroom. She felt like she was running a hospital, as she checked on him and Zelda, and told Jack to take a hot shower. He was soaked to the skin and sneezing.

'How are you? Not sick, I hope,' she said to Daphne as she passed her on the way to Sam's room.

'I'm okay, but I have a science paper due tomorrow. Can you help me?' Maxine knew the question really was if her mother would do it for her.

'Why didn't we work on it this weekend?' Maxine asked her, looking stressed.

'I forgot I had it.'

'A likely story,' Maxine muttered, as the intercom rang in the front hall. It was the doorman; he said that a Dr. Charles West was downstairs for her, and Maxine's eyes flew open wide with a look of panic. Charles! She had forgotten. It was Tuesday. They had a date for dinner, and he was supposed to come by at seven. He was right on time, half her household was sick, and Daphne had a science paper due that Maxine was supposed to help her with. She was going to have to cancel, but it was incredibly rude at the last minute. She couldn't imagine going out, and she was wearing the clothes she'd worn to the office. Zelda was too sick for her to leave the kids with her. It was a nightmare. She looked stricken when she opened the door to Charles three minutes later, and he looked startled to see her in slacks and a sweater, with wet hair and no makeup.

124

'I'm so sorry,' she said the moment she saw him, 'I've had the day from hell. One of my kids is sick, the other one missed his ride home from soccer practice, my daughter has a science paper due tomorrow and our nanny has a fever. I'm going nuts, please come in.' He came through the front door, just as Sam wandered into the hall, looking green. 'This is my son Sam,' she explained just as Sam threw up again, and Charles stared at him in amazement.

'Oh my,' he said, and looked at Maxine with alarm.

'I'm sorry. Why don't you go in the living room and sit down? I'll be in, in a minute.' She rushed Sam into her bathroom, where he threw up again, and then she ran back to the hallway and cleaned up with a towel. She got Sam into her bed, as Daphne walked into the room.

'When can we do my paper?'

'Oh my God,' Maxine said, ready to cry or have hysterics. 'Never mind your paper. There's a man in the living room. Go talk to him. His name is Dr. West.'

'Who is he?' Daphne appeared baffled, and her mother looked crazy. She was washing her hands, and trying to comb her hair at the same time. It wasn't working.

'He's a friend. No, he's a stranger. I don't know who he is. I'm having dinner with him.'

'Now?' Daphne looked horrified. 'What about my paper? It's half of my final grade for the semester.'

'Then you should have thought about it sooner. I can't do your paper. I have a date, your brother is throwing up, Zelda is dying, and Jack is probably going to catch pneumonia from standing in the rain at a bus stop for an hour.'

'You have a *date*?' Daphne stared at her. 'When did that happen?'

'It didn't. And it probably never will at this rate. Will you please go talk to him?' As she said it, Sam said he was going to throw up again, and she ran him into the bathroom, as Daphne went to meet Charles with a look of resignation. She managed to toss over her shoulder on the way out that if she flunked, it wasn't her fault, since her mother wouldn't help with the paper. 'Why is it *my* fault?' Maxine shouted back at her from the bathroom doorway.

'I feel better,' Sam announced, but he didn't look it. Maxine put him back in her bed, with towels around him, washed her hands again, and gave up on her hair. She was about to leave the room to see Charles, when Sam looked at her mournfully from the bed. 'How come you have a date?'

'I just do. He invited me to dinner.'

'Is he nice?' Sam looked worried. He couldn't even remember the last time his mother had gone out. Nor could she.

'I don't know yet,' she said honestly. 'It's no big deal, Sam. Just dinner.' He nodded. 'I'll be back in a minute,' she reassured him. There was no way she was going out to dinner.

She reached the living room finally in time to hear Daphne telling Charles all about her father's yacht, plane, penthouse in New York, and house in Aspen. It wasn't exactly what Maxine wanted her to talk about on the first date, although she was grateful Daphne had left out London, St. Bart's,

Morocco, and Venice. She gave Daphne a quelling look and thanked her for entertaining Charles. Maxine turned to him then and apologized profusely for Sam's performance when he walked in. What she really wanted to apologize for was Daphne bragging about her father. When she showed no sign of getting up, Maxine told Daphne she needed to get started on her science paper. Daphne was reluctant to leave, but finally did so. Maxine felt like she was going to have hysterics.

'I'm so sorry. My house isn't usually this insane. I don't know what happened. Everything went nuts today. And I'm sorry about Daphne.'

'What are you sorry about? She was just talking about her father. She's very proud of him.' Maxine suspected Daphne was trying to make Charles uncomfortable intentionally, but she didn't want to say that. It was bratty of her, and she knew better. 'I didn't realize you'd been married to Blake Williams,' he said, looking a little daunted.

'Yeah,' Maxine said, wishing they could start the evening over, without the scene from *The Exorcist* on the way in. It would have helped too if she'd remembered they had a date for dinner. She hadn't written it down, and it had gone right out of her head. 'That's who I was married to. Would you like a drink?' She realized as she said it that she had nothing in the house except some cheap white wine Zelda used for cooking. Maxine had meant to buy some decent wine over the weekend but had forgotten that too.

'Are we going to dinner?' Charles asked bluntly. It didn't look like it to him, with a sick kid, another one with a paper due, and Maxine looking frazzled beyond belief.

'Would you hate me if we didn't?' she asked honestly. 'I don't know how it happened, but I forgot. I had a crazy day today, and I somehow neglected to write it down when we made the date.' She looked near tears, and he felt sorry for her. Normally, he would have been furious, but he didn't have the heart to be. The poor woman looked overwhelmed. 'This could be why I don't date. I'm not very good at it.' To say the least.

'Maybe you don't want to date,' he suggested. It had occurred to her too, and she suspected he was right. It just seemed like too much trouble, and too hard to manage. Between her work and her kids, her life was full already. There was no room for anyone else, or the time and effort it took to date.

'I'm sorry, Charles. I'm usually not like this. I run a pretty tight ship.'

'You can't help it if your son and nanny got sick. Would you like to try again? How about Friday night?' She didn't want to tell him that Zelda would be off then. If she had to, she'd ask her to work. Between the root canal the week before, and tonight, Zelda owed her one anyway, and she was a good sport about things like that.

'That would be terrific. Would you like to stay? I have to cook dinner for the kids anyway.' He had a reservation for them at La Grenouille, but he didn't want her to feel bad, so he didn't mention it to her. He was disappointed, but he told himself he was an adult, and he could handle a broken date if he had to.

'I'll stay for a little while. You've got your hands full. You don't have to cook me dinner. Would you like me to have a look at your son, and the nanny?' he offered kindly.

She smiled gratefully at him. 'That would be really nice. It's just the flu. But that's more your bailiwick than mine. If they get suicidal, I'll step in.' He laughed. He had been feeling suicidal himself watching the chaos in her house. He was not used to children, and the confusion that surrounded them. He led a quiet, orderly life, and he preferred it that way.

She walked Charles down the hall to her bedroom, where Sam was tucked into her bed, watching TV. He looked better than he had all afternoon. And he looked up when his mother walked in. He was surprised to see a man with her.

'Sam, this is Charles. He's a doctor, he's going to take a look at you.' She was smiling at her son, and Charles could see how crazy she was about her kids. It would have been hard to miss.

'Is that your date?' Sam asked with suspicion.

'Yes, it is,' Maxine said, looking embarrassed. 'His name is Dr. West.'

'Charles,' he corrected with an easy smile as he approached the bed. 'Hi, Sam. Looks like you're feeling pretty crummy. Have you been throwing up all day?'

'Six times,' Sam said proudly. 'I threw up in the taxi coming home from school.' Charles glanced at Maxine with a sympathetic grin. He could imagine the scene.

'That doesn't sound like fun. Can I touch your tummy?' Sam nodded and pulled up the top of his pajamas, as his brother walked in.

'You had to call a doctor for him?' Jack looked instantly worried.

'He's her date,' Sam explained as Jack looked confused.

129

'Who's her date?' Jack asked.

'The doctor,' Sam told his brother, as Maxine introduced Jack to Charles, who turned to smile at him.

'You must be the soccer player.' Jack nodded, wondering where the mysterious doctor/date had come from, and why he hadn't heard about him. 'What position do you play? I played soccer in college. I was better at basketball, but I thought soccer was more fun.'

'Me too. I want to play lacrosse next year,' Jack volunteered as Maxine watched them.

'Lacrosse is a tough sport. You get a lot more injuries in lacrosse than in soccer,' Charles said, as he stood up after examining Sam, and then he looked down at the little boy with a smile. 'I think you're going to make it, Sam. I'll bet you feel better by tomorrow.'

'Do you think I'll throw up again?' Sam looked worried.

'I hope not. Just take it easy tonight. Would you like some Coke or ginger ale?' Sam nodded, assessing Charles with interest. As Maxine watched them, she realized how unfamiliar it was to all of them to have a man in their midst, but it was nice. And he had a sweet way with them. She could see that Jack was checking him out too. And a minute later, Daphne walked back in. They were all standing in their mother's bedroom, which seemed suddenly too small with so many people in it. 'Where are you hiding the sick nanny?' Charles asked her.

'I'll show you,' Maxine said, and led him out of the room, as Sam giggled and started to say something, and Jack put a finger to his lips to silence him. Maxine and Charles could hear them giggling and whispering as they walked away, as Maxine turned to Charles with an apologetic grin. 'This is a little different for them.'

'So I gather. They're nice kids,' he said easily, as they walked into the kitchen and then the hallway beyond. Maxine knocked on the door to Zelda's room, quietly opened it, and offered to have Charles take a look at her. She made the introductions from the doorway. Zelda looked instantly confused. She had no idea who Dr. West was or why he was there.

'I'm not that sick,' she said, looking embarrassed, thinking Maxine had called him just for her. 'It's just the flu.'

'He was here anyway, and he just took a look at Sam.' Zelda wondered if he was a new pediatrician she didn't know about. It never occurred to her that Maxine had a dinner date with him. And he told her pretty much the same thing he had told Sam.

A few minutes later, Maxine and Charles were standing in her kitchen, and she handed him a Coke, a bowl of chips, and some guacamole she found in the fridge. He said he was going to leave in a few minutes and let her take care of her kids. She had enough on her hands. She sat down at the kitchen table with him and they chatted for a few minutes. He had certainly had his trial by fire, and had met them all. Sam throwing up as he walked in was certainly one way to introduce Charles to her children, though not the one she would have chosen. As far as Maxine was concerned, he had passed with flying colors. She wasn't sure how he felt about it, but he had certainly been a good sport. This was by no means a standard first date. Far from it.

'I'm sorry tonight was such a mess,' she apologized again.

'It worked out fine,' he said easily, thinking longingly for a minute of the dinner they would have had at La Grenouille. 'We'll have a nice time on Friday night. I guess you have to be flexible when you have kids.'

'Usually, not as flexible as this. I'm pretty well organized most of the time. Today just got out of hand. Mostly because Zellie was sick too. I count on her a lot.' He nodded. It was obvious that she had to have someone to rely on, and her ex-husband wasn't around. After what Daphne had told him, he could see why. He had read about Blake Williams over the years. He was a major figure in the jet set, and didn't sound like a family man. Maxine had said as much over lunch.

Charles went to say goodbye to the children before he left, and told Sam he hoped he'd feel better soon.

'Thanks,' Sam said, and waved goodbye. And a moment later, Maxine let Charles out.

'I'll pick you up at seven on Friday,' Charles promised, and she thanked him again for being so nice about tonight. 'Don't worry about it. At least I got to meet all your kids.' He waved as he got in the elevator, and a moment later she collapsed on her bed next to Sam with a sigh, as the others walked in.

'So how come you didn't tell us you had a date?' Jack complained.

'I forgot about it.'

'Who is he anyway?' Daphne looked suspicious.

132

'Just a doctor I met,' Maxine said, looking exhausted. She didn't want to have to justify it to them. Tonight had been bad enough. 'And by the way,' she said to her daughter, 'you shouldn't brag about your father like that. It's not nice.'

'Why not?' Daphne looked instantly defiant.

'Because talking about his yacht and his plane isn't cool. It could make people uncomfortable.' Which of course was precisely why she had done it. Daphne shrugged and walked out of the room.

'He's okay,' Sam pronounced.

'Yeah, maybe,' Jack said, sounding unconvinced. He didn't see why his mother needed a man around. They were doing fine the way they were. It didn't shock them that their father went out with women, even a lot of them. They weren't used to seeing a man in their mother's life, and none of them liked the idea. It worked fine for them having her to themselves. And there was no reason why that should change, in their opinion anyway. Their mother got the message loud and clear.

It was eight o'clock by then and none of them had eaten, so Maxine went out to the kitchen to see what she could dig up. As she was pulling out salad and some cold meats and eggs, Zelda walked in in her bathrobe, looking puzzled.

'Who was that masked man, Tonto?' she asked Maxine, and her employer laughed.

'I guess the correct answer to that is the Lone Ranger. Actually, he's a doctor I met. I had a date with him, and I completely forgot. Sam threw up all over the front hall as he walked in. It was quite a scene.'

'Think you'll ever see him again?' Zelda asked with interest. She thought he'd seemed nice. And

133

good looking.

She knew that Maxine hadn't had a date in a long time, and this one looked promising to her. He seemed the right type, he was nice-looking, and she thought the fact that they were both physicians was a good beginning to establish common ground.

'Supposedly he's taking me out on Friday night,' Maxine said in answer to her question. 'If he recovers from tonight.'

'That's interesting,' Zelda commented, poured herself a glass of ginger ale, and went back to bed.

Maxine made pasta, cold cuts, and scrambled eggs, and they had brownies for dessert. She cleaned up the kitchen, and then went to help Daphne with her paper. They didn't finish until twelve o'clock. It had been a hell of a day, and a long night. And when she finally slipped into her bed next to Sam, she had a minute to think about Charles. She had no idea what would come of it, or if she'd see him again after Friday night, but in its own way, tonight hadn't been so bad. He hadn't run out the door screaming at least. That was something. And for now, it was enough.

CHAPTER 8

On Friday night, when Charles appeared to pick her up, everything worked like a Swiss clock. The house was deserted. Zelda was off. Daphne was spending the night with friends, as was Sam, having recovered from the flu, and Jack was at a party at a friend's before a bar mitzvah the next night. Maxine had bought scotch, vodka, gin, champagne, and a bottle of Pouilly-Fuissé. She was ready for him. She was wearing a short black dress, her hair in a neat bun, diamond earrings, and a string of pearls, and the house was silent.

When she let him in on the dot of seven, Charles entered with the look of a man heading across a minefield. He looked around, listened to the deafening silence, and stared at her in amazement.

'What did you do with your kids?' he asked nervously, and she smiled at him.

'I put them up for adoption, and fired the nanny. I was sad to let them go, but you have to have priorities in life. I didn't want to spoil another evening. They went very quickly.' He laughed and followed her into the kitchen, where she poured him a scotch and soda at his request, and carried a silver bowl of nuts into the living room. The silence was almost eerie. 'I'm really sorry about Tuesday, Charles.' It had been a scene right out of a movie. Or real life. A little too much so.

'It was kind of like hazing when I was in college.' Getting put in the trunk of a car with alcohol poisoning might have been easier and more fun, but he was willing to give it another shot. There was a lot about Maxine that he liked. She was a serious, intelligent woman with a booming career in the medical field, highly respected, and she was beautiful as well. It was a combination that was tough to beat. The only thing about her that unnerved him somewhat were her kids. He just wasn't used to that, and didn't feel a need for children in his life. But they were part of the package with her. And this time, at least, she had gotten them out of the way, and they would be able to enjoy an adult evening, which was what he preferred.

La Grenouille had very kindly given him another reservation for eight o'clock that night, and hadn't held Tuesday's last-minute cancellation against him. He went there often and was a good client. Maxine and Charles left her apartment at a quarter to eight, and reached the restaurant precisely on time, and were given an excellent table. The evening had been perfect so far, he observed, but the night was young. Nothing would have startled him now, after the introduction he'd had to her life three days before. For a minute there, he had been tempted to run. But now he was glad he hadn't. He liked Maxine a lot, and she was great to talk to.

For the first half of dinner, over scallops, soft shell crab, followed by pheasant and Chateaubriand, they discussed their work, and current medical issues that were pertinent to both of them. He liked her ideas, and was impressed by her accomplishments. And they were just starting on their soufflés when he mentioned Blake.

'I'm surprised your children aren't more critical of him, since you say he's such a no-show with them and is never around.' He realized that that was a real testimonial to her, since she could easily have turned them against him, and most women would, given how little he helped her.

'He's basically a nice man,' she said simply. 'Wonderful, in fact. And they see that. He's just not very attentive.'

'He sounds very selfish, and incredibly self-indulgent,' Charles observed, and Maxine conceded that he wasn't wrong.

'It would be hard not to be,' Maxine said quietly,

'given what happened with his success. Very few people could resist that and keep a level head. He has a lot of toys, and he likes to have fun. All the time, in fact. Blake doesn't do anything that's not fun, or high risk. That's just his style, it always was. The other path he could have chosen was to pour his money into philanthropy. And he does a fair amount of that, but he's not involved in charity in any hands-on kind of way. Basically, he figures that life is short, he's been lucky, and he wants to have a good time. He was adopted, and I think in a funny way, even though he had nice adoptive parents who loved him, he's always been insecure about life, and about himself. He wants to grab everything he can, before someone takes it away from him, or he loses it. That's a tough pathology to fight. The constant fear of abandonment and loss, so he grabs everything with both hands, and loses in the end anyway. Kind of a self-fulfilling prophecy.'

'He must be very sorry he lost you,' Charles said cautiously.

'Not really. We're good friends. I see him with the kids whenever he's in town. I'm still part of his life in a different way, as a friend and the mother of his kids. He knows he can count on me. He always could. And he has plenty of girlfriends, who are a lot younger and a lot more fun than I am, or ever was. I was always too serious for him.' Charles nodded. He liked that about her, and she suited him just fine. He found her relationship with her ex-husband strange. He almost never spoke to his ex-wife. Without children to bind them to each other, after the divorce there was nothing left, but a fair amount of animosity between them. Mostly,

137

there was nothing. It was as if they had never been married. 'When you have children,' Maxine said quietly, 'you're kind of stuck with each other forever. And I have to admit, if we didn't have that, I would miss him. This works for all of us, especially the kids. It would be sad if their dad and I hated each other.' Possibly, Charles thought as he listened to her, but maybe easier for the next man or woman in their lives. Blake was a tough act to follow, for anyone, and in her own way, so was she, although she was very modest.

There was nothing arrogant or pompous about Maxine, in spite of her very successful psychiatric career, and even the books she had written. She was very low key, and he liked that about her. He wasn't nearly as much so, and he knew that about himself. Charles West had a fairly good opinion of himself, and wasn't shy by any means about his own accomplishments. He hadn't hesitated to try to strong-arm her into doing things his way over the Wexler boy, and only backed off later when he found out who Maxine was, and how expert she was in her field. Only then had he conceded that she knew better, particularly after Jason's third suicide attempt, which had left Charles unnerved and feeling foolish. He usually hated to admit he was wrong, but had no other choice in that case. Maxine was powerful, but both feminine and gentle. She didn't need to throw her weight around, and rarely did, except when a patient's life was at stake, but never to feed her ego. In many ways, to Charles, she seemed like the perfect woman, and he had never met anyone like her.

'How do your children feel about your dating?' he asked her as they finished dinner. He didn't quite dare ask her what they had said about him, although he wondered. It had been clear on Tuesday night that they had been startled to see him. And she obviously hadn't prepared them, since she had forgotten their date completely. His appearance on the scene had taken everyone by surprise, including Maxine when he walked in. And in turn, with everything that had happened after that, they had surprised the hell out of him. He had told a friend about it the next day, who had roared with laughter at Charles's description of the chaotic scene, and had said in no uncertain terms that it would do him good and loosen him up a little. 'Couldn't happen to a nicer guy' had been his comment. As a rule, Charles preferred not to go out with women with children. He found it hard to spend time together when they were so wrapped up in their children's lives. Usually at least they had ex-husbands who took the kids half the time. Maxine had no one to take the heat off her, except a nanny, who was human and had her own problems. There was a lot resting on Maxine's shoulders, and being with Maxine would be a challenge for him because of that.

'They were pretty surprised,' Maxine said honestly. 'I haven't dated in a long time. They're used to the women in their father's life, but I don't think it has even occurred to them that there might be someone in mine one day.' And she hadn't adjusted to the idea either. The men she had gone out with briefly had been of so little interest to her, and so unappealing that she had given up the concept.

The doctors she met always seemed pompous to her, or she had nothing in common with them, and they found the demands of her practice and home life too taxing. Most men didn't want a woman or a wife who went to the hospital for emergencies at four in the morning, and had that many demands on them outside the home. Blake hadn't loved it either, but her medical career had always been important to her, and her children even more so. Her cup was very full, and as Tuesday night had proven, it didn't take much for it to run over. There wasn't much room, if any, for anyone else. And he suspected that that suited her children. It had been clearly written on all their faces when he met them, that they wanted her to themselves, and he was not welcome in their midst. They didn't need him. And he suspected she didn't either. She didn't have that desperate quality of most women her age, who wanted more than anything to meet a man. What she conveyed instead was that she was happy, fulfilled, and doing fine on her own. And that appealed to him too. He had no desire to be anyone's savior, although he did want to be the hub of a woman's life. And with Maxine, he never would be. There were both positives and negatives to that.

'Do you think they'd adjust to your being involved with someone?' he asked casually, checking it out, and Maxine thought about it for a moment.

'Probably. Maybe. It would depend on the person, and how well they adjusted to my kids. Those things work two ways, and take some effort from both sides.' Charles nodded. It was a reasonable answer.

'What about you? Do you think you'd adjust to having a man in your life again, Maxine? You seem pretty self-sufficient.'

'I am,' she said honestly, sipping at a delicate mint infusion, which was the perfect end to a great meal. The dinner had been delicious, and the wines he had chosen superb. 'To answer your question, I don't know the answer to that. I could only make the adjustment for the right man. I'd have to really believe it could work. I don't want to make another mistake. Blake and I were just too different. You don't notice it as much when you're young. After a certain point, when you're grown up and know who you are, it really matters. You can't kid yourself at our age, that something will work when it really doesn't. It's a lot harder to make the gears mesh later on, because there are more of them. It's all good fun when you're a kid. Later, it's another story. And it's not so easy to find the right match, there are a lot fewer candidates, and even with the good ones, there's a lot of baggage. It has to be worth the effort of making the adjustment. And my children give me an excuse not to try. They keep me busy and happy. The trouble is that one day they'll grow up, and I'll wind up alone. I don't have to face that right now.' She was right, and he nodded. They were a buffer against loneliness for her, and an excuse to be lazy about letting a man into her life. Somewhere, he suspected she was scared to try again. He had the impression that Blake had taken a big part of her with him, and even if they were 'too different,' as she claimed, he had the feeling she still loved him. That could be a problem too. And who could compete with a legend who had become a billionaire and had that much charm? It was a hell of a challenge, one that few men would take on, and clearly hadn't.

They moved on to other topics then, more about their work, her passion for her suicidal adolescent patients, her compassion for their parents, her fascination with trauma caused by public events. By comparison, his practice was far less interesting than hers. He dealt with the common cold, a host of more mundane ailments and situations, and the occasional sadness of a patient with cancer whom he immediately referred to a specialist and lost sight of. His practice did not revolve around crisis the way hers did, although he occasionally lost a patient too, but it was rare.

He came back to the apartment afterward and had a glass of brandy from her newly stocked bar. She was totally equipped now to entertain a date, even if she never saw him again. She would be fully stocked for the next one, five or ten years from now. Zelda had teased her about it. She had a very proper bar as a result of her date with him, which worried her a little with the kids around. She was planning to lock up the booze, to keep it away from them and their friends. She didn't want to provide any temptation. Daphne had reminded her of that.

Maxine thanked him for a wonderful dinner, and a terrific evening. She had to admit it was nice being civilized, getting dressed up, and spending an evening talking to an adult. It was a lot more exciting than KFC or Burger King with half a dozen kids in tow, which was more her style. Although to look at her, in her pristine elegance, Charles thought she deserved to go to La Grenouille more often, and he hoped to have the opportunity to take her there again. It was his favorite restaurant in town, although he liked Le Cirque too. He had a great fondness for excellent French food, and the atmosphere that went with it. He liked pomp and ceremony far more than she did, and adult evenings. He wondered as he talked to her if going out with her children would be fun too. It was possible, but he was not yet convinced, even if they were cute kids. He preferred talking to her without distraction, or Sam throwing up at his feet. They both laughed about it as he left, and they stood chatting for a moment in the same front hall where it had happened.

'I'd like to see you again, Maxine,' he said comfortably. From his perspective, the evening had been a success, and from hers too, despite their disastrous first beginning. Tonight had been entirely the reverse. It was perfect.

'I'd like that too,' she said simply.

'I'll call you,' he said, and made no move to kiss her. She would have been shocked and put off if he did. That wasn't his style. He moved slowly and deliberately when he liked a woman, setting the stage for something to happen later on, if they both chose that. He was in no rush, and never liked to push women too hard or too soon. It had to be a mutual decision, and he knew Maxine was nowhere near that point. She had been off the dating scene for too long, and had never really been in it. The concept of a relationship was not even on her mind. He would have to bring her around to that slowly, if he decided it was what he wanted. He wasn't sure about it yet either. She was nice to talk to and spend time with, the rest remained to be seen. Her kids were still a big hurdle for him to get over.

143

She thanked him again and gently closed the door. Jack was asleep in his room by then, after the party he'd gone to, as was Zelda in hers. The apartment was quiet as Maxine got undressed, brushed her teeth, and got into bed, thinking about Charles. It had been nice, there was no question about that. But it felt weird to her to be out with a man. It was so grown up, and so polite. And so was he. She couldn't imagine hanging around with him on a Sunday afternoon, with her kids around her, as she did with Blake when he was in town. But then again, he was their father, and his life wasn't home-centered either. He was only a tourist passing through their lives, although an appealing one. Blake was a comet in their skies.

Charles was solid, and they had a lot in common. He was very serious, and he appealed to that side of her. But he wasn't light-hearted or playful or a lot of fun. For a moment, she missed that in her life, and then realized that you couldn't have everything. If she ever got seriously involved with anyone again, she had always said she wanted someone solid she could rely on. Charles was certainly that kind of man. Then she thought to herself with a smile, beware of what you wish for. Blake was crazy and fun. Charles was responsible and adult. It was a shame that nowhere on the planet there was a man who could be both—a kind of grown-up Peter Pan, with good values. It was a lot to ask, and probably why, she told herself, she was still alone, and maybe always would be. You couldn't live with a man like Blake, and you might not want to with a man like Charles. Maybe it didn't matter, no one was asking her to make that choice. It was just dinner after all, good food and fine wines with an intelligent man. This wasn't about marriage.

CHAPTER 9

Blake was in London, meeting with his investment counselors about three new companies he was planning to take over. He was also meeting with two architects, one to make changes in the London house, the other to completely remodel and refurbish the palace he had bought in Morocco. There were a total of six decorators involved in both projects, and it was exciting for him. He was having a ball. He was planning to be in London for a month, and take the children to Aspen after Christmas. He had invited Maxine to join them, but she had decided not to come, and said he needed time alone with the children, which seemed silly to him. They always had a good time when she came along.

Most of the time, she just overlapped for a day here and there when he loaned her his boat, or one of his houses. He was generous to a fault, and loved knowing that she was having a good time with their children. He often loaned his homes to friends as well. There was no way he could use all of them full time. And he couldn't understand why Maxine had made such a fuss about his letting Daphne use the New York penthouse with her friends. She was old enough not to make a mess in the apartment, and there were people to clean it up if she did. He thought Maxine was being paranoid thinking that they would get into mischief there alone. He knew his daughter was a good girl, and how much trouble could they get into at thirteen? After five phone calls about it, he had finally given in to Maxine's wishes, but it seemed a shame to him. The New York penthouse stood empty most of the time. He was in London far more often, as it was more central to all the other places where he liked to spend his time. He was planning to go to Gstaad for a few days of skiing before he went back to New York, to warm up for Aspen. He hadn't skied since a quick trip to South America in May.

In his first few days back in London after seeing his children for Thanksgiving, Blake had been invited to a Rolling Stones concert. They were one of his favorite groups, and he and Mick Jagger were old friends. He had introduced Blake to a number of other players in the rock-star world, and several remarkable women. Blake's brief affair with one of the biggest female rock stars in the world had made headlines everywhere, until she spoiled everything and married someone else. That wasn't his game, and he was honest about it. He never pretended to anyone that he wanted to get married, or was even open to it. He had far too much money now. Marriage was much too dangerous for him, unless he married someone who had as much as he did, and those were never the women he went after. He liked them young, lively, and unencumbered. All he wanted to do was play. He didn't hurt anyone. And when it was over, they left with jewels, furs, cars, presents, and the best memories they ever had. And then he moved on to the next one, and started all over again. And when he got back to London, he was free at the moment. He had no one to take to the Rolling Stones concert, so he went by himself, and to a fabulous party at Kensington Palace afterward. Every royal, model, actress, socialite, aristocrat, and rock star was there. It was everything that Blake loved, and his world.

He had talked to half a dozen women that night, met some interesting men, and was thinking about leaving, when he ordered one last drink at the bar, and saw a pretty redhead smiling at him. She had a diamond in her nose, was wearing a ruby bindi and a sari, had spiky hair, and tattoos running down her arms, and she was staring unabashedly at him. She didn't look Indian, but the ruby bindi between her eyebrows confused him, and the sari she wore was the color of a summer sky, the same color as her eyes. He had never seen an Indian woman with tattoos before. Hers were flowers running up and down her arms, and there was another on her taut flat stomach, which the sari exposed. She was drinking champagne, and eating olives from a glass bowl on the bar.

'Hello,' he said simply, his dazzling blue eyes meeting hers, and her slow smile grew broader. She was the sexiest woman he had ever seen, and it was impossible to tell her age. She could have been anywhere from eighteen to thirty, and he didn't care how old she was. She was gorgeous. 'Where are you from?' he asked her, expecting her to say Bombay or New Delhi, although the red hair was out of context too. She laughed at his question, showing perfect white teeth that went on forever. She was the most striking woman he'd ever seen.

'Knightsbridge,' she said, laughing at him. Her laughter was like bells in his ears, delicate and sweet.

'What about the bindi?'

'I just like them. I lived in Jaipur for two years. I loved the saris and the jewels.' Who didn't? And five minutes after he'd met her, Blake was crazy about her. 'Have you been to India?' she asked him.

'Several times,' he said easily. 'I went on an incredible safari, taking photographs of tigers last year, much better than anything I've seen in Kenya.' She raised an eyebrow then.

'I was born in Kenya. My family lived in Rhodesia before that. And then we came home. It's rather tedious here. I go back every chance I get.' She was British, and she had the accent and intonations of the upper classes, which made him wonder who she was, and who her parents were. It didn't usually interest him, but everything about this woman intrigued him, even her tattoos. 'And you are?' she inquired. She was probably the only woman in the room who didn't know who he was, and he liked that about her too. It was refreshing. And he sensed correctly that they had been attracted to each other instantly. Powerfully so.

'Blake Williams.' He provided no further information, and she nodded and finished her champagne. He was drinking vodka, on the rocks. It was his drink of choice at events like this. Champagne gave him a headache the next day, vodka didn't.

'American,' she said matter-of-factly. 'Married?' she asked with interest, which he found an odd question.

'No. Why?'

'I don't do married men. I don't even talk to

148

them. I went out with a horrible Frenchman who was married and lied about it. Once burned, forever wise, or something like that. Americans are usually pretty good about that. The French aren't. They always have a wife and a mistress tucked away somewhere, and cheat on both. Do you cheat?' she asked him, as though it were a sport like golf or tennis, and he laughed.

'Not generally. No, actually, I don't think I ever have. I have no reason to, I'm not married, and if I want to sleep with someone else, I end it with the woman I'm with. That seems a lot simpler to me. I don't like drama or complications.'

'Neither do I. That's what I mean about Americans. They're very simple and straightforward. Europeans are far more complicated. They want everything to be difficult. My parents have been trying to get divorced for twelve years. They keep getting back together and splitting up again. It's very confusing for the rest of us. I've never been married myself, and don't want to be. It seems like a terrible mess to me.' She said it very simply, as though talking about the weather or a trip, and he was amused. She was a very funny young woman, very pretty, and what the Brits called 'very fey.' She was like some sort of wood nymph or sprite in her sari and her bindi and tattoos. He noticed then that she was wearing an enormous emerald bracelet that got lost among her tattoos, and a huge ruby ring. Whoever she was, she had plenty of jewels.

'I'd have to agree with you about the mess people make. I'm actually very good friends with my ex-wife. We like each other even better than we did when we were married.' For him, it was true,

149

and he was sure Maxine felt the same way about it too.

'Do you have kids?' she inquired, offering him some of her olives. He dropped two in his drink.

'Yes, I do, three. A girl and two boys. Thirteen, twelve, and six.'

'How sweet. I don't want children, but I think people are very brave to have them. It seems rather frightening to me. All that responsibility, they get sick, you have to make sure they're doing well in school, have good manners. It's even harder than training a horse or a dog, and I'm terrible at both. I had a dog once that did its business all over my house. I'm sure I'd be even worse with kids.' He laughed at the picture she painted, as Mick Jagger wandered by and said hello to her, as did several other people. Everyone seemed to know her except Blake, and he couldn't understand why he had never met her before. He spent a lot of time on the London scene.

He told her about the house in Marrakech then, visibly excited about it, and she agreed that it sounded like a fabulous project. She said that she had nearly studied architecture and decided not to, she could never do the math. She said she'd been terrible in school.

A number of his friends came up to him and said hello then, as did quite a few of hers, and the next thing he knew when he turned to look for her, she had disappeared. Blake was frustrated and disappointed. He had liked talking to her. She was eccentric, intelligent, outspoken, and different, and beautiful enough to catch his eye. He asked Mick Jagger about her later, and he laughed at Blake.

'You don't know her?' He seemed surprised. 'That's Arabella. She's a viscountess. Her father is supposed to be the richest man in the House of Lords.'

'What does she do?' He assumed she did nothing, but he had gotten the sense from talking to her that she had some kind of job or career.

'She's a painter. She does portraits. She's very good. People pay her a fortune to do their portraits. She also does their horses and dogs. She's completely crazy, but she's actually very nice. She's sort of typically British eccentric. I think she was engaged to some very fancy Frenchman, a marquis or something. I don't know what happened, but she didn't marry him. She went out to India instead, had an affair with some very important Indian chap, and came home, with a hell of a lot of good-looking jewels. I can't believe you don't know her. Maybe she was in India when you were around. She's a lot of fun,' he confirmed.

'Yes, she is,' Blake said, somewhat in awe of what Jagger had said about her. It all fit. 'Do you know how I'd find her? I didn't get her number before she left.'

'Sure. Have your secretary call mine tomorrow. I've got her number. So does everyone else. Half of England has had their portrait done by her. You can always use that as an excuse.' Blake wasn't sure he needed one, but it was certainly a possibility. He left the party then, sorry she had left before him, and his secretary got him the number the next morning. It hadn't been difficult at all.

He sat looking at the piece of paper for a minute, and then called her himself. A woman answered, and he recognized the voice of the night

151

before.

'Arabella?' he said, trying to sound confident, and feeling awkward for the first time in a long time. She was more like a whirlwind than a woman, and far more sophisticated than the girls he usually picked up.

'Yes, it is,' she said, in her clipped British way. And then she laughed before she even knew who it was. It was the same tinkling of fairy bells that he had heard the night before. She was magic.

'This is Blake Williams. I met you last night at the party at Kensington Palace, at the bar. You left before I had a chance to say goodbye.'

'You looked busy, so I slipped away. How nice of you to call.' She sounded sincere, and pleased to hear him.

'I actually wanted to say hello more than goodbye. Are you free for lunch?' He cut to the chase, and she laughed again.

'No, I'm not,' she said regretfully. 'I'm doing a portrait, and my subject can only come in during lunch. The prime minister, his schedule is awfully tight. What about tomorrow?'

'I'd like that very much,' Blake said, feeling about twelve years old. She was twenty-nine and he felt like a child with her, even at forty-six. 'How about Santa Lucia at one?' It had been Princess Di's favorite restaurant for lunch, and everyone else's ever since.

'Perfect. I'll be there,' she promised. 'See you then.' And before he knew it, she was off the line. No chitchat, no further conversation. Just the bare bones necessary to make the appointment for lunch. He wondered if she'd show up in the bindi and the sari. All he knew was that he couldn't wait to see her. He hadn't been this excited about anyone in years.

Blake arrived at Santa Lucia promptly at one the next day, and stood at the bar waiting for her. Arabella walked in twenty minutes later, her short red hair sticking up straight, a miniskirt, high-heeled brown suede boots, and an enormous lynx coat. She looked like a character in a movie, and there was no sign of her bindi. She looked more like Milan or Paris, and her eyes were the electrifying blue he remembered. She beamed the moment she saw him, and gave him a warm hug.

'You're so nice to take me to lunch,' she said, as though that had never happened to her before, which was obviously not the case. She was very glamorous, and at the same time very unassuming, and Blake loved that about her. He felt like a puppy at her feet, which was rare for him, as the headwaiter took them to their table, and made as big a fuss over Arabella as he did over Blake.

The conversation flowed with ease over lunch. Blake asked her about her work, and he talked about his experience in the high-tech dot-com world, which she found fascinating. They chatted about art, architecture, sailing, horses, dogs, his kids. They exchanged thoughts about everything imaginable and left the restaurant at four o'clock. He said he'd love to see her work, and she invited him to the studio the next day, after her next session with Tony Blair. She said other than that, she had an easy week, and was of course leaving for the country on Friday. Everyone who was anyone in England went to the country on the weekend, to their homes or someone else's. When they left each other on the street, he could hardly

153

wait to see her again. He was suddenly obsessed with her, and sent her flowers that afternoon, with a clever note. She called the minute they arrived. He had sent orchids and roses, with lily of the valley tucked in. He had used the best florist in London, and had sent everything exotic he could think of, which seemed fitting for her. Blake thought she was the most interesting woman he had ever met, and sexy beyond belief.

He went to her studio late the next morning, just after Tony Blair left, and was totally startled by how Arabella looked. She was a woman of many faces, exotic, glamorous, childlike, a waif, one moment a beauty queen, and the next an elf. She opened the door to her studio wearing paint-splattered skintight jeans, high-top red Converse sneakers, and a white T-shirt, with an enormous ruby bracelet on one arm, and she was wearing the bindi again. Everything about her was a little crazy, but utterly fascinating to him. She showed him several portraits in progress, and some old ones she had done for herself. There were some beautiful horse portraits, and he thought the one of the prime minister extremely good. She was as talented as Mick Jagger had said.

'They're fantastic,' he said to her, 'absolutely wonderful, Arabella.' She opened a bottle of champagne, she said to celebrate his first visit to her studio, the first of many, she hoped, as she toasted him. He drank two glasses with her, in spite of his aversion to champagne. He would have drunk poison for her, and then he suggested they go back to his place. He wanted to show her his treasures now too. He had some very important art, and an absolutely spectacular house that he

154

loved and was very proud of. They found a taxi easily, and half an hour later, they were wandering through his house, as she screamed with excitement over the art she saw. He opened another bottle of champagne for her, but he drank vodka this time. He turned on the sound system, showed her the theater he had had built, he showed her everything, and by nine o'clock they were in his enormous bed, making mad, passionate love to each other. He had never had an experience like that with any woman, even on drugs, which he had experimented with lightly at one point, and never liked. Arabella herself was like a drug to him, and he felt as though he had gone to the moon and back, as they lay in his enormous bathtub together later, and she slid on top of him, and began riding him again. He moaned in exquisite agony as he came in her, for the fourth time that night, and he heard the magical sound of her laughter, as the impossible wood sprite he had discovered at Kensington Palace drove him to the edge of sanity and back. He didn't know what this was with her, love or madness, but whatever it was, he never wanted it to end.

CHAPTER 10

The following Friday night, Charles and Maxine managed another very grown-up dinner at La Grenouille. They both had lobster and an exquisite white truffle risotto that was almost like an aphrodisiac, it was so good. And once again,

Maxine had enjoyed the meal, even more this time. She liked their intelligent, adult conversations, and he didn't seem quite as serious as he had before. He had a sense of humor after all, although he kept it in check. Nothing about Charles ever seemed out of control. He said he preferred everything in his life planned and in good order, moderate, predictable. It was the kind of life Maxine had always wanted, which had been impossible with Blake. And it wasn't totally feasible for her either, with three children and the unpredictable elements in their lives, and the kind of practice she had, where the unexpected happened regularly. But their personalities were a good fit. He was far closer to what she wanted than Blake had been, and she told herself that if Charles was less spontaneous, that was reassuring in some ways too. She knew what to expect of him. And he was a nice person, which appealed to her too.

They were in the cab on the way home, after their second dinner date at La Grenouille. He had promised Le Cirque next time, and maybe after that Daniel or Café Boulud, all his favorite haunts, which he wanted to share with her, when her cell phone rang, and she assumed it was one of the kids, looking for her. She was off call to Thelma Washington that weekend. Instead, it was her service trying to locate her for Dr. Washington, which Maxine knew meant it was something serious with one of her regular patients. That was the only time Thelma called her on weekends. Otherwise, she handled everything herself, except the situations she knew Maxine would want to be told about and participate in. Thelma's voice came on the line after the service put her through.

'Hi. What's up?' Maxine said quickly, and Charles thought it was one of her kids. He hoped it wasn't an emergency. They had had such a pleasant evening, he didn't want anything distressing to intrude. Maxine was listening carefully, frowning, with her eyes closed, and it didn't look good to him. 'How many units of blood have you given her?' There was silence again as Maxine listened to the answer. 'Can you get a cardiothoracic guy in right away? Try Jones . . . Shit . . . okay . . . I'll be right in.' She turned to Charles with a worried look. 'I'm sorry. I hate to do this to you. One of my patients just came in, code blue. Can I hijack the cab to Columbia Presbyterian? I don't have time to go home and change. I can drop you off on the way.' Her mind was full of what Thelma had said to her. It was a fifteen-year-old girl she had been seeing for only a few months. She had attempted suicide, and was hovering near death. Maxine wanted to be there, to make whatever decisions she could. Charles looked instantly sobered, and said of course she could take the cab.

'Why don't I go with you? I can hang around and lend moral support if nothing else.' He could only guess how hard those cases were, and Maxine made a career of them. He couldn't imagine dealing with that every day, but he admired her for it. And medically, it was far more interesting than what he did, much more stressful, and more important in a way.

'I might be there all night. At least I hope I will.' The only reason she wouldn't be was if the patient died, which was a strong possibility right now.

'No problem. If I get tired of waiting I'll go

157

home. Hell, I'm a physician too, this isn't news to me.' She smiled. She liked having that in common with him. It was a strong bond to share medical careers. They gave the driver the hospital's address uptown, and sped north as Maxine explained the situation to Charles. The girl had cut herself, slashed her wrists, and stabbed herself in the heart with a kitchen knife. She had done a hell of a job. And by sheer miracle, her mother had found her fast enough to make a difference. The paramedics had been on the scene in minutes. They had given her two units of blood so far, her heart had stopped twice on the way in, and they had gotten it going again. She was hovering near death, but still alive. This was her second attempt.

'Christ, they don't go at it halfway, do they? I always thought kids did it for attention and made kind of half-assed attempts.' There was nothing half-assed about this. They talked about it quietly on the way, and Maxine sprang into action the moment they walked in. She was wearing a black cocktail dress and high heels. She dumped her black evening coat, put a lab coat over her dress, found Thelma, and met with the ER team. She examined her patient, contacted the heart surgeon herself, and talked to the attending and the chief resident. Her patient's wrists were already sewn up, and the heart surgeon was there fifteen minutes later, and whisked the comatose girl into surgery, as Maxine comforted the parents. While she did, Charles and Thelma conferred quietly in the hallway.

'She's something, isn't she?' Charles said in admiration. She was like a tornado of efficiency once she was working. And she was back to them in the hallway half an hour later. Thelma agreed with Charles completely, and liked the fact that he was so impressed and respectful of Maxine's work.

'How's she doing?' Thelma asked Maxine. She had stayed more to keep Charles company than for any other purpose. Maxine was in charge now.

'Hanging in. This is a close one,' Maxine said, praying not to lose her.

Eloise, her patient, was in surgery for four hours, and it was nearly five before Maxine knew anything conclusive. Much to her amazement, Charles was still with her. Thelma had gone home hours before.

The surgeon came into the doctors' lounge looking victorious, as he grinned at Charles and Maxine. 'I swear, there are miracles sometimes that none of us can explain. She missed a whole lot of important stuff with her little hack job. She just missed killing herself by a hair. A lot could still go wrong in the next few days, but I think she's actually going to make it.' Maxine let out a whoop of sheer pleasure and threw her arms around Charles's neck. He hugged her and smiled. He was exhausted, but medically, it had been one of the most interesting nights of his life, to see what they contended with, and what they were doing to solve it, and Maxine was in charge of it all.

She went to tell Eloise's parents, and shortly after six A.M., she and Charles left the hospital. Maxine was going to come back in a few hours. It would be touch and go for the next few days, but the worst was over. They had replaced Eloise's blood, and repaired her heart. Her parents were beside themselves with relief, and so was Maxine. Her optimism was still guarded, but she had a feeling they were going to win this one, and had snatched victory from the jaws of death.

'I don't know how to tell you how impressed I am with what you do,' Charles said softly. He had an arm around her shoulders, and she was leaning against him on the ride home. She was still exhilarated from the night's work, but she was tired too. They both knew that it would be several hours before she came down from the excitement, and by then she had to be back at the hospital, probably without sleep. She was used to it.

'Thank you,' she said, smiling at him. 'Thanks for staying with me. It was nice knowing you were there. I'm usually alone on nights like this. I hope we win this one. I have a feeling we will.'

'So do I. Your cardio guy is top notch.' Charles thought she was too.

'Yes, he is,' Maxine agreed.

The cab stopped in front of her building, and she suddenly realized how bone tired she was as she got out. Her legs felt like cement, and the high heels were killing her. She was still wearing the white lab coat over her evening dress, and carrying her black evening coat. Charles had worn a good-looking conservative dark suit, a white shirt, and a navy tie. She liked the way he dressed. And he still looked impeccable after the long night.

'I feel like I've been dragged through a bush backward,' she said, and he laughed.

'You don't look it. You were absolutely fantastic tonight.'

'Thanks, it's all about the team, no one person, and how the luck runs on any given night. You just never know how it will turn out. You do your best, and pray a lot. I always do.'

He looked at her with eyes full of fresh respect and admiration. It was six-thirty in the morning, and he suddenly wished he could go home and go to bed with her. He would have liked to sleep with his arms around her, after the night they had shared. Instead, he bent down, as he stood outside her building with her, and brushed her lips with his. It was sooner than either of them had planned to kiss, but tonight had changed a lot of things for both of them. They had somehow formed a bond. He kissed her again, harder this time, and she kissed him back as he slipped his arms around her and held her close to him.

'I'll call you later,' he whispered. She nodded, and went into her building.

She sat in her kitchen for a long time afterward, thinking about all of it, her patient, the long night, and Charles's kiss. It was hard to say which of the three had shaken her most. Her patient's suicide attempt undoubtedly, but she felt as though lightning had struck her when Charles kissed her. But it felt nice too. She had loved having him there for her. In so many ways, Charles seemed like everything she had ever wanted. And now that he was here, she was scared of what it meant, and how she would do it. She wasn't sure there was room in her life for him and her kids. She was worried about that.

It was nearly nine that morning when she finally got to bed. Her children were still asleep, and she was hoping she'd get some sleep before she had to get moving with them. And she wasn't prepared for Daphne's attack, when she finally got up after two hours' sleep, and was drinking a cup of coffee in the kitchen around eleven. Daphne was glaring at her in fury. Maxine had no idea why, but she was sure she'd find out soon.

'Where were you last night?' Daphne asked her. She looked livid.

'At the hospital. Why?' Maxine looked blank at the question. What was her problem?

'You were *not*! You were with *him*!' She said it like an angry lover. Hell hath no fury like a kid in the face of a parent's new boyfriend, or even the suspicion thereof.

'I was with "him" for dinner, as you put it,' her mother said calmly. 'I got a call on the way home, one of my patients coded, and I had to go in. I think we managed to save her, if nothing goes wrong today.' She often reported to them on the emergencies she had spent the night with. 'So what's your problem here?'

'I don't believe you. I think you were at his apartment all night, sleeping with him.' She spat the words at her mother in a rage, as Maxine looked at her in amazement. This was totally uncalled for, but it made Maxine realize what kind of resistance she might get from them over Charles. Or from Daphne at least.

'That could happen one day with him or someone else. And if anything gets that serious in my life, I'll give you a heads-up. But I can assure you, Daphne, I was at work all last night. And I think you're completely out of line.' She looked angry herself as she turned away, and Daphne looked momentarily mollified and then turned on her again.

'Why should I believe you?' she asked as Sam walked into the room, and looked at his sister with concern. She sounded like she was being mean to

162

their mom, which was the case.

'Because I've never lied to you,' Maxine said sternly, 'and I don't intend to start now. And I don't appreciate your accusations. They're rude, inaccurate, and unnecessary. So back off and behave yourself.' And with that, Maxine stormed out of the kitchen without saying another word to either child.

'Now look what you did,' Sam scolded his sister. 'You made Mom mad. And she's probably tired from being up all night, so now she'll be really crabby for the rest of the day. Thanks a lot!'

'You don't know *anything*!' Daphne said, and stormed out of the kitchen too, as Sam shook his head, and poured himself a bowl of cereal. This was clearly not going to be an easy day.

Maxine went back to the hospital at noon, and was delighted to find that Eloise was doing well. She had regained consciousness, and Maxine was able to talk to her, although she wouldn't say why she had made the attempt. Maxine was recommending a long-term hospitalization for her, and her parents had agreed. They didn't want to risk anything like it happening again, whatever it took.

Maxine was back with her children by two. Daphne had gone out with friends, allegedly Christmas shopping, but Maxine was sure her daughter was avoiding her, which suited her just fine. She was still furious at Daphne's accusations that morning. And as usual, Sam was very sweet about making it up to her. Together they went to watch Jack play soccer. And much to their delight, Jack's team won the game. By the time they all got back to the apartment at five o'clock, they were in

163

better spirits. Daphne was home by then and was very subdued.

When Charles called her at six, he said he had just woken up, and was stunned to hear she had run around all day.

'I'm used to this,' she laughed. 'There's no rest for the weary. At least not when you have kids.'

'I don't know how you do it. I feel like I was hit by a bus. I'm a total wuss. How's your patient doing?' He sounded sleepy and sexy.

'Remarkably well. Thank God these kids are young. A lot of the time we have a pretty decent shot at saving them, though not always.'

'I'm glad this one worked out.' He had a vested interest in it now. 'What are you doing tonight?'

'We're going to a movie at eight, probably pizza or Chinese before that.' And then she had an idea. She assumed he was too tired to join them, and she was beginning to drag too, but they always had family dinners on Sunday night that were more festive than during the week. 'How about joining us for dinner tomorrow?'

'You and your children?' He sounded hesitant, and less enthused than she would have hoped. It was a new concept for him.

'Yes, that would be the idea. We can order in Chinese, or something else if you prefer.'

'I love Chinese takeout. I just don't want to intrude on a family dinner.'

'I think we can handle it. How about you?' She was smiling, and he couldn't think of a good excuse not to.

'Okay,' he said, sounding as though he had just agreed to bungee-jump from the Empire State Building, and by his standards he had. Maxine

164

appreciated that he was willing to make the effort. It obviously scared him to death.

'See you tomorrow at six,' she said, as Daphne stood in the room and glared at her.

'Did you just invite him to dinner tomorrow?' Daphne asked as soon as her mother hung up.

'Yes, I did.' And she was not about to ask permission. The children had friends over all the time, whom Maxine welcomed with open arms. She had a right to have friends over too, even if she rarely if ever exercised the privilege.

'Then I'm not eating with you tomorrow,' Daphne snarled.

'Yes, you are,' Maxine said calmly, and reminded her that her friends should be welcome in the house too. 'I don't know why you're making such an issue of this, Daphne. He's a perfectly nice person. I'm not running off with him. And you deal with your father's girlfriends all the time.'

'Is he your boyfriend?' Daphne looked horrified, as Maxine shook her head.

'No, he's not, but that wouldn't be the most outrageous thing that ever happened. It's a lot more unusual that I haven't dated in years. You don't need to make such a big deal of this.' But maybe she did. She obviously felt threatened by Charles and the whole concept of a man near her mother. And Jack didn't like it either. 'Nothing's going to happen here, Daff. But for chrissake, lighten up. Let's just treat it like what it is. A friend coming to dinner. If it turns out to be more than that one day, I'll tell you. For now, all it is is dinner. Okay?' As she said it, she thought of his kissing her that morning. So Daphne wasn't entirely wrong. It was more than just dinner.

165

Daphne didn't say a word, she just walked out of her mother's room in silence.

When Charles showed up the next day, Daphne was in her room, and Maxine had to coax, beg, and threaten her to finally emerge for dinner. She came to the kitchen, but she made it clear with her body language and behavior that she was there under protest. She ignored Charles completely, and looked at her mother in fury. And when they served the Chinese food that arrived at seven, Daphne refused to eat. Sam and Jack more than made up for it. Charles congratulated Jack on winning the game the day before, and asked him the details of the play.

And after that, Sam and Charles struck up a lively conversation. Daphne looked at both her brothers like traitors, and was back in her room in twenty minutes. Charles mentioned it to Maxine while she was cleaning up the kitchen, and putting the leftovers away. Dinner had been good, and Charles had done very well. It was obviously an effort for him to talk to children, but he was trying. It was all completely unfamiliar to him.

'Daphne hates me,' he said, looking upset, eating another fortune cookie that had been left on the table.

'She doesn't hate you. She doesn't know you. She's just scared. I've never really dated, and I haven't brought anyone home for dinner. She's afraid of what this means.'

'Did she tell you that?' He looked intrigued, and Maxine laughed.

'No, but I'm a mother and an adolescent shrink. She feels threatened.'

'Did I say something to upset her?' He looked

166

worried.

'No, you were great.' Maxine smiled at him. 'She has just decided to take a position. Personally, I hate teenage girls,' Maxine said blithely, and this time he laughed, given what she did for a living. 'Actually, fifteen is worse. But it starts at thirteen. Hormones and all that stuff. They should be locked up until they're sixteen or seventeen.'

'That's a hell of a thing to say for a woman who makes a career of dealing with them.'

'Not at all. I know whereof I speak. They all torture their mothers at that age. Their dads are the heroes.'

'I noticed,' he said glumly. Daphne had bragged about hers the first time they met. 'How am I doing with the boys?'

'Great,' she said again, and looked into his eyes with a gentle smile. 'Thanks for doing this at all. I know it's not your thing.'

'No, but you are,' he said gently. 'I'm doing it for you.'

'I know,' she said softly, and before they knew what had happened, they were kissing in the kitchen, and Sam walked in.

'Uh-oh,' he said the moment he saw them, and they jumped apart, looking guilty, as Maxine opened the fridge and tried to look busy. 'Daff will kill you if she sees you kissing him,' he said to his mother, and she and Charles both laughed.

'It won't happen again. I promise. Sorry, Sam,' Maxine said. Sam shrugged, grabbed two cookies, and walked out of the room again.

'I really like him,' Charles said warmly.

'It's good for all of them to have you around, even Daphne,' she said calmly. 'It's a lot more real

167

than having me all to themselves.'

'I didn't realize I was here on a training mission,' Charles said with a groan, and she laughed again.

They sat in the living room and talked for a while afterward, and Charles left around ten. In spite of Daphne's hostility at dinner, it had been a very pleasant evening. Charles acted as though he had survived going over Niagara Falls in a barrel, and Maxine looked happy when she walked into her room and found Sam in her bed, already half asleep.

'Are you going to marry him, Mom?' he whispered, barely able to keep his eyes open as she kissed him.

'No, I'm not. He's just a friend.'

'Then why were you kissing him?'

'Just like that, because I like him. But that doesn't mean I'm going to marry him.'

'You mean like Dad and the girls he goes out with?'

'Yeah, kind of. It's no big deal.'

'He always says that too.' Sam looked relieved and then drifted off to sleep as she looked at him. The arrival of Charles on the scene had certainly shaken everyone up, but she still thought it was a good thing. And it was fun for her to have a man to go out with. It wasn't a crime, she reminded herself. They'd just have to get used to it. After all, Blake dated. Why couldn't she?

CHAPTER 11

Blake's time with Arabella in London before Christmas was absolutely magical. He had never been as happy or as besotted with anyone in his life. She had even done a small naked portrait of him. He loved every single moment he spent with her. He took her to St. Moritz for the weekend, and skied with her. They went to Paris for three days to Christmas shop, and stayed at the Ritz. They even went to Venice and stayed in the palazzo he had there. They were the most romantic times he had shared with any woman. And inevitably, he had invited her to come to Aspen with him after Christmas, to spend the vacation with him and his children. He and Arabella were spending Christmas Eve together in London. She wanted him to meet her family, but he wanted to be alone with her and savor every moment. He wasn't big on meeting anyone's family. Things usually went awry when he did, and it raised false expectations. In Arabella's case, he just wanted her to himself, and she was more than willing. She had been staying in his London house with him since they met. And they had already been in the tabloids together numerous times.

Daphne had spotted them in *People* magazine, and had showed it to her mother, with a disapproving look. 'Looks like Dad's in love again.'

'Give him a break, Daff. It's never serious with him. He's just having fun.' Daphne was being tough on both her parents these days, Blake as well as Maxine.

169

'He said he'd come alone on the vacation this time.' That was what Daphne really wanted, time alone with him, to be the only woman in his life. And knowing Blake, Maxine knew that wasn't going to happen. And she thought the new woman in his life looked very pretty. She was happy with Charles, and it didn't bother her at all. It never did. 'I hope he doesn't bring her,' Daphne reiterated, and Maxine said she thought he probably would. It seemed better to warn her and let her get used to the idea.

Arabella had already accepted Blake's invitation to Aspen. She had never been there, and she loved the idea of spending the holiday with his adorable children. She had seen photographs of them, and he had told her all about them. She helped him shop for gifts for Daphne, and together they had picked out a beautiful little diamond tennis bracelet at Graff's that Arabella assured him would be perfect for her. She said it was fit for a princess. He had gone back to the store and picked out a gift that was suitable for a viscountess, a spectacular sapphire bracelet. And when he gave it to her, she was thrilled. They celebrated on Christmas Eve, and flew to New York in his plane the next day. They arrived at his New York apartment late in the afternoon on Christmas Day, and he called Maxine as soon as they got in. She and the children had just gotten back from celebrating Christmas with her parents, and the kids were ready to leave the next day. She had been packing for them for two days.

'I see you've been busy,' she teased him. 'Daffy and I have been reading about you in *People*.' She didn't tell him that Daphne wasn't pleased.

'Wait till you meet her. She's terrific.'

'I can hardly wait,' Maxine laughed. Usually the women in his life didn't last long enough for her to meet. And this had only been going on for a few weeks. She knew Blake, and she didn't believe him when he said this was different. He always said that. She couldn't imagine him being serious about anyone, although this woman was older than his usual fare, but she was still only twenty-nine, a kid as far as Maxine was concerned. And then Maxine volunteered her news. 'I'm seeing someone too,' she said nonchalantly.

'Well, that's a new trend. Who's the lucky guy?'

'An internist I met through a patient.'

'Sounds perfect. Is he nice?'

'I think so.' She didn't wax poetic, which he knew was typical of her. Maxine was reserved about everything.

'What do the kids say about it?' He was curious to know.

'Ah . . .' she sighed, 'that's another story. Daphne hates him with a passion, Jack isn't thrilled, and I don't think Sam really cares.'

'Why does Daff hate him?'

'He's a guy. They all figure they should be enough for me, and they are. But this is nice for a change. It gives me a grown-up to talk to between patients and car pools.'

'Sounds good to me.'

And then Maxine thought she should warn him about their daughter. 'She's on the warpath about you too.'

'She is?' He sounded surprised. 'What about?' He couldn't imagine. He was very naïve.

'Your new romance. She seems to be very

possessive about both of us these days. She said you promised to come to Aspen alone this time. Are you?'

He hesitated. 'Uh . . . no . . . actually not. Arabella is with me.'

'I figured. I told Daffy that was probably the case. You may be in for a bit of a shitstorm. Brace yourself.'

'Great. I'd better tell Arabella. She's been looking forward to meeting them.'

'The boys will be fine. They're used to your women. Just tell her not to take Daphne's attitude too much to heart. She's thirteen, it's a tough age.'

'Apparently,' he said, but he was confident that Arabella could win anyone over, even Daphne. He didn't think it was a big deal. 'I'll pick them up tomorrow morning at eight-thirty,' he told Maxine.

'I'll have them ready for you,' she promised. 'I hope everything goes okay.' Daphne hadn't relented about Charles yet, but she had only seen him in passing, and he had kept away for the holiday. He didn't like Christmas, had no family of his own anymore, and had gone to his house in Vermont. Maxine was meeting him there after the kids left with Blake. She was driving up the next day, and was a little nervous about it. It was going to be a honeymoon of sorts for them, and it had been a long time for her, but they had been dating for six weeks. She couldn't put it off forever. Sleeping with him seemed like a huge step.

Blake picked the children up in the morning as promised, and Maxine didn't go downstairs to see him. She told the children to give him her love. She didn't think it was fair to intrude on him with Arabella. Sam clung to his mother for a moment, and she told him he could call her on her cell phone anytime, and warned the older ones to keep an eye on him and sleep with him at night. Daphne already looked upset, since her mother had told her that Blake had Arabella with him. 'But he promised . . .' she had wailed, in tears, the night before, as Maxine reassured her that it didn't mean he didn't love her or want to spend time with her, he just liked having a woman around too. And they both knew that whoever Arabella was, she wouldn't be around for long. His women never were, and why would she be the exception to the rule? Daphne hugged her mom, and ran to catch the elevator where Jack and Sam were waiting.

The apartment was deadly quiet after they left. Maxine and Zelda tidied up together, and Zelda changed their beds before leaving for the theater for a matinee. And then Maxine called Charles in Vermont. He was anxious for her to come up. She was looking forward to seeing him, but nervous about their plans. She felt like a born-again virgin thinking about going to bed with him. And he had already been apologetic about his 'cabin in the mountains,' as he called it, knowing the kind of luxury she had experienced with Blake. He said that his house in Vermont was spartan and very plain. It was near a ski resort, and he was looking forward to skiing with her, but he pointed out that it was by no means St. Moritz, or Aspen, or any of the places she knew so well.

'Stop worrying about it, Charles,' she reassured him. 'If that was important to me, I'd still be married to Blake. Remember, I left. I just want to spend time with you. I don't care how simple the cabin is. I'm coming up for you, not the house.'

173

And she meant it.

He was enormously relieved to be alone with her for a change. It was still stressful for him being around her children. He had bought them all CDs for Christmas, by bands their mother had suggested, and some DVDs for Sam. He had no idea what they liked, and picking out gifts for them had made him nervous. He had bought Maxine a serious-looking Chanel scarf, which he thought was pretty, and she loved it. He had given it to her the last time they had dinner before he left for Vermont, four days before Christmas. He preferred leaving town before people got serious about the holidays. That just wasn't for him, which she thought was too bad. But it was easier for her that way with the children. Daphne would have had a major meltdown if he'd been around for Christmas and expected to spend time with them, so everything worked out for the best.

Maxine had given him a Hermès tie and a matching pocket scarf. He put them on for dinner that night. It was a comfortable relationship for both of them, not too serious, with plenty of room for them to continue to pursue their own careers and lives. Maxine didn't know how much things would change if she slept with him. She couldn't imagine him staying at the house with her children, and Charles had already said he would never do that. He would have been too afraid Daphne would kill him in his sleep. And besides that, he didn't think it was respectable to sleep with her with her children around, and Maxine agreed.

She left the city at noon, and was planning to be away until New Year's Day. And she expected to be in Vermont by six o'clock that night. Charles

174

called her on the road twice, to make sure she was all right. It was snowing north of Boston, but the roads were clear, although it got heavier when she got to New Hampshire, and by then she had heard from her children. Daphne had called her the minute they landed in Aspen, and sounded frantic.

'I *hate* her, Mom!' she whispered. Maxine listened and rolled her eyes. 'She's *awful*!'

'Awful how?' Maxine tried to keep an open mind, although she had to admit, some of Blake's women had been pretty dicey. Maxine had gotten philosophical about it in the last five years. They never lasted long anyway, so it wasn't worth getting upset about, unless they did something dangerous for the children. But they were too old for that now anyway, they weren't babies.

'She has tattoos up and down her arms!' Maxine smiled at the vision.

'So did the last one, and on her legs, and that didn't bother you. Is she nice?' Maybe she was being rude to the children. Maxine hoped not, but she didn't think Blake would let that happen. He loved his kids, even if he liked his women.

'I don't know. I won't talk to her,' Daphne said proudly.

'Don't be rude, Daff. It's not nice, and it'll just upset your father. Is she being nice to the boys?'

'She did a bunch of dumb pictures for Sam. She's a painter or something. And she wears this stupid thing between her eyes.'

'What kind of thing?' Maxine envisioned her with an arrow and a suction cup glued to her forehead.

'You know, like Indian women. She's such a fake.'

'You mean, like a bindi? Come on, Daff, don't be so tough on her. So she's a little weird. Give her a chance.'

'I hate her.' Maxine knew Daphne hated Charles too. She was hating a lot of people these days, even her parents. It was of the age.

'You probably won't ever see her again after this vacation, so don't waste a lot of energy on it. You know how that goes.'

'This one's different,' Daphne said, sounding depressed. 'I think Dad loves her.'

'I doubt that. Dad's only known her for a few weeks.'

'You know how he is. He gets all crazy about them in the beginning.'

'Yeah, and then they go up in smoke and he forgets them. Just relax.' But she wondered after she hung up if Daphne was right and this one would be the exception. Anything was possible. She couldn't imagine Blake ever marrying again or staying with the same woman long term, but you never knew. Maybe one day he would. Maxine wondered how she would feel about that when it happened. Maybe not so great. Just like her children, she liked the way things were. Change was never easy, but maybe one day she'd have to face it. In Blake's life, and her own. That's what Charles was all about. Change. It was scary for her too.

The trip took longer than she expected because of the snow, and she got to Charles's place at eight o'clock. It was a small, neat little New England house with a peaked roof and a rustic fence around it. It looked like something on a postcard. He came out to greet her as soon as she drove up, and carried in her bags. There was a front porch with a swing and two rockers on it, and inside there was one big bedroom, a living room with a fireplace and a hooked rug, and a cozy country kitchen. She was disappointed to note that there would have been nowhere to put her kids, if it ever came to that. Not even a guest room where she could have crammed all three into one bed. It was a house suitable for a bachelor, or at most a couple, and nothing else, which was how he lived. And he liked it that way. He had made that clear.

The house was cozy and warm when she walked in, and he set her bags down in the bedroom, and showed her the closet where she could hang her things. It was an odd feeling being alone there with him. It seemed a little premature since she had never slept with him, and now they would be sharing a bed. What if she decided not to sleep with him? she asked herself. But it was too late now, she was there. She suddenly felt very brave coming up, and shy as he bustled around showing her where things were. Towels, sheets, washing machine, the bathroom, of which there was only one. And everything in his kitchen was immaculate and neat. He had cold chicken and some soup waiting for her, but after the long drive she was too tired to eat. She was happy sitting by the fire with him and a cup of tea.

'Did the children get off all right?' he asked politely.

'They're fine. Daphne called when they got to Aspen. She's a little upset because her father brought his new girlfriend along. He had promised not to this time, but he just met someone new, so he brought her with him. He gets a little overenthused in the beginning.'

'He's a busy guy,' Charles said, sounding disapproving. He was always uncomfortable when she mentioned Blake.

'The kids will adjust. They always do.'

'I'm not so sure Daphne is going to adjust to me.' He was still worried about that, and he wasn't used to the hellish fury of teenage girls. Maxine was much less impressed.

'She'll be fine. She just needs some time.'

They sat and talked by the fire for a long time, and the scene outside was one of sheer beauty. They stood on the porch, looking out at the fresh snow spread out all around them. It was magical, as Charles put his arms around her and kissed her. And just as he did, her cell phone went off. It was Sam, calling to kiss her goodnight. She gave him a kiss, said goodbye, and then turned to Charles again, and she could see he was unnerved.

'They seem to find you, even here,' he commented drily. 'Don't you ever get time off?'

'I don't want to,' she said softly. 'They're my kids. They're all I've got. They're my life.' It was precisely what he was afraid of, and why they frightened him so much. He couldn't imagine detaching them from her.

'You need more in your life than just them,' he said softly. He sounded like he was volunteering for the job, and she was touched. He kissed her again, and this time no one called, no one disturbed them. She followed him back inside, and they took turns in the bathroom getting ready for bed. It was faintly embarrassing and kind of funny, and Maxine giggled as she got into bed. She was wearing a long cashmere nightgown with a

178

matching robe over it, and socks. It was hardly romantic, but she couldn't imagine wearing anything else. He was wearing clean striped pajamas, and she felt like her parents as they lay in his double bed side by side.

'This feels a little weird,' she admitted in a whisper, and then he kissed her, and it didn't feel strange anymore. His hands slipped under her nightgown, and little by little they took their clothes off under the covers and tossed them to the floor.

It had been so long since she had slept with anyone that she had been afraid it would be scary and awkward, and instead he was a gentle, considerate lover, and it seemed like the most natural thing in the world. They held each other tight afterward, and he told her how beautiful she was and said that he loved her, and she was shocked to hear the words. She wondered if he felt obliged to say them to her because they had made love. He said he had been falling in love with her since they met. And she told him as gently as she could that she needed more time before knowing that. There was so much she liked about him, and so much that she hoped to feel as she grew to know him better. She felt safe with him, which was important to her. She trusted him, and as they whispered in the dark, he made love to her again. And afterward, happy, comfortable, sated, and totally at peace, she fell asleep in his arms.

CHAPTER 12

The next morning Maxine and Charles bundled up and went for a long walk in the snow. He made breakfast for her, pancakes and Vermont maple syrup, with crisp strips of bacon. She looked at him tenderly, and he kissed her across the table. This was what he had been dreaming of since they met. Time like this was hard to come by in her life. Her children had already called her twice before breakfast. Daphne had declared full-scale war on her father's new love. And as he listened to Maxine's side of the conversation, Charles frowned. And she was shocked by what he said when she hung up.

'I know this may sound crazy to you, Maxine, but don't you think they're too old to be at home?'

'You were thinking maybe they should join the marines, or apply early to college?' After all, Jack and Daphne were only twelve and thirteen.

'I was in boarding school when I was their age. It was the best experience I ever had. I loved it, and it prepared me for life.' Just hearing him say it, Maxine was horrified.

'Never,' she said firmly. 'I would never do that to my kids. They've already lost Blake, more or less. I'm not going to abandon them too. And why? So I can have a better social life? Who cares about that? These are the years when kids need their parents, need to learn their values, bounce problems off them, and learn how to deal with issues like sex and drugs. I don't want some boarding-school teacher teaching my kids about those things. I want them to learn that from me.' She was shocked.

'But what about you? Are you willing to defer having a life until they leave for college? That's what it means if you have them around all the time.'

'This is what I signed on for when I had them,' she said gently. 'That's what parents are for. I see the results in my office every day when parents aren't there for their kids. Even if they are, things can go wrong. If you check out, and dump them in boarding school at these ages, I think you're asking for trouble.'

'I turned out okay,' he said defensively.

'Yes, but you opted not to have kids,' she said bluntly. 'That says something too. Maybe you missed something in your childhood after all. Look at the British, they send their children away at six or eight, and some of them are screwed up because of it and talk about it later as adults. You can't send a child away at that age, and not have it take a toll. People have trouble attaching after that. And I wouldn't trust teenage kids away at school. I want to be around to see what they're up to, and to share my values with them.'

'It sounds like a huge sacrifice to me,' he said sternly.

'Not at all,' she said, wondering if she really knew him. There was definitely a piece missing in Charles, when it came to kids, and she thought it was too bad. Maybe it was the piece that made her hesitate about him even now. She wanted to love him, but she needed to know that he could love her kids too, and surely not by lobbying to send them away to boarding school. The very thought of it

181

made her shudder. He could see that, and immediately backed off. He didn't want to upset her, although he thought it would have been a great idea, if she were willing. She wasn't. That was clear.

They went skiing that afternoon in Sugarbush, and it was easy and fun skiing with him. She had never been as proficient as Blake, but she was a good skier, and she and Charles were at the same level and enjoyed the same runs. They were both relaxed and happy afterward, and she had put aside their little disagreement that morning about boarding school. He was entitled to his own point of view, as long as he didn't force the issue with her. She didn't hear from her children that night, and Charles was relieved. It was nice spending uninterrupted time with her. He took her out to dinner, and when they got back, he made love to her in front of the fire. She was amazed at how comfortable and at ease she was with him. It was as though they had been sleeping together forever, and that night they curled up in his bed. It was snowing outside, and Maxine felt as though time had stopped, and they were alone together in a magical world.

*   *   *

In Blake's house in Aspen, things were less peaceful than they were in Vermont. The stereo was blasting, Jack and Sam were playing Nintendo games, friends dropped by, and Daphne was determined to make Arabella's life as miserable as she could. She made rude, cutting comments, and snide remarks about the outfits Arabella wore.

182

And whenever Arabella cooked, Daphne refused to eat. She asked her if she'd been checked for AIDS since she got her tattoos. Arabella had no idea how to deal with her, but she told Blake she was determined to hang in. He insisted they were good kids.

He wanted it to work with his kids. Daphne was doing everything possible to see that it wouldn't. And she was trying to rile the boys up against Arabella, but so far it hadn't worked. They thought she was okay, although her tattoos and her hair were a little weird.

Jack paid virtually no attention to Arabella, and Sam was polite. Sam had inquired about the bindi, and his father had told him that Arabella had worn them since she lived in India, and he thought it looked really pretty. Sam conceded that he did too. Daphne shrugged and told Arabella that they had seen so many women come and go in their father's life that they just couldn't be bothered anymore to get to know them. She assured Arabella he'd get rid of her within the next few weeks. It was the only comment she made that actually got under Arabella's skin, and Blake found her in their bathroom in tears.

'Sweetheart . . . baby . . . Bella darling . . . what's the matter?' She was crying as though her heart would break, and the one thing he couldn't stand was crying women, particularly those that he loved. 'What happened?' Arabella wanted to tell him that his bitch of a daughter had happened, but she restrained herself, out of love for him. She was genuinely in love with him, and he was crazy about her too.

Arabella finally repeated the comment Daphne

had made that had reduced her to tears. 'It just scared me, and all of a sudden I was wondering if you really were going to dump me when we get back to London.' She looked at Blake with huge eyes and started crying again, as he put his arms around her.

'No one is dumping anyone here,' Blake reassured her. 'I'm nuts about you. I'm not going anywhere, and if I have anything to say about it, neither are you. For a long, long time. I hate to say it, but my daughter is jealous of you.' He talked to Daphne about it later that afternoon, and asked why she was being so mean to Arabella. It really wasn't fair, and she had never done that to any of his girlfriends before.

'What's it about, Daff? I've had lots of women around, and let's be honest, some of them were just plain stupid.' Daphne laughed at his honesty. There had been some really dim-witted ones, beautiful but dumb, and Daphne had never gone after them, or even made fun of them.

'Arabella's different,' Daphne said reluctantly.

'Yeah, she's smarter and nicer than the rest of them, and a more reasonable age. So what's your problem?' He was annoyed at her, and it showed. She was making Arabella's life miserable for no reason.

'That's the point, Dad,' Daphne answered. 'She's better than the rest of them . . . so I hate her . . .'

'Explain that to me.' He was completely baffled.

Daphne spoke in a soft voice, and suddenly looked like a child again. 'I'm scared she might stick around.'

'So? What if she does, as long as she's nice to

184

you?'

'What if you marry her?' Daphne looked sick at the thought, and her father looked stunned.

'Marry her? Why would I want to do that?'

'I don't know. People do.'

'I don't. Been there, done that. I was married to your mom. I have three great kids. I don't need to get married again. Arabella and I are just having fun. That's all. Don't make such a big deal of it. We're not, why should you?'

'She says she loves you, Dad.' Daphne's eyes were huge. 'And I heard you tell her that you love her too. People who love each other get married, and I don't want you to marry anyone, except Mom.'

'Well, that's not going to happen,' he said matter-of-factly. 'Your mother and I don't want to be married to each other, but we love each other like this. And there's plenty of room for a woman in my life, whom I don't want to marry, and all of you. You don't need to worry about it. You have my word, Daff. You won't ever be seeing me get married. To anyone. Is that better?'

'Yeah. Maybe.' She still didn't look sure. 'What if you change your mind?' She had to admit, Arabella was pretty good looking, and smart and funny. In some ways, she seemed like the perfect woman for him, which was what terrified Daphne.

'If I change my mind, I'll discuss it with you first. I give you my permission to do whatever you have to, to talk me out of it. Is that a deal? But you don't need to be mean to Arabella now. It's not fair. She's our guest, and she's having a miserable time.'

'I know,' Daphne said with a victorious smile.

She had worked hard at it.

'Cut it out. You can be nice to her. She's a nice girl. And so are you.'

'Do I have to, Dad?'

'Yes, you do,' he said firmly. He was beginning to wonder if Daphne was going to do this to all his women now. She had made several unpleasant remarks about her mother's friend Charles too. She seemed to want her parents staying solo these days, which was not very realistic. Blake was happy that Maxine finally had someone. She deserved a little comfort and companionship in her life. He didn't begrudge it to her. But Daphne sure did, and was willing to do almost anything about it. He didn't like seeing her behave that way. She had turned into a little bitch overnight, and he wondered if Maxine was right about the age. He sure wasn't looking forward to a lot of this. It was going to make it hard to take her on vacations, since he almost always had someone with him, and it didn't even occur to him not to.

'I want you to make an effort with her now. For me,' he admonished her, and Daphne grudgingly agreed.

The results of his talk with her weren't obvious on the first night, but two days later, she had improved slightly. She answered when Arabella spoke to her, and she had stopped making remarks about her tattoos and her hair. It was something at least. And Arabella hadn't cried about it in days. The trip had turned out to be stressful for him, which it never was when he was with his kids, and he was almost sorry he'd brought Arabella along, for her sake, not for his kids'.

He was skiing peacefully with Arabella one

afternoon, and he had to admit, it was nice to get away from the children. They stopped several times to catch their breath on the harder runs, and he leaned over and kissed her. And they went back to the house that afternoon to make love. Arabella confessed that she could hardly wait till they got back to London, although she was glad to have met his children. But a little went a long way, and she felt as though she was constantly organizing things for them to do. It was also obvious that she and Daphne would never be friends. The best she could hope for was an uneasy truce, which was what she had gotten so far. It was still a vast improvement over Daphne's behavior in the beginning. But Blake didn't envy his ex-wife if this was what she had to deal with whenever her current boyfriend was around. He was amazed the guy put up with it. He suspected Arabella wouldn't have for long, if Daphne hadn't finally backed off.

For the first time ever, he was relieved to take them back to Maxine in New York. She had driven down from Vermont that day, and had just gotten home when Blake dropped them off at the apartment. Arabella was waiting for him at the penthouse, and they were leaving for London that night.

Sam immediately threw his arms around his mother with a shout of delight and almost knocked her down. And Jack and Daphne looked happy to be home too.

'How was it?' she asked Blake with a relaxed look. She could see in his eyes that it had been less than perfect, and he waited until Daphne left the room before he answered.

'Not as easy as it used to be,' he said with a

rueful grin. 'Watch out for Daff, Max, or you'll wind up an old maid.' She laughed at the warning. It was the least of her worries, and she'd had a great time with Charles in Vermont. She had come back relaxed and happy, and closer to him than she had been to anyone in years. In many ways, they were so much alike, they were a perfect match. Their medical careers meshed perfectly, they were both meticulous, neat, and organized. With no one else around, it was perfect. The challenge was going to be to see what happened when they were all home again.

'Did she ease up at all?' Maxine inquired about their daughter. And Blake shook his head.

'Not really. She stopped making the overtly outrageous comments she had in the beginning, but she managed to make Arabella's life miserable in every other subtle way. I'm surprised she stayed.'

'I take it she doesn't have kids of her own. That always helps,' Maxine said, and he shook his head.

'She'll probably have her tubes tied after this. I wouldn't blame her. But that works for me too,' he said, laughing, and Maxine groaned in sympathy.

'Poor woman. I don't know what we can do. Thirteen-year-old girls are famous for this kind of behavior. It's going to get worse before it gets better.'

'Call me when she gets out of college,' Blake said, as he got ready to leave. He stopped in the kids' rooms to see all of them, kissed them goodbye, and then lingered at the door for a minute with Maxine.

'Take care of yourself, Max. I hope this guy is good to you. If he isn't, tell him he'll have to deal with me.'

'Say that to Arabella too,' she said, hugging him, sorry that Daphne had given them such a hard time on the vacation. 'Where are you going now?'

'London for a few weeks, then Marrakech. I want to get the work on the house started. It's not really a house, it's more of a palace. You have to come over and see it sometime.' But she didn't know when that would be. 'I'll probably be in St. Bart's by the end of January. I'll pick up the boat there and float around for a while.' She knew the story. The kids probably wouldn't see him for a long time. More than likely not until their summer vacation. They were used to it, but it still made her sad for them. They needed to see more of Blake than they did. 'I'll stay in touch.' Sometimes he did, and sometimes he didn't, but she knew where to look for him, if she had to.

'Take care of yourself,' she said, hugging him at the elevator.

'You too,' he said, hugged her back, and was gone. It was always a strange feeling for her when she said goodbye to him. It made her wonder at times what life would have been like if they'd stayed married. He would have been gone all the time, just as he was now. It just wasn't enough for her, to have a husband in name only. What she needed was what she had finally found, a man like Charles, who would stick around. He was the ultimate grown-up.

CHAPTER 13

When Blake and Arabella got back to London, they both had a lot to do. He had meetings, and two houses to work on, and she had a portrait to do. It was a full two weeks before they could get out of town. And when they did, Blake was relieved. It was freezing in London, and he was tired of winter. Aspen and New York had been cold too, although at least in Aspen he could ski. But he was anxious to get to Morocco. Arabella had never been, and he couldn't wait to share it with her. She was as excited as he was the day they left. They were going to stay at the La Mamounia, and he was taking his architect with him. He already had blueprints for the house, and they looked fabulous to him. The project was going to take at least a year, which was fine with Blake. The best part was the planning, and the excitement of watching it take shape. And with Arabella's artistic sense, it was going to be fun sharing it with her. They chatted excitedly about it for the whole trip. And she was struck by the beauty of the place the moment they landed. They arrived at sunset, with a soft glow over the Atlas Mountains as they flew in.

A car was waiting to take them to the hotel and Arabella was dazzled as they drove through the city. The impressive Koutoubia Minaret was the first sign of Marrakech that caught her eye, and they drove through the central plaza, Jemaa el Fna, at twilight. It looked like the stage set for a movie. Even in her travels through India, she had rarely seen anything as exotic, there were snake charmers, dancers, acrobats, vendors selling things to drink, mules being led by their owners, men in long robes everywhere. It was straight out of *1001 Arabian Nights*. Blake was telling her that he wanted to take her to the souks, particularly the Souk el Zarbia, Medina, the walled city, and the Menara Gardens, which he said was the most romantic place in the world. There was a heady atmosphere all around them, and as she lowered the tinted windows to see better, the aroma of spices, flowers, people, and animals mingled to create an impression that had an aura all its own. The traffic around them was insane. There were mopeds and motorcycles darting among the cars, the traffic was crazy and disorganized, as horns sounded, people shouted, and street musicians added to the cacophony of sounds. Arabella turned to Blake with a wide, happy smile and her eyes dancing. It was even better than India for her, because she was sharing it with him.

'I *love* this!' she said excitedly, as he beamed at her. And he couldn't wait to show her his palace. He thought Marrakech was the most romantic place he'd ever been, and Arabella agreed. In spite of her travels in India, she loved this even more. Arabella came to life in exotic places in ways Blake had never seen her before.

They drove through the gigantic palm trees bordering the driveway, as they approached the peach-colored stucco of La Mamounia Hotel. Arabella had heard about it for years, and had always wanted to come here, and doing so with Blake was the best of all possible worlds. Men in white Moroccan outfits with red sashes greeted them, as Arabella noticed the carved wood and mosaic designs outside the hotel, and the manager appeared. Blake had already stayed there several times since buying the ancient palace, and had reserved one of the hotel's three luxurious private villas, which he was keeping until the remodeling and decoration would be complete.

Just to show Arabella, they walked into the main lobby where they stood on white marble floors, bordered in black marble, beneath a huge elaborate chandelier. They had entered the lobby through multicolored stained-glass doors, in red, yellow, and blue, as a bevy of men in white pajamas, gray vests, and red hats surrounded them and greeted Arabella and Blake. There were five luxurious restaurants and five bars for the guests' convenience, Turkish baths, and every possible amenity. And when the manager took them to Blake's private villa, a staff of servants were waiting for them there. The villa had three bedrooms, a living room, a dining area, a small kitchen for their use, and a separate full kitchen for a chef to prepare their meals, if they didn't wish to dine in the city or any of the hotel's restaurants. They had their own entrance, garden, and Jacuzzi, so if they didn't want to see anyone during their stay there, that was possible too. But Arabella was anxious to see the city with him. Blake had asked his driver to wait for them, and he and Arabella wanted to go out and explore, after they had a quiet meal in their garden. It was magical and exotic just being there.

They both showered and changed, and ate a light meal at the table in the garden, and then went out together hand in hand. They walked through the main square, kept their distance from the snake charmers, and took a carriage ride around the ramparts of the city. It was everything Arabella hoped it would be, and after sitting in the Jacuzzi in their private garden, and inhaling the heady fragrance of the flowers, they retired to their bedroom and made love for hours. It was nearly dawn when they fell asleep in each other's arms.

The next morning, their staff at the villa prepared an enormous breakfast for them. Blake showed her his plans for the palace he was rebuilding, and after breakfast they drove out to see it. It was even more fabulous than she expected. It had turrets and arches, and an enormous inner courtyard with beautiful old mosaics inset into the walls, and the rooms of the house were huge. It truly was a palace, and Blake's eyes danced as he walked through it with the architect and Arabella. She made some terrific suggestions for paint colors and the decor. And suddenly as he walked around, he knew he wanted to share it with her. He pulled her into his arms on a balcony overlooking the Atlas Mountains, and kissed her with the passion that had characterized their relationship from the first.

'I want this to be our love nest. It will be perfect for us. You can paint here.' He could see himself spending months there once it was finished. It was a perfect little town, with the restaurants, the bazaars with their exotic wares, and the beauty of nature beyond them. And there was a lively social life as well. Arabella had several French friends who had moved to Marrakech, and she and Blake had dinner with them before they left. It had been a terrific trip.

They dropped the architect off in London, and

then flew to the Azores, and from there to St. Bart's. Arabella loved his house there, and a week later they took off on his boat. It was the largest sailboat she had ever seen, and they headed for the Grenadine Islands, just north of Venezuela. She had had to reorganize all her portrait sitting sessions to be with him, and travel with him, but it was worth it. She lay naked on the sun deck with him, as they glided quietly through the transparent green waters. It was February by then, and they both agreed it was the perfect life. It was snowing everywhere else in the world but eternal summer for them. Best of all, it was the summer of their love.

* * *

Maxine was walking through snowdrifts then on the way to her office, and she was busier than ever. She'd had a number of new referrals, and a rash of school shootings around the country had her flying to several cities to consult with teams of psychiatrists and local authorities about how to deal with the children who'd been involved.

In her personal life, things were going well with Charles. The winter was flying by. And even Daphne was settling down. She and Charles might never be best friends, but she had stopped making overtly rude comments about him, and once in a while she even let her guard down when he was around, and they had a good laugh. He was making a superhuman effort with her kids. It was easiest for him with Jack and Sam, and he had taken both of them to several basketball games. Daphne was too busy with her own social life to join them, although he always invited her as well.

Maxine was extremely careful not to let them know that she and Charles were sleeping with each other. He never stayed at the apartment, except when all the kids were staying with friends. She tried to stay at his apartment once or twice a week, but she always came home before the children got up to go to school. It made for short nights for them, and very little sleep for her, but she thought it was important to do that. And once in a while, they went away for a weekend. It was the best they could do.

They had been dating for two and a half months on Valentine's Day, and Charles had made a reservation at La Grenouille. It was their favorite restaurant for dinner, and he called it their cafeteria and took her there at least once a week. He was a regular at their family dinners now on Sunday night, and he even cooked for them now and then.

Maxine was touched when she got two dozen red roses from him at the office on Valentine's Day. The note said simply 'I love you. C.' He was a very sweet man. Her secretary brought them in with a big smile. She liked Charles too. And Maxine wore a new red dress for dinner with him that night. He told her she looked great when he picked her up, and Sam made a face when Charles kissed her when he arrived, but they were used to it by now.

It was a perfect evening, and Charles came upstairs afterward. She poured him a glass of brandy, and they sat in the living room, as they often did, talking about what was going on in their lives. He was fascinated by her work, and after the

195

recent school shootings, she was scheduled to speak to Congress again. This time he was going to come. He told her he was proud of her, and then he reached up and took her hand. The children were all sound asleep.

'I love you, Maxine,' he said gently, and she smiled at him. She had finally broken through that barrier herself, particularly once she felt that he was making a real effort with her kids.

'I love you too, Charles. Thank you for a lovely Valentine's Day.' She hadn't had one like that in years. Their relationship worked perfectly for her. Not too much, not too little, he didn't monopolize her time, and she could count on seeing him several times a week. And she still had plenty of time for her work and her children. It was exactly what she wanted.

'The last two months have been wonderful,' he said peacefully, 'the best in my life, I think.' He had far more in common with her than he had had with his wife in twenty-one years. He had realized long since that Maxine was the woman he had been waiting for all his life. He had made up his mind in the last two weeks, and he was going to share his thoughts with her tonight.

'It's great for me too,' she said, as she leaned over and kissed him. They had left the lights off in the living room, it was relaxing and romantic that way, and she could taste the brandy on his lips.

'I want to spend more time with you, Maxine. We both need to get more sleep,' he teased. 'You can't keep getting up at four A.M. when we spend the night together.' They had decided against it that night in fact, because she had early patients to see the next day and so did he. Listening to him,

196

she was suddenly afraid he wanted to move in. And she knew only too well that that would traumatize her kids. They had finally gotten used to her dating him. Living together would have been too much, and it wasn't her style. She liked the fact that she had her apartment, and he had his.

'I think this works for now,' she said quietly, and he shook his head.

'Not for me. Not in the long run. I don't think either of us are the dating type, Maxine. And I think we're old enough to know what we want and when it's right.' Her eyes opened wide as she listened to him. She didn't know what to say, or even what he was saying to her. 'I knew it with you right away. We're like two peas in a pod . . . twins . . . we're both doctors. We have the same views about many things. I love your company. I'm getting used to your kids . . . Maxine . . . will you marry me?' She gave a sudden gasp at what he said and was silent for a long minute while he waited, looking down at her in the light from the street shining into the room. He could see her eyes wide with fright. 'It's going to be okay. I promise. I know this is right.' She wasn't as sure. Marriage was forever. She had thought it would be with Blake too, and it wasn't. How could she be sure of that now with Charles?

'Now? It's so soon, Charles . . . it's only been two months.'

'Two and a half,' he corrected. 'I think we both know it's right.' She thought that too, but even if it was, it was too early for her kids. She knew that for sure. She couldn't tell them she was marrying him. Not yet. They'd go nuts.

'I think the children need more time,' she said

197

gently. 'And we do too. Forever is a long time, and neither of us wants to make a mistake. We've done that before.'

'We don't want to wait forever either. I want to live with you,' he said softly, 'as your husband.' It was what so many women wanted, a man who offered marriage in months, and meant it. And she knew Charles did. But she had to mean it too, and she wasn't ready. 'What do you want to do?'

She was thinking quickly. She was surprised to realize that she didn't want to turn him down, but she wasn't ready to marry him yet either. She had to be sure. 'I'd like to wait to tell the children till June. That's six months from when we started. That's respectable. They'll be out of school then, and if it throws them for a loop, they can deal with it over the summer. It's too soon to tell them now.'

He looked mildly disappointed, but he was aware that she hadn't turned him down, and that pleased him immeasurably. He had been nervous about it. 'And get married when?' He held his breath, waiting for the answer.

'August? That would give them two months to get used to the idea. Enough to adjust, but not enough time to really stew about it. And that's a good time for us too, before they go back to school.'

'Does everything in your life revolve around your kids, Maxine? Isn't anything just about you, or us?'

'I guess not,' she said apologetically. 'But it's important that they feel comfortable about this, or it'll be harder for us,' especially for him if they objected. She was afraid they still might, even in June. They weren't going to be thrilled about it, she knew. They had just barely accepted him, and it didn't even occur to them that she might remarry. They had stopped worrying about that in the beginning, when she reassured them that she wouldn't, and she had believed it then. And now she was going to turn everything upside down with this announcement. 'I want my kids to be happy too.'

'They will be eventually, once they get used to the idea,' he said firmly. 'I guess I can live with a wedding in August, and telling them in June. I was hoping we could tell people right away.' He smiled at her. 'This is very exciting. But I'm willing to wait!' He pulled her close to him then, and he could feel her heart beating. She was feeling skittish and scared and excited all at once. She loved him, but this was so different from what she had had with Blake. But then again, she and Charles were older and this made more sense. Charles was the kind of solid, reliable man she had always wanted, not a madman like Blake, however charming he was, that you could never count on. Charles was no rogue, he was a man. And this felt right, even if it was surprising. She had been shocked when he asked.

This all seemed so soon to Maxine, but she agreed with him. At their age, they knew what worked and what they wanted. Why waste more time?

'I love you,' she whispered, and he kissed her.

'I love you too,' he said afterward. 'Where do you want to get married?'

'What about my house in Southampton?' It came to her when he asked the question. 'It's big enough for all of us to stay there, and we can tent the garden.' Between the two of them, they knew a fair amount of people.

'That sounds perfect.' They had gone out there for the weekend twice, and he loved it. Suddenly he looked worried. 'Do we have to take the children on the honeymoon with us?' he asked, and she laughed, and shook her head.

'No, we don't.' And then she had a thought. 'Maybe Blake would lend us his boat. It would be perfect for a honeymoon.' Charles frowned as she said it.

'I don't want to spend my honeymoon on your ex-husband's boat,' he said firmly, 'no matter how big it is. You're my wife now, not his.' He had been jealous of Blake from the first, and Maxine backed off immediately.

'I'm sorry. That was stupid of me.'

'Maybe Venice,' he said dreamily. He had always loved it. She didn't suggest that they borrow Blake's palazzo there. Charles had obviously forgotten that he had one.

'Or Paris. That might be romantic.' It was one of the few cities where Blake didn't have a house.

'We'll figure it out. We have until June to make plans.' He wanted to get her an engagement ring too, and he wanted her to help pick it out. But now she couldn't wear it till June, since they wouldn't tell the children until then. He was sorry about that. But it would be August before they knew it, he realized. In six months, she would be Mrs. Charles West. He loved it. And so did she. Maxine West. It had a nice sound.

They sat and whispered and made plans. They agreed that he would sell his apartment and move in with her. Given his small apartment and the size

200

of her family, it was the only arrangement that made sense. After they talked, she wished they could make love, but they couldn't. Sam was in her bed, sound asleep. She agreed to go to his apartment the following night, 'to seal the deal' as he said. They could both hardly wait now until they could spend the whole night together, and get up in the morning under one roof. And she would have everyone she loved in one place. It sounded great to her too.

They kissed for a long time before he left. He was tender and loving and kind. And as he got into the elevator, he whispered to her, 'Goodnight, Mrs. West.' She beamed at him, and whispered, 'I love you,' to him. And as she locked the door and walked to her bedroom, she turned it around in her mind. It wasn't at all what she had expected, but now that they had decided, it sounded like a wonderful plan to her too. She just hoped the kids would take the news well. She was glad Charles had agreed to wait. She loved the whole idea. He was the kind of man she should have married in the beginning. But if she had, she wouldn't have the great kids she did. So in the end, everything had worked out right. And she had Charles now. That was all that mattered.

CHAPTER 14

Although Charles and Maxine didn't tell the children their plans and kept them private for the moment, having made them between themselves changed everything subtly anyway. Charles suddenly had a proprietary air about him whenever he was around Maxine or the kids, and Daphne was quick to pick it up.

'Who does he think he is?' she complained one day when he had told Jack to take off his cleats and change his shirt before they went out to dinner. Maxine had noticed it too, but she was pleased that Charles was trying to fit in and take his place, even if awkwardly. She knew his intentions were good. Being stepfather to three children was a big leap for him.

'He means well,' Maxine said to Daphne, excusing him far more easily than her daughter was willing to.

'No, he doesn't. He's just bossy. Dad would never say that. He wouldn't care what Jack wears out to dinner, or if he wore his cleats to bed.'

'Maybe that's not such a good thing,' Maxine suggested. 'Maybe we need a little more order around here.' Charles was very proper, and liked everything neat and in control. It was one of the things they had in common. Blake was the opposite extreme.

'What is this? A Hitler Youth Camp?' Daphne snapped at her and stormed off. It made Maxine glad they had waited to announce their engagement and marriage the following summer. The children weren't ready to hear it yet. She was hoping that in the coming months, they would accept it a little more each day.

March was a busy month for Maxine. She attended two conferences at opposite ends of the country, one in San Diego on the effects of national traumatic events on children under twelve, where she was the main speaker.

And another on suicidality in adolescents, in Washington, D.C. Maxine was part of a panel that opened the conference, and she gave a separate lecture of her own on the second day of the event. And then she had to rush home to New York for spring break with her kids. She had hoped to convince Blake to see them during their spring vacation, but he said he was in Morocco, working on the house, up to his ears in construction and plans, and too busy to take a break. It was disappointing for her children and stressful for her to take a week off with them. Thelma handled her patients for her when she did.

Maxine took her children skiing in New Hampshire for a week during their break. And unfortunately, Charles couldn't get away. He was busy with his practice, so Maxine went to New Hampshire with her children, and a friend for each, and they had a ball. When she told Charles what she was doing, he confessed to being enormously relieved that he was too busy to join them. Six children were far too many for his nerves. Three already seemed like a lot to him. Six sounded insane. Maxine loved it, and called him from New Hampshire with reports several times a day. And the day after they returned, she left for the conference in Washington, D.C. Charles came down to visit her for one night, and they finally met in her bed at midnight. It had been a very busy week.

It ruffled his feathers a little when she was so busy, but in theory he understood. She was a woman with a demanding medical practice, and three young kids, who were hers to bring up on her own, with no help or guidance from Blake. She couldn't even reach him most of the time, no longer tried, and made every decision on her own.

Blake was wrapped up in his latest house adventure, and his life of 'fun,' while she worked her tail off, and took care of their kids. The only one who helped her was Zelda, no one else ever did. Maxine felt eternally grateful and in her debt. Neither Charles nor Blake had any concept of what it took to keep her life running smoothly and her kids attended to and in good shape. Charles's occasional suggestion that she take a month off, to relax and plan the wedding, only made her laugh. What? How? When? No way. She was swamped, and Blake was back to being the invisible man to their kids. He had been adorable with them in Aspen. But he had no plans to see them again before July or August. It was going to be a long time for them to wait, with everything on Maxine's shoulders until then.

And as spring and warm weather came, she saw more and more kids in crisis. Her sicker patients always responded negatively to spring and fall, particularly March, April, May, June, and September. In spring, all the people suffering from winter doldrums began to feel better. The weather was warmer, the sun came out, flowers bloomed, joy was in the air, and the truly sick ones felt more hopeless than ever. They were left like rocks on the beach when the tide went out, and they stuck out in their darkness, misery, and despair. It was a dangerous time for suicidal kids.

Much to her chagrin and despite all her efforts, two of her patients committed suicide in March, and a third one in April. It was a terrible time for her, and Thelma lost one of her patients too, an eighteen-year-old boy she had worked with for four years, and she was heartbroken for the family, and missed the boy herself. September was also an equally dangerous month, and statistically prime time for suicides in adolescent boys.

Thelma and Maxine commiserated about their lost patients over lunch, and Maxine shared the news of her secret engagement with her. It cheered them both, and was a sign of hope in their world.

'Wow! That is big news!' Thelma said, looking thrilled for her. It was a far happier topic than the reason they had lunch. 'How do you think your kids will react?' Maxine had told her they weren't telling them till June, and the wedding was planned for August.

'I'm hoping they'll be ready to hear it by then. June is only two months away, but they seem to be adjusting to Charles little by little. Basically, they like the way things have been, having me to themselves, with no man around to share me with, or interfere.' Maxine looked worried as she said it, and Thelma smiled.

'That makes them nice, well-adjusted, normal kids. It's a sweet deal for them having you alone, with no man for them to compete with for your attention.'

'I think Charles will be a great addition to our family. He's just the kind of man we always needed,' Maxine said, sounding hopeful.

'That will make it even harder for them,' Thelma said wisely. 'If he were a jerk, they could dismiss him, and so would you. Instead, he's a reasonable candidate and a solid citizen. That'll make him Public Enemy Number One, as far as they're concerned, for a while anyway. Fasten your seat belt, Max, something tells me you may hit some turbulence when you tell them. But they'll get over it. I'm really happy for you,' Thelma said with a broad grin.

'Thanks, me too.' Maxine smiled back at her, still nervous about her kids. 'And I think you're right about the turbulence. I'm not looking forward to it, so we put off telling them as long as we could.' But June was just around the corner, only two months away. And Maxine was getting anxious about the big announcement. For the moment, it made their wedding plans a little tense, and somewhat bittersweet. And a little bit unreal, until they told the kids.

She and Charles went to Cartier and picked out a ring in April. They had it sized, and Charles gave it to her formally over dinner, but they both knew she couldn't wear it yet. She kept it in a locked drawer of her desk at home, and took it out to look at it and try it on every night. She loved it. It was beautiful, and the stone sparkled unbelievably. She could hardly wait to wear it. Getting the ring made their plans feel more real. And she had already reserved the date for the caterer in Southampton in August. Their wedding was only four months away. And she wanted to look for a dress. She wanted to tell Blake too, and her parents, but not until after they told the kids. She felt she owed them that.

She, Charles, and the children spent the Easter weekend in Southampton, and had a very nice time. Maxine and Charles whispered about their wedding plans at night, giggling like two kids, and took romantic walks on the beach hand in hand while Daphne rolled her eyes. It was May when

Maxine had an unexpectedly serious talk with Zellie. She'd had a bad day. A friend of hers had died in an accident, and for the first time ever, she talked mournfully about her regrets about never having had children of her own. Maxine was sympathetic and figured it would pass. It had just been a very bad day.

'It's not too late,' Maxine said, trying to cheer her up. 'You could still meet someone and have a baby.' It was getting late, but it was not over for her yet. 'Women have babies a lot later than they used to, with a little help.' She and Charles had talked about it too, and Maxine would have liked that, but Charles felt her three were enough. He felt too old to have his own, which Maxine thought was too bad. She would have loved to have another baby, if he'd been willing. But he wasn't.

'I think I'd rather adopt,' Zelda said practically. 'I've been taking care of other people's kids all my life. I don't have a problem with that. I love them like my own.' She smiled, and Maxine hugged her. She knew that was true. 'Maybe I should look into adoption sometime,' Zelda continued vaguely, and Maxine nodded. It was one of those things people say to make themselves feel better, but don't necessarily mean. Maxine was fairly certain it was that.

Zelda knew nothing of Maxine's upcoming marriage. But they were planning to tell the children in three weeks when they got out of school. Maxine was apprehensive about it, but excited too. It was time to share their big news with them. Zelda didn't mention the idea of adoption again, and Maxine forgot about it. She assumed Zelda had too.

It was the last day of school, in early June, when Maxine got a call from the school. She was sure it was just a routine call of some kind. The kids were due home in an hour, and she was seeing patients at her office. The call was about Sam. He had been hit by a car when he was crossing the street to get to his car pool. He had been taken to New York Hospital by ambulance. One of the teachers had gone with him.

'Oh my God, is he all right?' How all right could he be, if they'd taken him away by ambulance? Maxine was panicked.

'They think his leg is broken, Dr. Williams . . . I'm so sorry, it was chaotic on the last day. He hit his head too, but he was conscious when they left. He's a brave little guy.' Brave? Fuck them. How could they let that happen to her son? She was shaking when she hung up, and rushed back into her office. She'd been seeing a seventeen-year-old boy, who had been a patient for two years, and had taken the call at her secretary's desk. She explained to her patient what had happened, and he told her how sorry he was. She apologized for ending the session, and had her secretary cancel the rest of her afternoon. She grabbed her handbag, and realized she should call Blake too, although there was nothing he could do. But Sam was his son too. She called his house in London, and the butler told her he was in Morocco, and might be at his villa at La Mamounia. When she called the hotel in Marrakech, they took the message but refused to confirm if he was there. His cell phone was on voice mail. She was frantic, and then she called Charles. He said he'd meet her at the emergency room. And with that, she flew out the door.

It was easy to find Sam in the ER. He had a broken arm and leg, two broken ribs, and a concussion, and he looked as though he were in shock. He wasn't even crying. And Charles was wonderful with him. He went into the operating room with Sam when they set the leg and arm. They couldn't do anything about the ribs but wrap them, and the concussion was mild fortunately. Maxine was beside herself as she waited. And later that afternoon, they let her take him home. Charles was still with her, and Sam was holding both their hands. It tore at her heart to see the condition he was in, and they settled him in her bed. They had painkillers to give him, and he was very groggy. Jack and Daphne were beside themselves when they saw him. But he was all right, he was alive, and all the damage would repair. The mother who had been carpooling called and apologized profusely, they had never seen the car coming. The driver had been devastated too. But not as much as Maxine. She was grateful it wasn't worse.

Charles stayed and slept on the couch, and took turns watching Sam with her. They both canceled their patients for the next day, and Zelda kept running in to check on Sam too. Maxine went into the kitchen for a cup of tea at midnight. It was her shift with Sam, and she ran into Daphne, who glared at her.

'Why is he sleeping here?' she demanded, referring to Charles.

'Because he cares about us.' Maxine was tired, and in no mood for Daphne's comments. 'He was great with Sam at the hospital. He was in the operating room with him.'

'Did you call Dad?' Daphne asked pointedly, and Maxine had had enough.

'Yes, I did actually. He's in goddamn Morocco, and no one can find him. He hasn't returned my calls. So what else is new? Does that answer your question?' With that, Daphne looked hurt and stormed off to her room. She still wanted her father to be something he wasn't, and never would be. They all did. Jack wanted his father to be a hero, and he wasn't. He was just a man. And everyone, including Maxine, wanted him to be responsible, and somewhere where one could find him. He never was. And this time was no different. It was precisely why they were divorced.

It took Maxine five days to locate him in Morocco. He said there had been an earthquake there, a bad one. And suddenly Maxine vaguely remembered hearing about it. But all she'd thought about for the last week was Sam. He had been miserable with the ribs, and had a headache for several days from the concussion. The arm and leg weren't as bad since they were in casts. And Blake sounded upset when she told him.

'It would be nice if you were somewhere where I can call you, for a change. This is ridiculous, Blake. If anything happens, I can never find you.' She was not amused, and very angry at him.

'I'm really sorry, Max. All the phone lines were down. My cell phone and email haven't worked till today. It was a nasty earthquake, and a lot of people got killed in villages not far from here. I've been trying to help out, organizing airlifts of supplies.'

'Since when have you been playing Good

Samaritan?' She was seriously pissed at him. Charles had been there for her. As usual, Blake hadn't.

'They need help. There are people wandering the streets with no food, and bodies all over the place. Look, do you want me to fly in for Sam?'

'You don't need to. He's okay,' she said, calming down. 'But it was scary for all of us. Particularly him. He's asleep now, but you should call him in a few hours.'

'I'm sorry, Max,' he said, sounding sincere. 'You've got enough on your hands without dealing with that too.'

'I'm all right. Charles was here.'

'I'm glad,' Blake said quietly, and she realized that he sounded tired too. Maybe he really was doing something useful in Morocco, although it was hard to believe. 'I'll call Sam later. Give him a kiss from me.'

'I will.'

And he did in fact call Sam several hours later. Sam was thrilled to talk to his dad and told him all about it. He said Charles had stayed in the operating room with him, and held his hand. He told Blake that his mom was upset and the doctor wouldn't let her come in, which was true. She had nearly fainted, worrying about her son. Charles had been the hero of the day. And Blake promised to come and see Sam soon. By then, Maxine had read all about the earthquake in Morocco. It was a big one, and two villages had literally been destroyed and everyone in them killed. There was even extensive damage in the cities. Blake had been telling the truth. But she was still upset that she hadn't been able to reach him for their son. It

211

was typical of Blake. He never changed. He would be a rogue to the end of his days. Or a flake anyway. Thank God she had Charles.

He was still sleeping on the couch by the end of the week, and he had been there for all of them every night after work, and he had been so good with Sam. They both agreed that it was a good time to share their plans with the kids. It was time. It was June, and school was out.

Maxine gathered everyone in the kitchen on Saturday morning. Charles was there with her, which she wasn't entirely convinced was a good idea, but he wanted to be there when she told them, and she felt she owed it to him. He had proven himself with Sam, she couldn't shut him out now. And the children could unburden themselves later to her, if they had anything to say about it.

She sounded a little vague at first, talking about how kind Charles had been to them in the last several months. She looked at each of her children as she said it, as though trying to convince them as well as remind them. She was still afraid of their reaction to the news. And then there was nothing left to do but say it.

'So Charles and I have decided to get married in August.' There was dead silence in the room and absolutely no reaction as they stared at their mother. They looked like statues.

'I love your mother, and you,' Charles added, sounding stiffer than he meant to. But he had never done anything like this before, and they were a daunting group. Zelda was hovering in the background.

'Are you kidding?' Daphne was the first to react, and Maxine answered her seriously.

212

'No. We're not.'

'You hardly know him.' She spoke to her mother and ignored Charles.

'We've been dating for almost seven months, and at our age we know when it's right.' She paraphrased Charles, and Daphne got up from the kitchen table and walked out of the kitchen without another word. They heard her bedroom door slam a minute later.

'Does Dad know?' Jack asked.

'Not yet,' his mother answered. 'We wanted to tell you first. Then I'm going to tell Dad, and Grandma and Grampa. But I wanted you to be the first to know.'

'Oh,' Jack said, and then disappeared too. His door didn't slam, it just closed, as Maxine's heart sank. This was even harder than she thought.

'I think it will be good,' Sam said quietly, looking at them both. 'You were very nice to me at the hospital, Charles. Thank you.' He was being polite, and he looked less upset than the others, but he wasn't thrilled either. He could easily figure out that he wouldn't be sleeping with his mother anymore. Charles was going to take his place. It was upsetting for them all, and as far as they were concerned, their life had been fine before Charles. 'Can I watch TV in your room now?' Sam asked. None of them had asked details of the wedding, or even when it would be exactly. They didn't want to know. And a moment later, Sam had left on his crutches, which he was managing very well. Charles and Maxine were alone in the kitchen, and Zelda spoke up from the doorway.

'Congratulations,' she said softly. 'They'll get used to it. It's kind of a shock. I was beginning to

213

suspect that's what you two had in mind.' She smiled, but she looked a little sad too. It was a big change for them all, and they were used to the way things were, and liked them that way.

'It won't change anything for you, Zellie,' Maxine reassured her. 'We'll need you just as much. Maybe more.' Maxine smiled.

'Thanks. I wouldn't know what to do with myself if you didn't.' Charles looked at her and smiled. She seemed like a nice woman to him, although he didn't love the prospect of running into her in his pajamas late at night when he moved in. He was in for a whole new life, with a wife, three kids, and a live-in nanny. His privacy was a thing of the past. But he still thought this was right. 'The kids will adjust,' Zelda reassured them again. 'They just need some time.' Maxine nodded.

'It could have been worse,' Maxine said encouragingly.

'Not much,' Charles said, looking discouraged. 'I was kind of hoping some of them would be pleased. Maybe not Daphne, but at least the boys.'

'No one likes change,' Maxine reminded him. 'And this is a big one for them. And for us.' She leaned over and kissed him, and he smiled at her ruefully as Zelda went back to her room, to leave them alone.

'I love you,' he said to her. 'I'm sorry your kids are upset.'

'They'll get over it. One day we'll laugh about it, like our first date.'

'Maybe that was an omen,' he said, looking worried.

'No . . . it's going to be great. You'll see,' Maxine said, and kissed him again. And Charles silently

214

hoped she was right as he took her in his arms. He was sad that her kids weren't happy for them.

CHAPTER 15

The children stayed in their rooms for the next several hours after the shock of their mother's announcement, and Charles decided to go home. He hadn't slept there in days, and he thought it was a good time to leave Maxine alone with her children. He left, still looking upset, and Maxine reassured him again that they'd adjust, but he wasn't as sure. He wasn't backing out, but he was scared. And so were the kids.

Maxine collapsed into a chair at the kitchen table after he left, with a cup of tea, and she was relieved to see Zelda wander into the kitchen from her room.

'At least someone around here is still talking to me,' she said to Zelda, as she poured herself a cup of tea too.

'It's mighty quiet around here,' Zelda commented as she sat down across from Maxine. 'It's going to take some time for the dust to settle.'

'I know. I hate to upset them, but I think it's a good thing.' Charles had proven himself to her again with Sam's accident. He was everything she had hoped he would be, and the kind of man she had needed in her life for years.

'They'll get used to it,' Zelda reassured her. 'It's not easy for him either,' she said, referring to Charles. 'You can tell he's never been around kids.' Maxine nodded. You couldn't have everything.

And if he had children of his own, they might not have liked that either. This was simpler.

Maxine cooked dinner for the children that night, and everyone pushed their food around their plates. None of them could eat, including Maxine. She hated the look on their faces. Daphne looked as though someone had died.

'How can you do that, Mom? He's a creep.' It was a mean thing to say about him, and Sam intervened.

'No, he's not. He's nice to me. And he'd be nice to you, if you weren't so mean to him.' What he said was true, and she didn't say it, but Maxine agreed. 'He's just not used to kids.' They all knew that was true.

'When he took me to the basketball game, he tried to tell me I should go to boarding school,' Jack said, with a worried look. 'Are you going to send us now, Mom?'

'Of course not. Charles went to boarding school, and he loved it, so he thinks everyone should go. I'd never send you guys away.'

'That's what you say now,' Daphne commented. 'Wait till you're married to him, and he makes you.'

'He's not going to "make" me send you away. You're my kids, not his.'

'That's not how he acts. He thinks he owns the world,' Daphne said, glaring at her mother.

'No, he doesn't.' Maxine stood up for him, but she was glad that her children were venting. At least it got everything out in the open between them. 'He's used to running his own life, but he's not going to run yours. He wouldn't want to, and I won't let him.'

216

'He hates Dad,' Jack said matter-of-factly.

'I don't think that's true either. He may be jealous of him, but he doesn't hate him.'

'What do you think Dad will say?' Daphne asked with interest. 'I'll bet he'll be sad if you get married, Mom.'

'I don't think so. He's got ten million girlfriends. Is he still with Arabella?' She hadn't heard anything about her recently.

'Yeah,' Daphne said, looking glum. 'I just hope he doesn't marry her. That's all we need.' They all sounded as though something terrible had happened. This had certainly not been good news to them. She had expected it, but it was hard anyway. Only Sam seemed to think it was okay, but he liked Charles better than the others.

Charles called her after dinner to see how they were. He missed her, but it had been a relief to get home. The past week had been tough for all of them. First Sam's accident, and now this. And Maxine felt trapped in the middle.

'They're okay. They just need some time to get used to the idea,' she said sensibly.

'Like what? Twenty years?' He was very upset about it.

'No, they're kids. Give them a few weeks. They'll be dancing at our wedding like everyone else.'

'Have you told Blake?'

'No, I'll call him later. I wanted to tell the kids first. And I'm going to call my parents tomorrow. They will be thrilled!' Charles had met them once and liked them very much. He liked the idea of marrying into a family of physicians.

The children were lackluster for the rest of the

evening. They stayed in their rooms and watched DVDs. Sam was sleeping in his own room again. And it was funny to think, as she lay in her bed that night, that in two months Charles would be living here. It was hard to imagine living with anyone again after all these years. And Sam was right, he wouldn't be able to sleep in her bed. She was going to miss it. In spite of the fact that she loved Charles, the good news had a downside for everyone, even her. Life worked that way. You traded some things for others. But it was hard to sell that to kids. And sometimes, even to herself.

She called Blake just after midnight, which was morning for him. He sounded busy and distracted, and she could hear machines and shouting in the distance. It was hard talking to him.

'Where are you? What are you doing?' she said loudly.

'I'm in the street, trying to help clear things. We airlifted in some bulldozers to help them. They're still digging people out. Max, there are kids walking around the streets here with nowhere to go. Whole families got wiped out, and children are still looking for their parents. There are injured people lying everywhere, because the hospitals are full. You can't imagine what it's like.'

'Yes, I can,' she said sadly. 'I've gone to natural disaster scenes for work. There's nothing worse.'

'Maybe you should come over here and help. They need people to advise them what to do about the children, and how to handle things afterward. In fact, you're just what they need. Would you ever consider it?' he said, sounding pensive. His house was still standing, and he could have left, but he liked the country and the people so much and wanted to do all he could to help.

'I would, if someone hires me to. I can't just fly over there and start telling them what to do.'

'I could hire you.' He wanted to do whatever it took.

'Don't be silly. I'd do it for free for you. But I'd need to know what kind of advice they want from me. What I do is very specific. It's about managing the children's trauma, immediately, and long term. Let me know if there's anything I can do.'

'I will. How's Sam?'

'He's okay. He's doing pretty well on his crutches.' And then she remembered why she had called him. He had distracted her for a minute with his stories about the earthquake damage and the horror of orphaned children wandering the streets. 'I have something to tell you,' she said solemnly.

'About Sam's accident?' He sounded worried. She had never heard him sound like this. For once, he was thinking about someone other than himself.

'No. About me. I'm getting married. To Charles West. We're getting married in August.' He was quiet for a minute.

'Are the kids upset?' He expected them to be.

'Yes.' She was honest with him. 'They like things the way they are. They don't want anything to change.'

'That's understandable. They wouldn't like it if I got married either. I hope he's good to you, Max,' Blake said, sounding more serious than he had in years.

'He is.'

'Then congratulations.' He laughed then and sounded more like himself. 'I guess I didn't expect it to happen so soon. But it'll be good for you, and

219

the kids. They just don't know it yet. Listen, I'll call you when I can. I have to go now. There's too much going on here to talk for long. Take care of yourself and kiss the kids . . . and Max, congratulations again . . .' And before she could even thank him, he was gone. She hung up the phone, and went to bed. She was thinking about Blake in the devastation after the earthquake in Morocco and all he was doing to help orphans and wounded people, clear away rubble, and fly in medicines and food. For once, he was doing more than just putting his money to good use, he was rolling up his sleeves to do the work himself. It didn't sound like the Blake she knew, and she wondered if he was finally growing up. If so, it was long overdue.

*   *   *

Maxine called her parents in the morning, and finally someone was thrilled with the news. Her father said he was delighted and he liked him, and that Charles was just the kind of man he had hoped she would find and marry one day. And it pleased him that he was a physician too. He told her to congratulate Charles, and offered his best wishes to her, which was the proper way to do it. And then her mother got on the phone, and asked all about the wedding.

'Are the children excited?' she asked, as Maxine smiled and shook her head. They didn't get it.

'Not exactly, Mom. It's a big change for them.'

'He's a very nice man. I'm sure in the long run they'll be very glad you married him.'

'I hope so,' she said, sounding less sure than her

220

mother.

'Both of you will have to come to dinner soon.'

'We'd love that,' Maxine said. She wanted Charles to get to know them better, particularly since he had no family himself.

It was nice for everyone that her parents were so happy for them, and that they approved. It mattered a great deal to Maxine, and she hoped it would to Charles too. It would help to balance the children's lack of enthusiasm.

*   *   *

Charles had dinner with her and the children that night, and it was a quiet meal. There were no unpleasant outbursts, and no one said any-thing rude, but they weren't happy either. They just got through it, and went to their rooms. This wasn't the way Charles had hoped it would be.

Maxine told him about her call to her parents, and he looked pleased.

'At least someone around here likes me,' he said, looking relieved. 'Maybe we should take them to La Grenouille.'

'They want to have us over first, and I think they should.' She wanted to get him used to their traditions, and bring him into her family.

And then, after dinner, she had an idea. She unlocked her desk drawer and took out the ring she had been waiting to wear for months. She asked Charles to put it on her finger, and he looked thrilled. It finally made what they'd been saying real. They were engaged to be married, no matter how unhappy her children appeared to be about it. It was a wonderful thing, and Charles

221

kissed her as they both looked down at the ring. It sparkled as brightly as her hopes for their marriage, and their love for each other, which hadn't dimmed in the last difficult days. Nothing had changed. This was just one of those rough patches they knew they had to get through. And Maxine had foreseen it more than he. He was delighted she still loved her ring, and him. They were getting married in nine weeks.

'We have to get busy now working on the wedding,' she said, feeling excited and young again. It was nice not having to keep it secret anymore.

'Oh my God,' he said, teasing her. 'How big is it going to be?' She had already ordered the invitations. They were going out in three weeks, and they still had to make their final lists, and she said something about signing up for the registry at Tiffany. 'Do people do that for second weddings?' he asked, looking surprised. 'Aren't we a little old for all that?'

'Of course not,' she said, looking giddy. 'And I still have to find a dress.' She needed to find one for Daphne too. Maxine was faintly nervous that she'd refuse to come to the wedding, so she wasn't going to push it.

As they made their lists that night, they agreed to invite two hundred people to the wedding, which might leave them with around a hundred and fifty, which sounded right to both of them. And she said that she had to invite Blake. Charles balked at that.

'You can't invite your ex-husband to the wedding. What if I invited my ex-wife?'

'That's up to you, and it's fine with me if that's

222

what you want. For me, Blake is family, and the children would be very upset if he wasn't there.' Charles groaned as he listened.

'That is not my definition of extended family.' He knew by then that he had fallen into a very unusual group of people. There was nothing ordinary or 'normal' about them, and it was even stranger to realize that he was marrying the former wife of Blake Williams. That took them out of the norm right there. 'Do whatever you want,' he finally said. 'I can sense that we're going to be pushing the outer edges of the envelope here. Who am I to tell you what to do? I'm only the groom.' He was only half-teasing, and it still seemed remarkable to him that his future wife was telling him that her ex-husband would be hurt if he wasn't invited to their wedding. Unless he wanted a major battle on his hands, and stepchildren who would hate him even more than they did, he felt he had no choice but to give in.

'He isn't going to walk you down the aisle, is he?' Charles asked, looking worried.

'Of course not, silly. My father will do that.' Charles looked relieved. And she knew, without Charles admitting it, that he had always had an issue about Blake. It was hard for any man to feel he measured up to him. If money was the yardstick for success used by most people, then Blake was at the top of the heap. But that didn't change the fact that he was irresponsible, and always had been, and was never there for her children. Blake was fun to be with, and she would always love him. But Charles was the man she wanted to be married to, without question.

He kissed her when he left that night, and they

had discussed most of the details. They both laughed with pleasure as she flashed her ring.

'Goodnight, Mrs. West,' he said softly, and as he said it, she realized that she'd probably have to keep 'Williams' for work. It would be too complicated to change it for all her patients, and all the professional things she did, so even though she would be Mrs. West socially, she would still be Dr. Williams, and carry Blake's name forever. There were some things you just couldn't change.

CHAPTER 16

Blake called Maxine in the office between patients, and it had already been a crazy day for her. She had dealt with three new referrals, and she had just been arguing with the caterer in Southampton about the price of the tent for their wedding. The price was insane, but there was no question that they needed one. Her parents had offered to pay for it, but at her age she didn't feel right letting them do it. On the other hand, she didn't want to get screwed over by the caterer either. Tents were expensive, especially with the clear sides she wanted. It would be too claustrophobic otherwise. She still sounded annoyed when she took Blake's call.

'Hi,' she said brusquely. 'What's up?'

'Sorry, Max. Bad time? I'll call you back if you want.' She glanced at her watch, and saw that it was already late for him. She wasn't sure if he was in London again, or still in Morocco, but either way it was late in the evening, and she could hear in his voice that he was tired.

'No, no, it's fine. I'm sorry. I have a few minutes before my next patient. Are you okay?'

'I am. But no one else is around here. I'm still in Imlil, about three hours outside Marrakech. Amazingly, they have a mobile phone mast, though not much else, so I could call you. I've gotten involved with these kids here, Max. What's happened to them is just awful. They're still pulling people out of the rubble, where they've been buried with all the dead members of their families for days. Others are just wandering around the streets looking dazed. They're dirt poor here in the villages, and something like this just wipes them out. They're assessing that more than twenty thousand people were killed.'

'I know,' Maxine said sadly. 'I've seen the stories in the *Times* and on CNN.' It struck her that she couldn't reach him when her own son got hurt, but suddenly he was trying to heal the woes of the world. At least it was better than his flitting from party to party on his jet all over the world. Disaster scenes weren't unfamiliar to her because of her work. But it was the first time she had heard him so upset about something that didn't involve him directly. But he was seeing it first-hand. She had been in situations like that herself, in natural disasters where she'd been sent to consult, both in the States and abroad.

'I need your help,' he said. He was bone tired; he had hardly slept in ten days. 'I'm trying to organize assistance for the children. I've met some very interesting and powerful people over here, since I bought the house. The government systems are so overwhelmed that the private sector is trying

225

to see what they can do to bail them out. I've taken on a huge project for the kids, and I'm doing it myself. I need some advice about what kind of assistance they're going to need, both long term and now. It's right up your alley. I need your expertise, Max.' He sounded tired, worried, and sad.

She exhaled sharply as she listened. That was a tall order. 'I'd love to help,' she ventured. She was impressed by the magnitude of what he was doing, but she had to be realistic about it too. 'I'm not really sure I can advise you over the phone,' she said sadly. 'I don't know the available government systems to access there, and you really have to see those things firsthand. It's not about theory in a disaster like that. You have to be there, like you are, to figure it out and do it right.'

'I know,' he said. 'That's why I called. I didn't know what else to do.' He hesitated for a split second. 'Will you come over, Max? These kids need you, and so do I.' She was stunned when she heard what he said. Although he had mentioned the idea in their earlier conversation, she had no idea he was so serious about this, or that he would actually ask her to come. Her schedule was jam-packed for the next month. She was going on vacation, as she always did, with the kids in July, and with the wedding coming up in August, her life was insane.

'Shit, Blake . . . I'd love to, but I don't see how I can. I've got a really full patient load right now, and some of them are very sick.'

'I want to send you my plane. Even if you only stay for twenty-four hours, it would be a huge help. I need your eyes here, instead of mine. I've got the money to make a difference, but I don't know my ass from a hole in the ground, and you're the only one I trust. Tell me what to do here. Otherwise, I'm just whistling in the dark.' He had made an amazing request, and she didn't see how she could do it. On the other hand, he had never asked her for anything like this before. And she could tell that his heart was fully in it. He was committed to do everything he could to help, both hands on, and with his funds. And it was the kind of work that she found most rewarding too. There was no question that it would be heartbreaking and backbreaking going into a disaster like that, but it was what she loved most, and an opportunity to make a real difference. She was proud of him for what he was doing, and listening to him talk about it brought tears to her eyes. She wanted to tell his children about it, so they could be proud of their dad.

'I wish I could,' she said slowly. 'I just don't see when or how.' She would have loved to go to Morocco, to help and advise him. She admired his good intentions and hard work. She could tell that this was different for him and she wanted to help him. She just couldn't see how right now.

'What if you cancel your Friday? I have the plane there on Thursday, you could fly overnight. That would give you three days here over the weekend. You fly back Sunday night, and you're back in your office on Monday.' He had been trying to work it out for hours, and there was silence at her end.

'I'm off this weekend,' she said pensively, and Thelma was already covering for her. She could ask her for another day. But Maxine was well aware that going to Morocco for three days was a crazy thing to do, given all she had on her own plate.

'I just don't know who else to ask. These kids' lives will be ruined if someone doesn't do the right stuff for them now. A lot of them are going to be screwed anyway.' They had been injured and maimed and blinded, brain-damaged, and lost limbs when their homes and schools collapsed on them. An incredible number had been orphaned. He had seen a newborn baby being rescued, still alive, as they pulled it from the rubble, while Blake watched and cried.

'Give me a couple of hours to figure this out,' Maxine said quietly as her buzzer went off to tell her that her next patient had arrived. 'I've got to think about it.' It was Tuesday. If she went, she had two days to get organized. But natural disasters never gave you notice, or time to plan. She had left before on a few hours' notice. And she wanted to help him out, or at least refer someone good to advise him. There was an excellent association of psychiatrists she knew in Paris who specialized in this kind of thing. But the thought of going to help excited her too. And she hadn't done anything like this in a while. 'When can I call you?'

'Anytime. I haven't been to bed all week. Try my British cell phone, and my BlackBerry. They both work here now, some of the time at least . . . and Max . . . thanks . . . I love you, babe. Thanks for listening and giving a damn. Now I understand what you do. You're an incredible woman.' He had new respect for her after all he'd just seen first-hand. He felt as though he'd grown up overnight, and she could hear it. She knew that this was genuine, and a whole new side of Blake that was

228

emerging at last.

'The same to you,' she said softly. There were tears in her eyes again. 'I'll get back to you as soon as I can. I don't know if I can come, but if I can't, I'll find you someone first rate who will.'

'I want you,' he begged her. 'Please, Max . . .'

'I'll try,' she promised, hung up the phone, and opened the door to her patient. She had to force her mind back to present time to listen closely to what the twelve-year-old girl was saying. She was a cutter, and had lines running up and down both arms. She had been referred to Maxine by her school, and was one of the victims of 9/11. Her father was one of the firefighters who had died, and she was part of an ongoing study Maxine had been doing for the city since it happened. The session was longer than usual, and afterward Maxine hurried home.

All her children were hanging out in the kitchen with Zelda when she got there, and she told them about their dad and what he was doing in Morocco. Their eyes shone as she told them, and she mentioned that he had asked her to join him. They were excited to hear about it and said that they hoped she would.

'I don't see how I can,' she said, looking stressed and distracted, and then walked out of the kitchen to call Thelma. She couldn't cover for Maxine on Friday since she was teaching a class at the NYU Medical School that day, but she said her partner could step in for Maxine on Friday instead, if she went. And Thelma was doing the weekend anyway.

Maxine made some other calls, checked her computer to see what appointments she had on Friday, and by eight o'clock she had made a decision. She hadn't even stopped for dinner. This was the least she could do, and Blake was making it easy for her by sending his plane. This was what life was about. She had always loved the line from the Talmud, and thought of it often, 'To save one life is to save a world entire.' And she realized that perhaps Blake had finally figured that out too. It had taken him one hell of a long time. At forty-six, he was turning into a real human being.

She waited until midnight to call him. It was very early morning for him by then. She had to try several times on both his cell phones, and finally got through. He sounded even more exhausted than he had the day before. He told her he had been up all night, again. It was the nature of the beast in those situations, Maxine knew, and what everyone had to do. If she went, she would be doing that too, so as not to lose any more time than they already had. There was no time to waste or spend on food or sleep. Blake was living that now.

She cut to the chase. 'I'll come.' He started crying when she said it. They were tears of relief, exhaustion, terror, and gratitude. He had never seen or experienced anything like this. 'I can come Thursday night,' she continued.

'Thank God . . . Max, I can't thank you enough. You are one hell of a woman. I love you . . . thank you with all my heart.' She told him about the kind of reports she would need when she got there, and what she wanted to see. It was up to him to get her access to government officials, get her into hospitals, and help her meet with as many of the children as possible, wherever they were being gathered. She wanted to make the best possible use of every minute she was there, and Blake wanted that too. He promised to take care of everything at his end, and he thanked her another dozen times before they hung up.

'I'm proud of you, Mom,' Daphne said softly when her mother hung up. She had been standing in the doorway, listening to her end of the conversation, and there were tears rolling down her cheeks.

'Thanks, sweetheart.' Maxine stood up and came to hug her. 'I'm proud of your dad too. He doesn't know anything about this stuff, and he's doing everything he can.' Daphne saw clearly in one of those rare special moments that her parents were both good people, and it had touched her heart, just as Blake's call had touched Maxine's. They talked about it for a while, as Maxine made hasty lists of what she'd need for the trip. And she emailed Thelma confirming that she was going and needed her partner to cover her practice for her on Friday.

Maxine realized that she had to call Charles too. They had been planning to spend the weekend in Southampton and meet with the caterers and the florist. He could do it without her, or they could postpone it for a week. It wouldn't make much difference, the wedding was still two months away. But it was too late to call him that night. She climbed into bed and lay there wide awake for hours, thinking of all she wanted to do when she got to Morocco. Suddenly, this was her project too, and she was grateful to Blake for sharing it with her. It felt as though her alarm went off five minutes after she fell asleep. And she called Charles right after breakfast. He hadn't left yet for his office, and she had to be in hers in twenty minutes. Since school was out, all the children were sleeping, and Zellie was puttering around the kitchen, getting ready for the onslaught that would come later.

'Hi, Max,' he said happily, pleased to hear her when he answered. 'Everything okay?' He had learned that calls from her at unusual times didn't always mean good news. Sam's recent accident had taught him that. Life was different when you had kids. 'Sam all right?'

'He's fine. I just wanted to give you a heads-up. I have to go away this weekend.' She sounded rushed and a little more brusque than she meant to, but she didn't want to be late for her office, and she knew he didn't either. They were both punctual to a fault. 'I have to cancel the meetings with the caterer and florist in Southampton, unless you want to go without me. Otherwise, I can do it next week. I'm going away.' She realized she sounded disjointed as she spoke.

'Something wrong?' She flew around to conferences all the time, but rarely on weekends, which, as much as possible, she considered sacred for her kids. 'What's up?' He seemed confused.

'I'm going to Morocco to meet Blake,' she said bluntly.

'You're *what*? What does *that* mean?' He was stunned, and he didn't like the sound of it at all. Maxine was quick to explain.

'Not like that. He was there when they had the big earthquake. He's been trying to organize rescue missions, and resources for the kids. It sounds like a huge mess, and he has no idea what he's doing. This is his first foray into humanitarian

232

work like that. He wants me to come over, look at some of the kids, meet with the various international and government agencies involved, and give him some advice.' She made it sound as though he had asked her to pick up a head of lettuce at the supermarket. Charles sounded shocked.

'You're doing that for *him*? Why?'

'Not for him. It's the first sign of being a human being and an adult he's shown in forty-six years. I'm proud of him. And the least I can do is give him some advice, and help them out.'

'That's ridiculous, Max,' Charles said, fuming. 'They've got the Red Cross. They don't need you.'

'It's not the same thing,' she bristled. 'I don't dig out survivors, drive an ambulance, or minister to the injured. I advise governments on how to deal with trauma in children. That's exactly what they need. I'm only going for three days. He's sending the plane for me.'

'Are you staying with him?' Charles asked, sounding suspicious. He acted as though she had said she was taking a cruise with Blake on his yacht. She had done that before too, with the children, but he was harmless. And they shared children, which justified almost anything to her. But in any case, this was different, whether Charles understood that or not. This was work, and that was it. Nothing else.

'My guess is I won't be staying anywhere, if this is anything like other earthquake disaster scenes I've been to. I'll be camping out in a truck, and sleeping standing up. I probably won't even see Blake when I get there, or not much.' It seemed ridiculous to her that Charles would make a

233

jealous scene over something as obvious and benign as this.

'I don't think you should go,' he said, digging in his heels. He was livid.

'That wasn't the question, and I'm sorry you feel that way,' Maxine said coolly. 'You have nothing to worry about, Charles,' she said, trying to sound gentle and be understanding about it. He was jealous. It was sweet. But this was one of her specialties and the kind of work she did all over the world. 'I love you. But I'd like to go over and lend a hand. It's only coincidental that the one who asked me to go is Blake. Any of the agencies involved could have called me too.'

'But they didn't. He did. And I don't see why you're going. For chrissake, when his son got hurt, it took you nearly a week to find him.'

'Because he was in Morocco, and they had an earthquake,' she said, sounding exasperated. This was seeming more unreasonable to her by the minute.

'Yeah, and where has he been for the rest of his children's lives? At parties and on yachts and chasing women. You told me yourself, you can never find him, and that's not because of earthquakes. The guy is a jerk, Max. And you're running halfway around the world to make him look good while he rescues a bunch of earthquake survivors? Give me a break. Screw him. I don't want you to go.'

'Please don't do this,' Maxine said through clenched teeth. 'I'm not running off with my ex-husband for an illicit weekend. I am going to consult about starting up a program for thousands of children who have been left orphaned and

234

injured and are going to be traumatized for the rest of their lives if someone doesn't do the right stuff in the beginning. It may not make much difference, depending on how they implement it, and what kind of funding is available to them, but it could make some. And that's my only interest here, not Blake, but helping those kids, as many as I can.' She made it very clear to him, but he wasn't buying it. Not for a minute.

'I had no idea I was marrying Mother Teresa,' he said, sounding even angrier than before, much to Maxine's utter frustration and chagrin. The last thing she wanted was a fight with Charles over this. It was pointless, and would just make things harder for her. She had made a commitment to Blake, and she was going. It was what she wanted to do, whether Charles liked it or not. He didn't own her, and he had to respect her work, and even her relationship to Blake, such as it was. Charles was the man she loved, he was her future. Blake was her past, and the father of her children.

'You're marrying a psychiatrist specializing in suicidality in adolescents, with a subspecialty of trauma in children and adolescents. I think that's pretty clear. The earthquake in Morocco is right up my alley. The only reason you're upset about it is because of Blake. Can we be grown-ups here? I wouldn't make a fuss if you were doing it. Why can't you be reasonable about me?'

'Because I don't understand the kind of relationship you have with him, and I think it's sick. You two have never cut the cord, and you may be a psychiatrist, Dr. Williams, but I think your bond to your ex-husband is twisted, that's what I think.'

235

'Thanks for your opinion, Charles. I'll take it into consideration some other time. Right now, I'm late for my patients, and I'm going to Morocco for three days. I made a commitment, and I'd like to do it. And I would appreciate it if you would be a little more adult about it, and trust me with Blake. I'm not going to have sex with him amid the rubble.' She was raising her voice, and so had he. They were fighting. About Blake. This was crazy.

'I don't care what you do with him, Maxine. But I can tell you one thing, I'm not going to put up with this kind of thing after we're married. If you want to run off to earthquakes and tsunamis and God knows what else halfway around the world, that's fine with me. But don't plan on doing it with your ex-husband and have me stick around. I think this is just an excuse for him to get you over there and hang out with you. I don't think it has a goddamn thing to do with Moroccan orphans or anything of that nature. The guy isn't enough of a human being to give a damn about anyone but himself, and you've told me that yourself. This is just an excuse and you know it.'

'Charles, you're wrong,' she said quietly. 'I've never known him to do anything like this either, but I have to respect what he's doing. And I'd like to help him if I can. I'm not helping *him*. I'm doing what I can for *those children*. Please try to understand that.' He didn't answer her, and they both sat there fuming. It bothered her that he had such an issue about Blake. It was going to make things very difficult for her and the children in the future if he didn't get over it. She hoped he would soon. And in the meantime, she was going to Morocco. She was a woman of her word. And hopefully, Charles would calm down. They hung up, but nothing had been resolved.

Maxine stood staring at the phone for a moment afterward, upset by the conversation. And she jumped at the voice behind her. In the heat of her fight with Charles, she hadn't heard Daphne come in. 'He's an asshole,' Daphne said, with a voice from beyond the grave. 'I can't believe you're going to marry him, Mom. And he hates Dad.' Maxine disagreed, but she could understand why her daughter felt that way.

'He doesn't understand the kind of relationship I have with him. He never talks to his ex-wife. They don't have kids.' But it was more than that with Blake. In their own way they still loved each other, it had just transformed into something else, a kind of familial bond that she didn't want to lose. And she didn't want a showdown with Charles over it. She wanted him to understand, and he didn't.

'Are you still going to Morocco?' Daphne asked with worried eyes. She thought her mother should, to help out her dad and all those kids.

'Yes, I am. I just hope Charles calms down over it.'

'Who cares?' Daphne said, pouring cereal into a bowl, as Zellie started making pancakes for her.

'I do,' Maxine said honestly. 'I love Charles.' And she hoped that one day her children would too. It wasn't unheard of for children to resent a stepparent, particularly at these ages. There was nothing unusual about it, she knew, but it was damn hard to live with.

Maxine was a full half hour late at her office, and continued to run late all day. She hadn't had time to talk to Charles again. She was swamped, seeing patients, and canceling whatever appointments she could for the end of the week. She called Charles as soon as she got home, and was discouraged to find that he was still upset. She reassured him as much as possible, and asked him if he wanted to come over for dinner. He stunned her by saying that he'd see her when she got back. He was punishing her for the trip that had been generated by Blake, and he didn't want to see her before she left.

'I'd love to see you before I go,' she said gently. But Charles wasn't ready to give it up. She hated leaving knowing that he was still angry at her, but he refused to relent. Maxine thought it was childish of him, but decided to let him calm down while she was away. There was no other choice. When she called him later, she found he had even turned off his phone. He was stewing and taking it out on her.

She had a pleasant dinner with her children that night, and after another crazy day in the office on Thursday, she called Charles again in the evening, before she left. This time he answered his phone.

'I just wanted to say goodbye,' she said as calmly as she could. 'I'm leaving for the airport.' They were flying out of Newark where Blake always landed his plane.

'Take care of yourself,' Charles said gruffly.

'I emailed you Blake's cell phone and BlackBerry, and you can try mine. I think it'll work while I'm there,' she said, trying to be helpful.

'I'm not going to call you on his phone,' Charles said, sounding angry again. It still rankled him that she was going. It was going to be a miserable weekend for him. She understood why, and she felt badly about it, but she was sorry he couldn't seem to get past it and be more understanding. She was excited now about the trip, and what she'd be doing. There was always a kind of professional high in those situations, even though they were heartbreaking. But helping in national disasters like that made one feel like one's life had some meaning. She knew it was good for Blake too, and it was a first for him, which was part of why she was going. She didn't want to let him down, and she wanted to reinforce the turn his life seemed to be taking. It was just too much for Charles to understand. And Daphne was right. He hated Blake, and had been jealous of him from the first.

'I'll try and call you,' Maxine reassured him, 'and I left Zellie your numbers in case anything happens here.' She assumed he'd be in town, since she wouldn't be around.

'Actually, I'm thinking about going to Vermont,' Charles replied. It was beautiful there in June. She would have loved it if he had the kind of relationship with her children where he would see them even without her, since he was going to become their stepfather in two months, but he didn't. And she knew that, in her absence, the children wouldn't want to see him either. It was a shame. They still had a long way to go before both factions were at ease with each other. They needed her to be the bridge between them. 'Be careful, disaster sites like that can be dangerous. And that's North Africa, not Ohio,' he admonished her before they hung up.

'I will, don't worry.' She smiled. 'I love you, Charles. I'll be back on Monday.' She was sad when she hung up. This had definitely been a hiccup between them. She hoped it wouldn't be more than that, and she was sorry she hadn't seen him before she left, because he refused to. It seemed childish and petty to her that he was being so stubborn about it. As she went to kiss her children goodbye, she observed to herself that in the end, no matter how old they were or how grown up they pretended to be, all men were babies.

CHAPTER 17

Blake's plane took off from Newark airport on Thursday night, just after eight P.M. Maxine settled back comfortably in one of the luxurious seats, and she was planning to use one of the two bedrooms to get a good night's sleep. The rooms had king-size beds, beautiful sheets, and warm comforters and blankets, and there were big fluffy pillows. One of the two flight attendants on board brought her a snack, and shortly after that, a light dinner of smoked salmon and an omelette they had prepared on board. The purser gave her the details of the flight, which would take seven and a half hours. They would arrive at seven-thirty A.M. local time, and a car and driver would be waiting to take her to the village outside Marrakech where Blake and several other rescue workers had set up camp. The International Red Cross was there too in full force.

Maxine thanked the purser for the information, ate the light meal, and went to bed by nine. She knew she'd need all the rest she could get before she got there, and it was easy to do in the luxury of Blake's plane. It was handsomely decorated in beige and gray fabrics and leathers. There were cashmere blankets on every seat, mohair couches, and thick gray wool carpets throughout the plane. The bedroom was done in a pale yellow, and Maxine fell asleep the moment her head hit the pillow. She slept like a baby for six hours, and when she woke up, she lay in bed, thinking about Charles. She was still upset that he was so angry at her, but she knew that going to Morocco had been the right decision.

She combed her hair and brushed her teeth, and put her heavy boots back on. She hadn't used them for a while and had retrieved them from the back of her closet, where she kept clothes for situations like this. She had brought rough gear with her, and suspected she'd be sleeping in what she wore for the next few days. She was actually excited about what she was going to do, and hoped she could make a difference, and be of some assistance to Blake.

She emerged from the bedroom looking fresh and rested, and enjoyed the breakfast the flight attendant served her. There were fresh croissants and brioche, yogurt, and a basket of fresh fruit. And she did some reading after she ate, as they started to descend. She had pinned a caduceus to her lapel when she got up, which would identify her as a physician at the disaster site. And she was ready to roll when they landed, her hair in a neat braid, and wearing an old tan safari shirt under a heavy sweater. She had T-shirts, and a rough jacket too. Jack had checked the weather for her online before she packed. And she had a water canteen that she filled with Evian before she left the plane. There were work gloves clipped to her belt, and surgical masks and rubber gloves in her pockets. She was ready to work.

As Blake had promised, there was a Jeep and driver waiting for her when she got off the plane, and she carried a small shoulder bag with clean underwear in case there was a place for her to shower on site, and she had medicines in the event that she got sick. She had brought the surgical masks with her in case the stench of rotting bodies was too much, or they were dealing with infectious diseases. She had alcohol wipes with her too. She had tried to think of everything before she left. It was always a little bit like a military operation going into situations like that, even if there was utter chaos. She wore no jewelry except a watch. And she had left her engagement ring from Charles in New York. She was all business as she hopped into the waiting Jeep and they drove off. Her French was rudimentary, but she was able to talk to the driver on the way. He said many people had been killed, thousands, and many people were hurt. He talked about bodies lying in the streets, still waiting to be buried, which to Maxine meant diseases and epidemics in their immediate future. You didn't have to be a doctor to figure that out, and her driver knew it too.

It was a three-hour drive to Imlil from Marrakech. It took two hours to a town called Asni, in the Atlas Mountains, and nearly another hour to Imlil on rough roads. It was cooler on the way to Imlil than it had been in Marrakech, and the countryside was greener as a result. There were mud-brick villages, goats, sheep, and chickens

242

on the roads, men on mules, and women and children carrying bundles of sticks on their heads. There were signs of damaged huts, and the trauma of the earthquake from Asni to Imlil, and there were footpaths between all the villages, most of which had been destroyed. Open-backed trucks from other areas carried people from one village to another.

Once they began to approach Imlil, Maxine could see flattened mud huts everywhere, with men digging through the rubble for survivors, sometimes with their bare hands, for lack of tools with which to do it. They pawed through the debris looking for loved ones and survivors, often crying, as Maxine felt tears sting her eyes. It was hard not to feel for them, as she sensed and knew only too well that they were looking for their wives, children, siblings, or parents. It reminded her of what she would see when she finally reached Blake.

As they reached the outskirts of Imlil, she saw International Red Cross and Moroccan Red Crescent workers assisting people near the flattened mud houses. There seemed to be almost no structures left standing, and hundreds of people wandering by the side of the road. There were a few mules, and other livestock wandering loose, often interfering with traffic on the road. It was slow going on the last miles to Imlil. There were firemen and soldiers in evidence too. Every possible form of rescue worker had been deployed by the Moroccan government and other countries, and helicopters were buzzing overhead. It was a familiar sight from other disaster areas she had worked in.

Many of the villages lacked electricity and water at the best of times, conditions were rough, particularly farther up the mountains, past Imlil. Her driver was giving her details of the regions as they crawled through the villagers, refugees, and livestock on the roads. He said that people from Ikkiss, Tacheddirt, and Seti Chambarouch, in the mountains, had come down to Imlil for help. Imlil was the gateway to the central High Atlas, and the Tizane Valley, dominated by Jebel Toubkal, the highest mountain in North Africa, at nearly fourteen thousand feet. Maxine could already see the mountains ahead, dusted with snow even now. The population in the area were Muslims and Berbers. They spoke Arabic and Berber dialects, and Maxine already knew that only some of them would speak French. Blake had told her on the phone that he was communicating with people in the village in French and through interpreters. He had come across no one so far, except Red Cross workers, who spoke English. But after years of traveling, his French was pretty good.

The driver also explained that above Imlil was also the Kasbah du Toubkal, a governor's former summer palace. It was a twenty-minute walk from Imlil to get there. There was no other way except by mule. He said they were bringing the wounded in from the villages by mule as well.

The men they saw were wearing djellabas, the long hooded robes worn by the Berbers. And everyone looked exhausted and dusty, after traveling by mule, walking for hours, or digging people out of their homes. As they got closer to Imlil, Maxine could see that even buildings made of concrete blocks had been destroyed by the earthquake. Nothing was left standing, and they began to see the tents the Red Cross had erected as field hospitals, and shelter for the countless refugees. The more typical mud huts were all in rubble on the ground. The concrete-block buildings had fared no better than the mud and clay homes. There were wildflowers by the side of the road, whose beauty seemed in sharp contrast to the devastation Maxine was seeing everywhere.

The driver told her that the United Nations headquarters in Geneva had also sent a disaster-assessment team to advise the Red Cross and the many international rescue teams who were offering to come in and help. Maxine had worked with the UN on several occasions, and realized that if she worked with any international agency on long-term solutions, it would most likely be with them. One of their great concerns at the moment was the fear of malaria spreading in the destroyed villages, as it was common in the area, spread by mosquitoes, and cholera and typhoid were real dangers too, from contamination. Bodies were being buried quickly, according to the traditions of the region, but with many bodies still unrecovered, the spread of disease as a result was a real concern.

It was more than a little daunting, even to Maxine, to see how much work there was to do, and how little time she had to advise Blake. She had exactly two and a half days to do whatever she could. Maxine was suddenly sorry she couldn't stay for weeks instead of days, but there was no way she could. She had obligations, responsibilities, and her own children to return to in New York, and she didn't want to push Charles more than she already had. But Maxine knew that rescue teams and international organizations would be working here for months. She wondered if Blake would too.

Once in Imlil, they saw more huts that had fallen down, trucks that had been overturned, fissures in the ground, and people wailing over their dead. It got steadily worse as they advanced into the village to where Blake had said he'd be waiting. He was working out of one of the Red Cross tents. And as they drove slowly toward the rescue tents, Maxine was aware of the hideous, acrid stench of death that she had experienced before in similar situations, and that one never forgot. She pulled one of the surgical masks out of her bag and put it on. It was as bad as she had feared, and she had to admire Blake for being there. She knew the whole experience must be a shock to him.

The Jeep drove her into the central part of Imlil, where houses were collapsed, rubble and broken glass were everywhere, bodies were lying on the ground, some covered with tarps, some not, and people were shuffling around still in shock. There were children crying, carrying other younger children or babies, and she saw two Red Cross trucks where volunteers were serving food and tea. There was a medical tent with a huge Red Cross on it, and smaller tents set up in a camp. The driver pointed to one of them, and then followed her as she approached it on foot over rough ground. Children stared up at her with matted hair and filthy faces. Most of them were barefoot, and some had no clothes on as they had fled in the night. The weather was warm, mercifully, and she took her sweater off and tied it around her waist. The smell of death, urine, and feces was everywhere as she walked into the tent, looking for

246

a familiar face. There was only one person she would know here, and she found him within minutes, talking to a little girl in French. Blake had learned most of his French in nightclubs in St. Tropez, picking up women, but it seemed to work, Maxine thought, and she smiled the moment she saw him. She was standing next to him within seconds, and when he looked up, he had tears in his eyes. He finished what he was saying to the little girl, pointed her to a group of others, being cared for by a volunteer from the Red Cross, and stood up and hugged Maxine. She could hardly hear what he said over the rumble of bulldozers outside. They had been flown in from Germany by Blake. And rescue teams were still digging to get people out.

'Thank you for coming,' he said, sounding like a drowning man. 'It's so awful. So far, there are more than four thousand children who seem to be orphans. We're not sure yet, but there are going to be a lot more before it's over.' More than seven thousand children were dead. And almost twice as many adults. Every family had been decimated and sustained losses. And he said the next village up the mountain was worse. He had been there for the past five days. There were almost no survivors there, and most had been brought here. They were shipping the elderly and the severely wounded to hospitals in Marrakech.

'It looks pretty bad,' she confirmed. He nodded, holding her hand in his own, and gave her a tour of the camp. There were crying children everywhere, and every volunteer seemed to be holding a baby. 'What's going to happen to them?' Maxine asked. 'Has anything official been organized yet?' She knew they would have to wait for confirmation that parents were dead and family members couldn't be found. It would be a mess until then.

'The government and the Red Cross and Moroccan Red Crescent are working on it, but it's still pretty chaotic right now. It's mostly word of mouth, and what people are telling us. I'm not involved in the rest of it, I've been concentrating on the kids.' Once again, it struck her as odd for a moment, since he had always spent so little time with his own, but at least his instincts were good, and his heart was in the right place.

She spent the next two hours roaming around the camp with him, talking to people in the best French she could muster. She offered her services at the medical tent, if they needed them, and she identified herself to the head surgeon as a psychiatrist, specialized in trauma. He had her talk to several women and an old man. One woman had been pregnant with twins and lost them both from a blow when her house collapsed around her, and her husband had been killed, buried under the rubble. He had somehow saved her life and lost his own, she explained. She had three other children, but no one could find them. There were dozens of cases like hers, and one beautiful young girl had lost both arms. She was crying pitifully for her mother, and Maxine just stood with her and stroked her hair, as Blake turned away in tears.

It was nearly sunset when she and Blake stopped at the Red Cross truck, and took steaming cups of mint tea. And as they stopped to listen, they both heard the mystical call to prayer that reverberated from the village, started by the main mosque. It was an unforgettable sound. She had promised to go back to the medical tent later that night, to outline some plans for helping them deal with trauma victims, but that meant almost everyone here, including the workers. They had seen some terrible tragedies firsthand. Maxine had chatted with the Red Cross volunteers for a few minutes. Everyone needed such basic care at this point that there was really no way to set up more sophisticated interventions. All you could do was talk to people one by one, and she and Blake hadn't sat down for hours. It was only as they sipped their tea that Maxine suddenly thought of Arabella, and asked him about her, and if she was still in his life. He nodded, and smiled.

'She had a commission and couldn't come on this trip. I'm glad she's not here. She's pretty squeamish. She faints if someone gets a paper cut. This wouldn't be for her. She's at the house in London.' She had moved in with him officially months before, which was a first for him too. Usually, women stayed with him for a while, and then just disappeared from his life. After seven months, Arabella was still around. Maxine was impressed.

'Is she a keeper?' she asked with a broad smile, finishing her tea.

'Could be,' he said, looking sheepish. 'Whatever that means. I'm not as ballsy as you are, Max. I don't need to get married.' He thought it was a brave thing to do, but he was happy for her, if that was what she wanted. 'I've been meaning to tell you, by the way. I want to give you and Charles your rehearsal dinner in Southampton. I feel like I owe you at least that.'

'You don't owe me anything,' she said gently,

with her surgical mask hanging around her neck. The smell was still awful, but she couldn't drink her tea otherwise. She had given a mask to Blake too, and surgical latex gloves. She didn't want him getting sick, and it was easy to do in a place like this. Soldiers had been burying bodies all day, while family members wailed. It was an eerie, torturous sound, mercifully drowned out by the bulldozers some of the time.

'I want to do that for you. It'll be fun. Have the kids settled down yet?'

'No,' she said honestly, 'but they will. Charles is a good man. He's just awkward with kids.' She told Blake about their first date then, and he laughed.

'I would have run like hell,' Blake confessed, 'and they're my kids.'

'I'm surprised he didn't.' Maxine was smiling too. She didn't tell him how furious Charles had been that she had come to Morocco. Blake didn't need to know that, and his feelings might have been hurt, or like Daphne, he might have concluded that Charles was a jerk. Maxine felt a need to protect them both. As far as she was concerned, they were both good men.

She went back to the medical tent for a while after that, trying to help them work out a plan, and she talked to some of the paramedics about signs of severe trauma to look for, but at this point it was like trying to dig through a mountain with a spoon, not very effective and pretty crude.

She was up for most of the night with Blake, as he had been for days, and in the end they both slept in the Jeep that had brought her there, piled on top of each other like puppies. She didn't even think about what Charles's reaction would have

250

been to that. It was entirely beside the point, and of no interest here. She could spend her time reassuring him when she got home. She had more important things to do now.

They spent most of Saturday with the children. She talked to as many of them as she could, and sometimes just held them, particularly the young ones. Many of them were getting sick, and she knew that some would die. She sent at least a dozen of them to the medical tent with volunteers. And it was dark before she and Blake stopped.

'What can I do?' Blake looked as helpless as he felt. Maxine was more used to this than he was, but it upset her too. There was such a huge need here, and so little at hand to fill it.

'Honestly? Not much. You're doing about as much as you can.' She knew he was pouring money and machinery into the rescue efforts, but by now they were finding only bodies, not survivors.

And then he shocked her with what he said next. 'I want to take some of the kids home,' he said softly. It was a normal reaction. Others in similar circumstances had reacted that way before. But she knew that in situations like this, adopting orphans was not as simple as Blake may have thought.

'We all do,' she said quietly. 'You can't take them all home.' The government was going to set up makeshift orphanages for them, and eventually feed them into their own system, and some might find their way into international agencies for adoption, but very few. Children like that usually stayed within their own countries and cultures. And most of the children around them were Muslims. They would be taken care of by their own. 'The hardest part of this work is having to

251

walk away. At some point, you've done all you can within the scope of your possibilities, and you have to go home. They stay.' It sounded harsh, but she knew that in most cases, that was true.

'That's my point,' he said sadly. 'I can't do that. I feel like I owe something here. I can't just set up a pretty house, and show up with a bunch of fancy people now and then. I feel like I owe more than that, as a human being. You can't just take forever,' he said. It was a new discovery for him, and it had taken him a lifetime to get there.

'What about helping them right here, instead of trying to take them home? You could get caught up in red tape forever.'

He looked at her strangely then, as something occurred to him, which might make more sense in the long run. 'What if I turn my house here into an orphanage? I could support, house, and even educate them. The house in Marrakech could probably house a hundred kids if we reconfigure it, and the last thing I need is another house. I don't know why I didn't think of it before.' He was smiling broadly, and there were tears in Maxine's eyes.

'Are you serious?' Maxine was stunned, and it sounded as though his plan might work. He had never done anything like it before. It was a totally selfless project, and a wonderful thing to do. And it was certainly feasible for him, if he wanted to do it. She was sure he could set the palace up as an orphanage, staff it, finance it, and change the lives of hundreds of orphaned children in the years to come. It would be a miracle for any one of those kids, and made far more sense than trying to adopt any of them himself. By turning over his house, setting it up properly, and financing the project he could help many, many more.

'Yes, I am serious,' he said, with his eyes boring into hers, and she was shocked at what she saw. Blake had grown up. He was finally an adult. There was no sign of Peter Pan, or the rogue.

'It's a fantastic idea,' she said with a look of admiration.

He looked excited about it, and she saw a light in his eyes she had never seen there before. She was very proud of him.

'Will you help me assess them as time goes on, as trauma victims? Kind of like a mini version of one of your studies. I want to get them whatever help I can. Psychiatric, medical, educational opportunities.'

'Sure,' she said softly. It was an amazing project. She was too moved to even tell him how impressed she was. And it would take her time and several visits to properly assess the situation for him.

They slept in the Jeep again that night, and she made rounds with him again all the next day. The children they saw were adorable and in such dire need that it made his idea of turning his house into an orphanage for some of them all the more poignant. And in the coming months, there would be much work to do. Blake had already called his architect that day, and was working on setting up meetings with government agencies to implement his plan.

She spent her last hour in the camp at the medical tent again. She had the feeling that she had done very little while she was there, but one always felt that way in situations like this. Blake walked her to the Jeep at the end of the day. He looked worn out. He had so much on his mind.

'When are you going back?' she asked him with a look of concern.

'I don't know. When they don't need me anymore. A few weeks, a month. I have a lot to organize here now.' They were going to need help for a long time, but eventually the worst of the crisis would be over, and he would go back to London, where Arabella was waiting patiently for him. He was so busy he had hardly had time to call her, but she was loving and adorable whenever he did. She told him how wonderful and what a hero he was and that she was in awe of him. And so was Maxine. She had been monumentally impressed by his efforts and plans for setting up an orphanage in his palace in Marrakech.

'Don't forget you have the boat for two weeks in July,' he reminded her. They both felt awkward talking about it here. A vacation on a superyacht seemed totally out of place in this context. She thanked him again for it. Charles would be joining them this time, albeit reluctantly, but she had insisted that it was one of their traditions, and the children would be upset if they didn't do it. And he was part of the family now. She said she didn't want to change anything for them just yet. It was too soon, and there was no room for them in his house in Vermont. 'And don't forget the rehearsal dinner. I'll have my secretary call yours. I want to do something fabulous for you and Charles.' She was touched that he'd thought about it, especially now. And she was looking forward to meeting the famous Arabella. Maxine was sure that she was much nicer than Daphne was willing to admit.

She hugged Blake before she left and thanked

him for the privilege of letting her come, and making it happen.

'Are you kidding? Thank you for coming all the way out here for three days to help me.'

'You're doing an incredible job, Blake,' she praised him. 'I'm so proud of you, and the kids will be too. I can't wait to tell them what you're doing.'

'Don't tell them yet. I want to get it all set up first, and I have a lot to do before it happens.' It was going to be a huge amount of work, coordinating both the construction of the orphanage and finding the right people to run it. A mammoth job.

'Just take care of yourself, and don't get sick,' she reminded him. 'Be careful.' They were going to start having epidemics of malaria, cholera, and typhoid soon.

'I will. I love you, Max. Take care of yourself, and kiss the kids for me.'

'I will. I love you too,' she said, as they hugged for a last time, and he waved as she sped off in the Jeep.

It was dark when she finally got on the plane. The flight crew were waiting for her, with a delicate meal prepared. She just couldn't touch it, after all she'd seen. She sat staring into the night for a long time. There was a bright moon at the tip of the wing, and a sky full of stars. And everything she had just seen and done for three days felt unreal. She thought about all of it, and about Blake and what he was doing, as they flew toward New York, and she finally fell asleep in her seat, and didn't wake until they landed in Newark at five A.M. The days she had just spent in Morocco felt more than ever like a dream.

255

CHAPTER 18

Maxine was at her apartment at seven. The children were still asleep, and Zelda was still in her room. Maxine showered and dressed for the office. She had slept well on the plane, so she felt rested, although she had a lot to think about and digest after her trip. It was a beautiful June morning, so she walked to the office and got there just after eight. She had an hour before her first patient was due in, and she called Charles to let him know she was home safely. He answered on the second ring.

'Hi, it's me,' she said softly, hoping he had calmed down.

'And who would that be?' he asked, sounding gruff. She had called him three times from Morocco, and never reached him, so she had left messages on his answering machine at home. It was just as well. She didn't want to fight with him long distance. He hadn't answered in Vermont either, and there was no machine to leave a message. She was hoping that he had mellowed out in the four days since she left.

'That would be the future Mrs. West,' she teased. 'At least I hope so.'

'How was it?' He sounded better, or so she thought. She'd know better when she saw him, and could read the expression in his eyes.

'Amazing, terrible, sad, heartbreaking. The way all those things are. The kids there are in terrible shape, but so are the adults.' She didn't tell him about Blake's plan to set up an orphanage, right off the bat. She thought that would be pushing it.

256

She talked about the earthquake damage in more general terms. 'As usual, the Red Cross is doing a great job.' And so was Blake, but she didn't say it. She wanted to be cautious with Charles and not get him riled up again.

'Are you exhausted?' he asked sympathetically. She would have to be. She'd been halfway around the world for three days, and he was sure living conditions had been miserable and the visit grueling while she was there. Although he was angry about why, and who had invited her, he was proud of her for going, although he had never said that to her.

'Not really. I slept on the plane.' He remembered then with a ripple of irritation that she had traveled on Blake's private jet.

'Would you like to go out to dinner tonight, or are you too jet-lagged?'

'I'd love it,' she said quickly. It was clearly a peace offering from him, and she was looking forward to seeing him.

'Our old standby?' He meant La Grenouille, of course.

'How about Café Boulud? It's not as formal, and it's closer to home.' She knew she might be tired later on, after a day in the office on the heels of the long trip. And she wanted to see her kids.

'I'll pick you up at eight,' he said quickly, and then, 'I missed you, Max. I'm glad you're home. I was worried about you.' He had thought about her all weekend in Vermont.

'I was fine.'

And then with a sigh, 'How was Blake?'

'He's trying very hard to make a difference, and it's not easy. It never is in those situations. I'm glad

I went.'

'We'll talk about it tonight,' he said brusquely. They hung up, and she glanced at the messages on her desk before her first patient showed up. It looked like nothing dramatic had happened over the weekend. Thelma had faxed her a brief report. None of Maxine's patients had had problems, or had to be admitted over the weekend. She was pleased. She worried about them too.

The rest of the day went smoothly, and she managed to be home by six o'clock so she could see the children after work. Zelda had gone to an appointment, and when she came back, she was wearing high heels and a suit, which was rare.

'Where have you been?' Maxine asked, smiling at her. 'You look like you had a hot date.' That hadn't happened to Zelda in years.

'I had to see a lawyer about something. No big deal.'

'Everything okay?' Maxine looked momentarily worried, but Zelda said it was fine.

Maxine told her children about the work their father was doing in Morocco, and they were extremely proud of him. She said she was too. She told them everything except about the orphanage. She had promised him that she would let him tell them about it, and she kept her word.

She even managed to be dressed on time when Charles showed up just before eight o'clock. He said hello to the children, who muttered greetings and disappeared into their rooms. They were a lot less friendly now that they knew about the wedding plans. He had become the enemy overnight.

Maxine ignored them, and they walked to the restaurant on East 76th Street. It was a warm balmy night, and she was wearing a blue linen dress and silver sandals, a far cry from her army surplus gear and combat boots that she had been in twenty-four hours before, in a different world with Blake. He had called her to thank her again that afternoon. He said he had already made some contacts to further his plans. He was embarking on it with the same determination, energy, and focus that had won him his success over the years.

They were halfway through dinner when Maxine told Charles about the rehearsal dinner Blake was giving for them the night before the wedding. Charles stopped and stared at her with his fork halfway to his mouth.

'What did you just say?' He had begun to relax and warm up to her again, when she hit him with that.

'I said that he wants to give the rehearsal dinner for us, the night before the wedding.'

'I guess my parents would be doing that if they were alive,' Charles said regretfully, as he set his fork down and sat back in his chair. 'Do you want me to do it?' He looked a little startled by the whole idea.

'No,' Maxine said, smiling at him. 'I think for a second wedding, it's pretty much up for grabs. Blake is like family anyway. The kids will be thrilled to have him do it.'

'Well, I'm not,' Charles said bluntly, pushing away his meal. 'Are we ever going to get rid of that guy, or is he just going to tag along forever? You told me you had a decent relationship, but this is ridiculous. I feel like I'm marrying him too.'

'Well, you're not. But he is the children's father. Trust me, Charles, it's better like this.'

'For who?'

'Well, for my kids.' And for her too. She would have hated to have an ex-husband she never spoke to, or where they were constantly fighting over the kids.

Charles was glaring at her. She had never seen someone as jealous, and she couldn't help wondering if it was because of who Blake was and what he had achieved, or because she'd been married to him. It was hard to tell.

'And I suppose if I say no to the rehearsal dinner, your children will think I'm a prick.' The answer to that was yes, but she was afraid to say that to Charles. 'This is a completely no-win situation for me.'

'No, it isn't. If you let him do it, the children will have a ball planning it with him, and he puts on a great party.' As she said it, Charles looked angrier by the minute. It had never occurred to Maxine that he would be that upset. Blake was her family, and she had hoped Charles would understand. 'Maybe I should just invite my ex-wife too.'

'That would be fine with me,' Maxine said gently, as Charles signaled for the check. He was in no mood for dessert, and Maxine didn't care. The jet lag had finally caught up with her, and she didn't want to fight with Charles about Blake, or anything.

He walked her back to her building in silence, and left her outside. He said he'd see her the next day, hailed a cab, and left without another word to her. Things were definitely stressful between them, and she hoped the wedding plans didn't make things worse. They were meeting with the caterer in Southampton that weekend. Charles had already told her he thought both the tent and the wedding cake were too expensive, which was annoying since she was paying for all of it herself. Charles was a little tight about things like that. But Maxine wanted everything beautiful for their wedding.

As she rode up in the elevator, she thought about telling Blake not to do the rehearsal dinner, but she knew that he'd be so disappointed. And the kids would be upset too, if they got wind of it. She hoped that Charles would get used to the idea, and even relax about Blake in time. And if anyone could soften Charles up, it was Blake. He had an easy way with everyone, and no one had ever been able to resist his charm and sense of humor. If Charles could, it would be a first.

In spite of his anger at her the night before, the next morning Maxine had to ask Charles to come by that night, to go over the guest list and details about the wedding. The caterer had called for more information, and wanted to know several things before their meeting on Saturday. Charles grudgingly came over after dinner, still in a bad mood from the night before. He was mad about the rehearsal dinner, and he still hadn't completely swallowed her trip to Morocco. There was a little too much Blake Williams in his life these days, even at his wedding. It was a lot for Charles to digest.

Charles sat down at the kitchen table with the children as they were finishing dessert. Zelda had made apple pie with vanilla ice cream, and he willingly had a piece, and said it was very good.

And just as they were about to leave the table, Zellie cleared her throat. It was obvious that she was going to say something, but they had no idea what it was.

'I . . . uh . . . I'm sorry to do this right now. I know with the wedding coming up, and . . .' She looked apologetically at Maxine, who was suddenly convinced Zelda was going to quit. That was all she needed right now. With the wedding in August, and Charles moving in, she wanted as much stability and continuity as possible for them. This was no time for a major change, or for someone important to them to leave their lives. And Maxine had relied on her for years. Zelda was family now. Maxine looked up at her in panic. The children stared, having no idea what to expect. And Charles looked nonplussed as he finished his pie. Whatever Zelda had to say had nothing to do with him, or so he thought. Who Maxine employed or didn't was entirely up to her. It wasn't his problem, and she seemed fine to him, and a pretty good cook. But in his mind, like anyone else, she could always be replaced. That wasn't how Maxine and her children felt about it, by any means.

'I . . . I've been doing a lot of thinking . . .' Zelda said, twisting a dish towel in her hands. 'You guys are growing up,' she said, looking at the children, 'and you're getting married,' looking at Maxine, 'and I just feel like I need something more in my life too. I'm not getting any younger, and I don't think my life is going to change anymore.' She smiled lopsidedly. 'I guess Prince Charming lost my address . . . so I've decided . . . I want a baby . . . and if that doesn't work for you guys, I understand, and I'll leave. But I've made up my mind.' For a long moment, they all stared at her, stunned. Maxine wondered for an instant if she had sneaked off to a sperm bank and gotten pregnant. It sounded like it to her.

'Are you pregnant?' Maxine asked in a choked voice. The children said nothing, nor did Charles.

'No. I wish I were,' Zelda answered with a rueful smile. 'That would be great. I thought about it, but the last time you and I talked about it, Max, I told you I've been loving other people's kids all my life. I have no problem with that. So why have morning sickness and get fat? And this way I can keep working. I'll have to. Kids aren't cheap,' she said, and smiled at them. 'I went to see a lawyer about adopting. I've seen him four times. A social worker came to do a home study here. I had the physical and I've been approved.' And through all of that, she hadn't said a word to Maxine.

'When are you thinking about doing this?' Maxine asked, holding her breath. She was not ready to have a baby in the house right now. Or maybe ever. This was a lot to swallow, with a new husband moving in too.

'It could take up to two years,' Zelda said, as Maxine breathed again, 'if I hold out for a designer baby.'

'A designer baby?' Maxine asked, looking blank. She was still the only one doing the talking. The others were too stunned.

'White, blue-eyed, healthy, both parents Harvard grads who decided that a baby doesn't work with their lifestyle. No alcohol or drugs, upper middle class. That can take a long time. Generally, these days, those girls don't get pregnant in the first place, or they have abortions, or they keep their babies. Babies like that are pretty rare. Two years is optimistic, particularly for

263

an unmarried middle-aged woman like me, working class. The designer babies go to people like you.' She glanced at Maxine and Charles, and Maxine could see Charles shudder and shake his head.

'No, thank you,' he said with a smile. 'Not for me. Or us.' He smiled at Maxine. He really didn't care if Zelda was planning to adopt a baby in two years, whatever kind it was, designer or otherwise. It was definitely not his problem. He was relieved at that.

'So you think two years from now, Zellie?' Maxine asked hopefully. By then, Sam would be eight, Jack and Daphne in high school at fourteen and fifteen, and she could worry about it then.

'No. I don't think I even have a shot at a baby like that. I considered international adoption, and I looked into it, but there are too many unknowns, and it's too expensive for me. I can't go sit in Russia or China, for three months, waiting for them to give me some random three-year-old from an orphanage, who might have all kinds of damage that I only figure out later. They don't even let you pick your baby, they pick it for you, and most of them are three or four years old. I want a baby, a newborn if possible, that no one else has screwed up.'

'Except in the womb,' Maxine warned her. 'You have to be very careful you know what you're getting, Zellie, and that there were no drugs or alcohol used during the pregnancy.' Zelda looked away for a minute.

'That's kind of my point,' Zelda said, looking back at her again. 'My best shot is a somewhat high-risk baby. Not a special-needs one like spina bifida or Down's or anything. I don't think I could handle that. But a relatively normal kid from a girl who might have done some drugs or had a few beers while she was pregnant.' She didn't look frightened at the prospect, but her employer did. Very.

'I think that's a big mistake,' Maxine said firmly. 'You have no idea what kind of problems you'd be getting into, particularly with a mother who did drugs. I see the results of that in my office all the time, and a lot of the kids I see were adopted and had drug-addicted biological parents. Those things are genetic, and the effects can be pretty scary later on.'

'I'm willing to take that on,' Zelda said, looking her in the eye. 'In fact,' she took a deep breath, 'I just did.'

'What do you mean?' Maxine frowned at her as Zelda went on, and now Charles was paying attention too, and so were the kids. You could hear a pin drop in the kitchen as Zelda spoke.

'There's a baby coming up, the mother is fifteen and was homeless for part of her pregnancy. She did drugs in the first trimester, but she's clean now. The father is in jail for dealing drugs and grand theft auto. He's nineteen and he's not interested in the baby or the girl, so he's willing to sign off. He already did, and that's a big deal too. Her parents won't let her keep the baby, they have no money, and she's a sweet kid. I met her yesterday.' Maxine realized that explained the suit and high heels Zelda had been wearing the day before. 'She's willing to give me her baby. All she wants are photographs once a year. She doesn't want to see it, which is great, so she's not going to pester me, or upset the baby. Three couples have already passed on this, so if I want him, he's mine. It's a boy,' she said with tears rolling down her cheeks, and a smile that broke Maxine's heart. She couldn't even imagine wanting a baby that much, to take so much risk, and take someone's child who might be damaged for life. She got up and put her arms around Zellie and hugged her.

'Oh, Zellie . . . I think that's a beautiful thing to want to do. But you can't take on a baby like that. You have no idea what you're getting into. You just can't do that.'

'I can and I am,' she said stubbornly, and Maxine could see she meant it.

'When?' Charles asked. He had gotten the gist, and it sounded disastrous to him.

Zellie took a breath. 'The baby is due this weekend.'

'Are you kidding?' Maxine nearly shrieked, and the kids looked stunned too. 'Now? Like in a few days? What are you going to do?'

'I'm going to love him for the rest of his life. I'm naming him James. Jimmy.' Maxine suddenly felt sick. This couldn't be happening to them. But it was. 'I don't expect you to back me in this. And I hate to do this on such short notice. I thought it would take me a lot longer, like a year or two. But they called me about this baby yesterday, and I said yes today. So I had to tell you.'

'They told you about this baby yesterday because no one else wants it,' Charles said coldly. 'This is a very foolish thing to do.'

'I think it's meant to be,' Zellie said wistfully, and Maxine wanted to cry. It sounded like a huge mistake to her, but who was she to decide other

266

people's lives? She wouldn't have done it, but she had three healthy kids, and who knew what she would do in Zellie's position? It was a very loving thing to do, even if a little crazy, and very high risk. She was brave to do it. 'If you want me to leave now, I will,' Zelda said quietly. 'I can't do anything else. I can't force you to let me have the baby here. If you let me, and want me to stay, I will, and we can see how it works for all of us. But if you want me to go, I'll make other arrangements and leave in the next few days. I'll have to figure out a place to live pretty quick, since the baby could be born over the weekend.'

'Oh my God,' Charles said, and got up from the table, looking pointedly at Maxine.

'Zellie,' Maxine said quietly, 'we'll work it out.' As she said it, all three of her children cheered in unison and jumped up to hug Zellie.

'We're having a baby!' Sam shouted, delighted. 'It's a boy!' He wrapped his arms around Zelda's waist, and she started to cry.

'Thank you,' she whispered to Maxine.

'Let's see how it goes,' Maxine said weakly. She had had her children's answer instantly, but she had Charles to deal with too. 'All we can do is try, and hope it works out. If it doesn't, we'll talk about it. How much mess can a baby make?' As she said it, Zelda wrapped her arms around Maxine's neck and hugged her so tightly Maxine could hardly breathe.

'Thank you, thank you,' she said through her tears. 'This is all I've ever wanted. A baby of my own,' Zelda said, crying.

'You're sure?' Maxine said seriously. 'You can still hold out for a baby that's not high risk.'

'I don't want to wait,' she said staunchly. 'I want him.'

'That could be a mistake.'

'It won't be.' She had made her mind up, and Maxine saw that there was nothing she could do to dissuade her. 'I have to go and get a crib tomorrow and some stuff.' Maxine had given Sam's crib away years before or she would have offered theirs. It was a stunning thought realizing that they could have a baby in their midst in the next few days. And as Maxine looked around, she realized Charles had left them. She found him in the living room, fuming, and when he looked at Maxine, there was murder in his eyes.

'Are you insane?' he spat at her. 'Are you crazy? You're going to take a crack baby into our home? Because you know that's what it is. No one in their right mind would want an infant with that profile, and the poor woman is so desperate, she'll take anything. And now it's going to be living with you! . . . and with *me*!' he added. 'How dare you make a decision like that without asking me first?' He was shaking with rage, and Maxine didn't completely blame him. She wasn't thrilled either, but they loved Zellie. Charles didn't. He barely knew her. And he had no concept of how much she meant to them. To him, she was just a nanny. She was family to Max and the children.

'I'm sorry I didn't ask you, Charles. I swear, it just slipped out. I was so moved by what she said, and I felt so sorry for her. I just can't ask her to leave so quickly, after twelve years, and my kids would be distraught. So would I.'

'Then she should have told you what she was doing. This is outrageous! You should fire her,' he

268

said coldly.

'We love her,' Maxine said gently. 'My children have grown up with her. And she loves them too. If it doesn't work out, we can always let her go. But with all these changes for my kids, our getting married, them getting used to you, Charles, I don't want her to go.' There were tears in Maxine's eyes. And Charles's were glacial and rock hard.

'And what am I supposed to do now? Live with a crack baby? Change diapers? This isn't fair.' It wasn't fair to her either. But she had to make the best of it for the kids. They needed Zellie too much to lose her now, crack baby or not.

'You probably won't even know it's here,' Maxine reassured him. 'Zellie's room is in the back of the apartment. Most likely the baby will be in her room much of the time for the first few months.'

'And then what? He sleeps with us, like Sam?' It was the first time he had made a snide remark about her children, and she didn't like it, but he was upset. 'There's a goddamn drama every day now with you, isn't there? One minute you're running off to Africa with him, the next he's giving our rehearsal dinner, and now you've invited the nanny to bring her adopted crack baby into the house. And you expect me to put up with that? I must be insane,' he said and then glared at her. 'No, you are.' He pointed an angry finger at her, and slammed out the front door.

'Was that Charles?' Zelda asked her, looking anxious, when Maxine walked back into the kitchen with a grim look. Everyone had heard the front door slam. Maxine nodded in answer without further comment. 'You don't have to do this, Max,' she said, looking apologetic. 'I can go.'

'No, you can't,' Maxine said, putting an arm around her shoulders. 'We love you. We're going to try and make this work. I just hope you get a good baby here, and a healthy one,' she said sincerely. 'That's all that matters now. Charles will adjust. We all will. This is just a little new for him right now,' she said, and then started to laugh. What next?

CHAPTER 19

Charles and Maxine went to Southampton that weekend, as planned. They met with the caterer for their wedding, walked on the beach holding hands, made love several times, and by the end of the weekend, Charles was calm again. Maxine had promised him that if Zelda's baby was too much for them, she would leave. Everything seemed fine between them again by the end of the weekend as they drove home. He had desperately needed some peaceful time with her, and her full attention, which meant a lot to him. And after being with her all weekend, he had perked up like a flower in the rain.

'You know, when we have time together like this,' he said, as they drove back to the city, 'everything makes sense again. But when I get caught up in that nuthouse of yours and your soap opera life, it just drives me insane.' She was hurt by what he said.

'It's not a nuthouse, Charles. And we don't lead a soap opera life. I'm a single mom with three kids and a career, and things happen. They happen to everyone,' she said reasonably, and he looked at her as though she really were insane.

'How many people do you know whose nanny brings home a crack baby on three days' notice? Excuse me. That doesn't sound normal to me.'

'I'll admit,' she said, smiling at him, 'it's a little off the wall. But things happen. She's important to us, and especially right now.'

'Don't be silly,' he said. 'They'd be fine without her.'

'I doubt that, and I sure wouldn't be. I rely on her more than you know. I can't do it all alone.'

'You have me now,' he said confidently, and Maxine laughed. 'Great, and how are you at laundry, ironing, getting dinner on the table every night, running car pool, making play dates, getting the kids to school, making snacks, packing lunches, supervising slumber parties, and taking care of them when they're sick?'

He got the message, but he didn't agree with her and never had. 'I'm sure they could be far more independent, if you'd let them be. There's no reason why they can't do most of that themselves.' And this from a man who had never had kids, and had barely ever seen one up close until hers. He had avoided them all his life. He had all the pompous, unrealistic views of people who have never had children, and could no longer remember being one themselves. 'Besides, you know my solution to all that,' he reminded her. 'Boarding school. You'd have none of those problems, and you wouldn't have a woman with a crack baby living in your house.'

'I don't agree with you, Charles,' she said simply.

271

'I am never sending my children away to school until they leave for college.' She wanted to make that clear to him now. 'And Zellie isn't adopting a "crack baby." You don't know that for sure. "High risk" does not mean the baby is addicted.'

'It could be,' he insisted, and he had gotten that message loud and clear about her negative view of boarding school for her children. Maxine was not letting go of her children, or sending them away. If he didn't love her so much, he'd have put his foot down. And if she didn't love him, she wouldn't have put up with the things he said. She just figured it was one of his quirks. But he had loved the peaceful, childless weekend he had just spent with her. Maxine, on the other hand, had loved it but had missed her kids. She knew that having no children of his own, it was something he would never understand, and she let it go at that.

They were having Chinese takeout with the children in the kitchen on Sunday night, when Zellie came running in.

'Oh my God . . . oh my God . . . it's coming . . . it's coming!' For a minute they'd all forgotten. Zelda looked like a chicken without her head as she ran around the kitchen.

'What's coming?' Maxine asked her blankly. She truly had no idea.

'The baby! The birth mom is in labor! I have to go to Roosevelt Hospital right away.'

'Oh my God,' Maxine said, and everyone got up and exclaimed over her excitedly as though she were having it herself. Charles sat at the table, eating calmly, and shook his head.

Zelda was dressed and out the door five minutes later, and the rest of them talked about it and then went to their rooms. Maxine sat at the table and glanced at Charles.

'Thanks for being a good sport,' she said gratefully. 'I know this isn't fun for you.' She was sorry it had happened at all, but she was trying to make the best of it. There was no other choice. Or only choices she didn't want, other than this one, welcoming Zellie's baby.

'It's not going to be fun for you either, when that baby is screaming the house down. If it's born drug addicted, it's going to be a nightmare for all of you. I'm glad I'm not moving in for another two months.' So was she.

*   *   *

And as it turned out, much to her chagrin, Charles wasn't wrong. The birth mother had done far more drugs than she admitted, and the baby was born addicted to cocaine. He spent a week in the hospital being detoxed, while Zelda sat with him every day and rocked him. And when he came home, he screamed night and day. Zellie sat with him in her room. He was a poor eater, he hardly slept, and she couldn't put him down. All he did was scream. The poor little thing had come into the world in a very hard way, but into the arms of an adoring adoptive mother.

'How's it going?' Maxine asked her one morning. Zelda looked like ten miles of bad road after another sleepless night. She was awake with the baby every night, for most of the night, holding him.

'The doctor said it could take a while for the drugs to get out of his system. I think he's a little better,' Zellie said, looking down at her son blissfully. She had totally bonded with Jimmy as though she'd given birth to him herself. The social workers had come to check on him several times, and no one could have faulted Zellie for how devoted she was to him. He just wasn't a lot of fun for anyone else. Maxine was relieved they'd be leaving on vacation in a few weeks, and with luck by the time they got back, Jimmy would have settled down. It was all she could hope for now. Zellie was a wonderful mom, and just as patient and loving as she had been with Jack and Sam when they were born. And little Jimmy was a lot harder to deal with.

In the meantime, plans for the wedding were under way. Maxine hadn't found a dress yet, and she needed one for Daphne too. Daphne refused to have any part of it, and was threatening not to go to the wedding at all, which was yet another challenge Maxine had to face. She didn't say anything about it to Charles. She knew how hurt he would have been. So she went shopping on her own, hoping to find dresses for both of them. She had already gotten khaki suits for the boys, and one for Charles too. At least that was done.

*   *   *

Blake had called from Morocco, told her all that he'd accomplished since she left. The new construction to transform his palace into a home for a hundred kids was already under way. He had turned staffing, and the running of the future orphanage, over to a group of very competent people, and he had done all he could for now. He planned to come back every month to make sure they were moving ahead as planned. So he was going back to London for the time being, and he told Maxine that everything was ready on the boat for them. She and the kids could hardly wait. It was their best vacation together every year. Charles was not as sure.

Blake had told Arabella about his plans for the orphanage too. She thought it was a wonderful thing to do.

He decided to surprise her when he flew back to London. He was coming home a week earlier than he'd said he would. He had done everything he could, and he had work to do now in London, setting up the financial arrangements for the orphanage, and a hundred orphans.

He arrived at Heathrow at midnight, was at his house forty minutes later, and let himself in. The house was dark, and Arabella had said she'd been working hard, so he assumed she was asleep. She'd said she had hardly been going out, and it was no fun without him. She was desperate for him to come home.

Blake was exhausted after the flight to London, and everything he'd been doing in the past weeks. He had a deep tan on his face and arms. Beneath where his T-shirt had been, his skin was white. All he wanted now was to get his hands on Arabella, and jump into bed with her. He was starving for her. He tiptoed into his bedroom, in case she was asleep. He saw her shape under the sheet, sat down next to her, and leaned down to kiss her, only to discover that there were two bodies, not one, and they were intertwined and half asleep. His eyes flew wide open, and he turned on the light for a better look. He couldn't believe what he was seeing, and at first he wanted to believe it was a mistake. It was no mistake. An extraordinarily handsome dark-skinned man sat up in bed with her, with a look of panic. Blake suspected it was one of the important Indian men she knew, or perhaps a new one. It didn't matter who he was. He was in Blake's bed with her.

'I'm terribly sorry,' the man said politely, instantly wrapped himself in the sheet that was floating loose on the bed, after what must have been a lot of activity, and swept out of the room as fast as he could. Arabella stared at Blake in horror and started to cry.

'He just dropped by,' she said faintly, which was clearly a lie, because he was packing two alligator suitcases in Blake's dressing room, so he must have been there for a while. He emerged five minutes later in a beautifully cut suit. He was a striking-looking man.

'Thank you, sorry,' he said to Blake. 'Goodbye,' he said to Arabella, and hurried downstairs carrying both his bags. A moment later, they both heard the front door slam. He had been staying with her, in Blake's house, with no shame whatsoever.

'Get out of my bed,' Blake said coldly. She was shaking and reached out to him.

'I'm so sorry . . . I didn't mean to . . . I won't do it again . . .'

'Get up, and get out,' Blake said plainly. 'You could at least have gone to your own place. Then at least I wouldn't have known. This was a little cheeky, don't you think?' She had gotten up and was standing before him in all her naked beauty.

She was a gorgeous girl, tattoos and all. The only thing she was wearing was her ruby bindi between her eyes. Blake was no longer amused. 'You have five minutes,' he said clearly. 'I'll send you whatever you forget.' He reached for the phone and called a cab. She disappeared into the bathroom and emerged in blue jeans and a man's T-shirt. She had on high-heeled gold sandals and looked sexy as hell. But he no longer wanted her. She was used goods. And a liar. A big one.

She stood looking at him with tears rolling down her cheeks, as he looked away. It was a nasty little scene. None of the women he had gone out with had ever been dumb enough to bring other men to his bed. And he had dated Arabella longer than anyone else. It had been seven months, and it hurt. He had trusted her, and was more in love with her than he had been with the others. It took every ounce of restraint not to call her ugly names as she clattered down the stairs. He went to the bar, and poured himself a stiff drink. He never wanted to see her again. She tried calling him later that night, and for days thereafter, and he didn't answer her calls. Arabella was history. She had gone up in a puff of smoke, bindi, tattoos, and all.

CHAPTER 20

Maxine's frantic search for the perfect wedding dress continued into early July. She was shopping for their trip, when she came upon the dress accidentally. It was just what she wanted, by Oscar de la Renta, a huge champagne-colored organdy skirt with a lavender satin sash and a tiny beaded beige bustier, and the way the dress fell, it had just the hint of a train, but not enough to look overdone. She found sandals to match and immediately decided to carry beige orchids. And by sheer luck, the next day she found a beautiful lavender silk strapless dress for Daphne. They were all set. She was excited and happy about her wedding dress, and Daphne's. But she decided to wait to show her till they got back from the trip. Daphne was still threatening not to come to the wedding. Maxine was hoping that Blake would convince her otherwise. He could jolly her into it like no one else.

When he called Maxine the day before the trip she mentioned it to Blake, and he promised to do his best with Daphne. He was calling just to let her know that the boat was ready and waiting for them in Monaco, its home berth. Zellie's baby was screaming, as usual, when he called. The baby was still having a tough time, and so was Zellie.

'What's that noise?' Blake asked, sounding puzzled, and Maxine laughed ruefully. It wasn't easy being around the house these days. It sounded like an alarm going off at all hours of the day.

'That's Jimmy,' Maxine explained. 'Zellie's

baby.'

'Zellie had a baby?' He sounded impressed. 'When did that happen?'

'Three weeks ago.' She lowered her voice so no one would hear her. She hated to admit that Charles was right, but the screaming couldn't last forever, she hoped. She was just grateful that Zellie's room was at the back of the apartment. The kid had lungs like Louis Armstrong. 'She adopted a baby who was born addicted to cocaine. She let me know her plans four days before he was born. She offered to quit, but I just couldn't let her go. We love her too much. We'd all be miserable without her.'

'Yeah, I know,' Blake said, still startled. 'How's Charles dealing with all this?'

'He's not loving it. We're still all getting used to each other.' She didn't tell him that he thought boarding school was a great idea. Blake didn't need to know that. 'It's a big adjustment.'

'I don't think I'd love it either,' Blake said honestly, and then told her everything was moving ahead in Morocco. It was a remarkable plan, and all was going well.

'When are you coming?' she asked him.

'Don't worry, I'll be there for the wedding. And everything's lining up fine for the rehearsal dinner.' He had rented a beautiful club for it. 'I'll come in a few days before.'

'Is Arabella coming with you?'

'Uh . . .' He hesitated, which Maxine thought was strange. 'Actually, no.'

'That's too bad. I was hoping to meet her. Will she be doing a portrait?'

'I don't know. And to be honest, I don't give a

279

rat's ass. I found her in my bed with a very good-looking Indian guy the night I came home. He had moved in too. I threw her out that night, and I haven't seen her since.'

'Shit, I'm sorry, Blake.' He made light of it, but she knew it must have hurt. She had lasted longer than any of the others. A lot longer. But he seemed to be taking it pretty well.

'Yeah, me too. It was a good run anyway. So I'm free as the breeze again, except for a hundred orphans in Morocco.' He laughed.

'Daphne will be pleased, about Arabella, I mean.'

'I'm sure she will. How is she doing with Charles?' he inquired.

'About the same. I hope the boat trip will help. It will give them time to get to know each other. He's a nice man, he's just very adult.'

'Zellie's baby ought to break him in.' They both laughed at that. 'Anyway, have a good time on the boat, Max. The Big Day is coming. Are you scared? No cold feet?' He was curious about it, and wished her well.

'No cold feet. I know I'm doing the right thing. I think he's right for me. I just wish the period of adjustment were a little easier, for everyone.' Trying to join the two factions was stressful for her. Blake didn't envy her.

'I don't think I could do it again,' Blake said honestly. 'I think Arabella may have cured me.'

'I hope not. You'll find the right one.' He had changed a lot in the last couple of months. She wondered if he was ready for a grown-up, instead of a toy. You never knew. It could happen. She hoped so for him. It would be nice to see him settle

280

down, and have more time for their children.

'I'll call you on the boat,' he promised, and then hung up.

*   *   *

That night, she and Charles had dinner with her parents. Charles had bought every kind of seasick medicine he could lay his hands on, and was still gritting his teeth about taking a vacation on Blake's boat. He was doing it for Maxine, and admitted to her parents that night that he was not looking forward to it.

'I think you'll enjoy it,' her father said breezily as the two men talked about medical issues, and golf. 'It's quite a boat. And you know, he's really a nice guy. Have you met him yet?' Arthur Connors asked his future son-in-law about the last one.

'No, I haven't,' Charles said with a tense look. He was sick of hearing about Blake, from the children, Maxine, and now her father. 'I'm not sure I want to. But I don't have much choice in the matter. He's coming to our wedding, and giving the rehearsal dinner.'

'That's just like him,' Arthur laughed. 'He's kind of a big kid in a man's body. He was all wrong for Maxine, and a lousy father, but he's a decent guy. Just irresponsible and made way too much money too young. It ruined him. He hasn't done a day's work since, just runs around with fast women and buys houses. I used to call him "the rogue."'

'That's not the kind of man you want your daughter married to,' Charles said sternly, feeling insecure again. Why did everyone like Blake so goddamn much? It wasn't right, given how

281

irresponsible he was. It wasn't good enough just to have fun and be amusing.

'No, he isn't,' Arthur agreed readily. 'I thought that when she married him. He was kind of a wild guy even then, with all kinds of crazy ideas. But he's a lot of fun.' He looked at Charles then and smiled. 'It's nice to have her married to a physician finally. I'd say you two are the perfect match.' Charles beamed at that. 'How are you doing with the kids?'

'It takes a little time to adjust, never having had any myself.'

'It must be nice for you now,' Arthur beamed, thinking of his grandchildren, whom he was crazy about. 'They're great kids.' Charles agreed with him politely, and a few minutes later, they went in to dinner. It was a very pleasant evening, and Charles looked relaxed and happy when they left. He liked her parents, which made Maxine happy too. At least that was one area that was easy for them. He hadn't quite mastered the children yet, and he was jealous of Blake. But he loved Maxine, as he reminded her often. And he even liked her parents. They both knew that the rest would fall into place in time, particularly once Zellie's baby stopped screaming. Hopefully, by the time they got back from the boat.

CHAPTER 21

Charles, Maxine, and her three children flew directly from New York to Nice. And as they left the house, Jimmy was still screaming.

282

It was an easy flight. Three of Blake's crew members and the captain were waiting at the Nice airport for them, and took them to the boat in two cars. Charles had no idea what to expect, but was a little surprised by the crisp uniforms, and the professionalism of the crew. This was obviously no ordinary boat. And Blake Williams was no ordinary man. She was called *Sweet Dreams*, and Maxine didn't tell Charles, but Blake had built the boat for her. And she was a very, very sweet dream. She was a two-hundred-forty-six-foot sailboat, the likes of which Charles had never seen. There was a crew of eighteen on board, and staterooms more beautiful than most houses, or any hotel. There was a fortune in art on the burnished wood walls. The children always had a ball when they were on board. They scampered around her like she was their second home, which in some ways she was.

They were delighted to see the crew, who were equally happy to see them. The crew were trained to meet every imaginable need, and spoil them in every possible way. No request was too menial or too small or ever ignored. It was the only time of the year when Maxine was totally pampered, and could completely relax. The crew entertained the children, and took out the toys at every stop. There were Jet Skis, and tiny sailboats, speedboats, and rafts to pull behind them, and a helipad for when Blake came on board. And there was a full-size theater to entertain them at night, a fully equipped gym for them to exercise in, and a masseur to give them all massages.

Charles sat on deck looking startled and uncomfortable, as the enormous sailboat left the dock. A stewardess offered him a drink, and another one offered him a massage. He declined both, as he watched Monaco shrink behind them, and they set sail toward Italy. Maxine and the kids were below unpacking and making themselves comfortable. Fortunately, none of them ever got seasick, and on a boat this size, Charles suspected he wouldn't either. He was watching the coast with binoculars when Maxine came upstairs to find him. She was wearing a pink T-shirt and shorts. Charles had already been politely told not to wear shoes on the teak deck. He was sipping a Bloody Mary and smiled at Maxine, as she cuddled up next to him and kissed his neck.

'Are you doing okay?' She looked happy and relaxed, and prettier than he'd ever seen her.

He nodded, with a sheepish smile. 'I'm sorry I made such a fuss about coming on the boat. I can see why you love it. Who wouldn't? I just felt odd because it's Blake's. It's a little like stepping into his shoes. He really is a tough act to follow. How am I ever going to impress you after you've had all this?' It was honest of him to say so, and humble, and it touched her. It was nice being on vacation with him, even if it was on Blake's boat. She was with Charles, not with Blake, which was exactly where she wanted to be, and with whom.

'You don't have to impress me that way. You impress me with you. Don't forget, I walked away from all this.'

'People must have thought you were crazy. I do.'

'I wasn't. We weren't right for each other. He was never around. He was a lousy husband. It's not about all this, Charles. And I love him, but he's a flake. He wasn't the right man for me, not in the end anyway.'

284

'Are you sure?' Charles looked doubtful. 'How can you be a flake and make enough money to have all this?' He had a point.

'He's good in business. And he's willing to risk anything to win. He's a good gambler, but that doesn't make him a good husband or father. And he gambled on me in the end, and lost. He figured he could never be there, do whatever he wanted, show up once in a blue moon, and not lose me. After a while, it just wasn't worth it to me. I wanted a husband, not just a name. All I had was his name.'

'It's not a bad name,' Charles commented, as he finished his drink.

'I'd rather have yours,' she whispered, as he leaned over and kissed her.

'I'm a very lucky man.' He was beaming as he said it.

'Even if I have three kids who give you a hard time, an all-consuming practice, a crazy ex-husband, and a nanny who adopted a crack baby on four days' notice?' she asked, looking him in the eye. She worried sometimes about his ability to tolerate her life. It was a lot wilder than what he was used to. Not as wild as Blake's by any means, but much more lively than anything he had ever known. But being with her excited him too, and in spite of his complaints, he was crazy about her. She could feel that now.

'Let me think about it for a minute,' he said in response to her list a moment before. 'No, in spite of that, I love you, Max. I just need some time to get used to all this. Especially the kids. I just don't feel comfortable with them yet.' That was honest of him too. 'I never thought I'd fall in love with a woman with three children. But they'll be gone in a few years.'

'Not for a while,' she reminded him. 'Sam is only six. And the other two still have high school to get through.'

'Maybe they'll skip a grade,' he teased her. She didn't like that he was so anxious for her children to grow up and leave. It was the one big concern she had about him. It was an important point to her. Up until now, she had lived for her kids, and she wasn't intending to change that for anyone, not even Charles.

She told him about Blake's Moroccan orphanage then, and warned him not to tell the children. Their father wanted it to be a surprise.

'What's he going to do with a hundred orphans?' Charles looked amazed. Why would anyone do a thing like that? Even with Blake's money, it seemed like a crazy thing to do.

'House them, educate them, take care of them. Send them away to college one day. He's setting up a foundation for the orphanage. It's a nice thing for him to do. It's an amazing gift to those kids. He can afford it, it won't make a dent in what he has.' That, Charles could believe, just from looking at the boat, and all he had read about Blake. He had one of the biggest fortunes in the world. It still amazed Charles that Maxine took nothing from him, and was content with her far more human-scale life. Not many women would have resisted the temptation to stick it to him when they left. And he suspected that was why she and Blake were such good friends, because he knew what a good person she was. Charles was well aware of it himself.

They lay on the sun deck for a while then, and the children joined them for lunch. They were planning to anchor outside Portofino that night. The boat was too big to go into port, and the kids were never that interested in going ashore. From there, they were going to Corsica for several days, Sardinia, Capri, and Elba on the way back. They had a nice trip planned, and they were going to spend most of it on the boat, at anchor.

Much to Maxine's surprise, Charles played card games with the children at night. She had never seen him so relaxed. Sam had just had both his casts off, and his ribs were feeling better, so he could get around the boat with ease. And Charles took him on one of the Jet Skis the next day. He looked like a kid himself. He went scuba diving with one of the crew members afterward, since he was certified. And he went snorkeling with Maxine after lunch. They swam to a small beach together, and they lay on the white sand. Jack and Daphne were watching them with binoculars, and Daphne set them down with a look of disgust when they kissed. Daphne was still giving him a tough time, but it was hard to avoid him on the boat. And eventually even she relaxed, particularly after he taught her how to water-ski. He was good at it, and taught her a few tricks that made it easier for her.

It delighted Maxine to see Charles warming up to her children. It had taken a long time, and they hadn't made it easy for him, except for Sam, who got along with everyone and felt sorry for him. He thought Daphne was being too mean, and said as much to Charles.

'You think so, eh?' Charles said, laughing. He had been in great spirits ever since they'd been on

287

the boat. Despite his earlier trepidation, he conceded to Maxine that it was the best vacation he'd ever had, and she had never seen him look more relaxed.

Blake had called them the second day out. He just wanted to be sure the trip was going well, and told Maxine to give Charles his best. She relayed the message, but a cloud crossed Charles's eyes again.

'Why don't you relax about him?' she suggested, and Charles nodded, and said nothing. No matter what she said to reassure him, he was still fiercely jealous of Blake. She could understand it, but it seemed so unnecessary to her. She was in love with Charles, not with Blake.

They talked about their wedding, and she got emails from the caterer and the wedding planner. Everything was under control.

They swam in beautiful coves off Corsica, and lay on white sandy beaches. And then they went on to Sardinia, which was far more social, and there were other big boats there as well. Maxine and Charles had dinner ashore, and the next day they left for Capri. It was always fun for the children there. They rode in a horse-drawn carriage, and did some shopping, and Charles bought her a beautiful turquoise bracelet that she loved. And he told her again on the way back to the boat what a good time he was having on the trip. They both looked happy and relaxed. Blake had given them a great gift with the boat. And the children were finally beginning to enjoy Charles, and not complaining as much about him to Maxine, although Daphne still said he was uptight. But compared to her father, everyone was. Charles was a grown-up to the core. But he still managed to have a good time, tell some jokes, and he danced on deck with Maxine one night, to some good music the crew had put on for them.

'It doesn't bother you to be on his boat with another man?' Charles inquired.

'Not in the least,' she answered. 'He's been on board with half the women on the planet. It's been over between me and Blake for a long time. I wouldn't be marrying you if that weren't the case.' Charles believed that was true, he just felt that everywhere he went, Blake was looking over his shoulder. There were photographs of him everywhere, a few of Maxine, and many of the kids. They were all in beautiful silver frames.

The weeks sped by too quickly, and suddenly it was the last night. They had anchored off St. Jean Cap Ferrat and were going in to Monte Carlo the next day, to fly home. It was a beautiful moonlit night, the children were watching a movie, and she and Charles sat on deck chairs, talking softly.

'I hate to go home,' she admitted. 'Leaving the boat is always like being cast out of the Garden of Eden. Reality hits hard after this.' She laughed as she said it, and he agreed. 'The next couple of weeks are going to be crazy before the wedding,' she warned him, but he didn't look worried or upset about it anymore.

'I figured they would be. I'll go hide somewhere if it gets to be too much for me.'

Maxine was planning to work for two weeks, and she had a lot to do in the office and many patients to see, before she took August off, for the wedding and the honeymoon. Thelma and her practice were covering for her again, as they always did.

When they got home, the wedding would be four weeks away. She could hardly wait. Maxine and her children were all moving to her house in Southampton on the first of August, and Charles was coming too. So were Zellie and her new baby, and Maxine hoped that would be okay. It was going to be a powerful dose of reality for Charles, but he said he was braced for it. They were both excited about the wedding, and her parents were staying with them for the wedding weekend too. It would give Charles someone to talk to, while Maxine tended to the final details. The only time Charles wouldn't be staying with them was the night before the wedding, after the rehearsal dinner. She had made him take a room at a hotel, so he wouldn't see her the morning of the wedding. She was superstitious about that, which he said was a nuisance, but he was willing to indulge her for one night.

'It might be the only decent night's sleep I get, with all the people you'll have in the house.' It was a far cry from his peaceful cabin in Vermont. Maxine never wanted to go there because they couldn't take the kids with them, unlike her rambling old house in the Hamptons, which housed them all and still left room for guests.

The captain pulled the boat into port in Monte Carlo early the next morning, and they were already moored there when everyone woke up. They had a last breakfast on board, and then the crew members were going to drive all five of them to the airport. Just before they left, Maxine stood looking up at the beautiful sailboat from the dock.

'You love her, don't you?' Charles asked as she nodded.

'Yes, I do,' Maxine said softly. 'I always hate to leave.' She looked at him then. 'I had a wonderful time with you, Charles.' She leaned over and kissed him, and he kissed her back.

'So did I,' he said as he slipped an arm around her waist, and together they walked away from the *Sweet Dreams*, and got into the car. It had been the perfect vacation after all.

CHAPTER 22

The next ten days in her office were crazy for Maxine. When she left in August, she would be gone for a month, but most of her patients would be too. Many of them were away for summer vacations with their parents. But she had several of the more acutely sick ones to see before she signed off to Thelma, and Maxine wanted to bring her up to date.

The two women had lunch together right after Maxine got back from the boat trip, and Thelma asked her about Charles. She had met him twice, but didn't really have a sense of him, other than that he was very reserved. She had met Blake once too and commented that the two men were as different as night and day.

'You sure don't go for a type,' Thelma teased her, 'and if you do, I'm not sure which one it would be.'

'Probably Charles. We're more alike. Blake was an early mistake,' Maxine said glibly, and then reconsidered. 'No, that's not true, or fair. It worked when we were young. I grew up, he didn't,

291

and it all went down the drain after that.'

'No, it didn't. You got three great kids out of it.' Thelma had two, and they were gorgeous. Her husband was Chinese, from Hong Kong, and the children had exquisite caramel-colored skin, and huge slightly Asian eyes. They were the best of both. Her daughter was a teenage model, and Thelma always said that her son broke every heart in school. As his mother had done, he was going to Harvard in the fall, and heading for medical school after that. Her husband was a physician too, a cardiologist and head of the department at NYU, and theirs was a marriage that worked. Maxine had been trying to get the four of them together for dinner for ages, but they hadn't been able to arrange it so far. They were all too busy.

'Charles seems very serious to me,' Thelma commented, and Maxine agreed.

'He is, but he has a sweet side to him too. He's very good with Sam.'

'And the others?'

'He's working on it.' Maxine smiled. 'Daphne is tough.'

'God save me from teenage girls,' Thelma said, and rolled her eyes. 'Jenna hates me this week. She has for two years actually. Sometimes I think she always will. I don't know what I do wrong most of the time, but as far as she's concerned, the minute I get up in the morning, I've fucked up. The only thing I do right is my shoes. She wears them all.' Maxine laughed at the description. She had the same problems with Daphne, although she was two years younger and not as angry yet. But she was getting there. It was going to be a long haul. 'How's your nanny doing with her baby, by the way?'

'He's still screaming. Zellie says the pediatrician thinks he's doing well, but it's a tough adjustment. I bought Charles earplugs for when we go to Southampton. I wear them myself. It's the only thing that works. Zellie's going to have hearing loss from holding him if that kid doesn't stop soon.' Maxine smiled affectionately as she said it.

'Sounds like fun,' Thelma said, and they both laughed. It was nice to take some time off and relax over lunch. Maxine didn't do it often, and she was so busy in her office she felt guilty about it, but Thelma was a good friend. She was one of the few psychiatrists Maxine trusted with her practice.

As planned, Maxine turned her practice over to her on the first of August, and they all left for Southampton in a caravan of cars. Hers, Charles's, and Zellie drove a rented station wagon. The children rode with Zellie, since Maxine's car was piled high with things for the wedding. And Charles drove alone in his impeccably detailed BMW. He didn't say it, but Maxine knew he didn't want the children in it. And they were happy riding with Zellie since the only place Jimmy slept and finally stopped crying was in the car. It was a blessed relief. And more than once when he was howling his little lungs out in the apartment, she had suggested that Zellie get the car out and drive around the block. Several times she had, and it worked. Maxine was only sorry she couldn't do that all night. He was a cute little guy with a sweet face. It was hard to bond with him because he cried so much, but it had slowly started to get better in the last week. There was hope. With any luck at all, he would be over it by the time Charles moved in after the honeymoon. He had postponed moving his clothes into the apartment until then.

Charles put his things in her bedroom as soon as they arrived at the house in Southampton. She gave him a closet, and filled her own with the things she'd brought from town. She put her wedding gown, carefully concealed and covered up in a closet in one of the guest rooms, along with Daphne's pale lavender dress, which she had yet to try on. So far she had refused, and claimed she was going to skip the wedding and stay in her room. She liked Charles better after the boat trip, but not enough to want to see them get married. She still told her mother that she was making a mistake and he was too dull and too uptight.

'He's not dull, Daffy,' Maxine said quietly. 'He's responsible and solid.'

'No, he's not,' her daughter insisted. 'He's boring and you know it.' But Maxine was never bored with him. He was always interested in her work, and they talked medicine most of the time. She and Thelma never did. But it was what she and Charles enjoyed most.

For the first week, Maxine had a thousand details to take care of, meetings with the caterer and the wedding planner. She talked to the florist almost every day. They were doing white flowers everywhere, and bringing in hedges and topiary trees with sprays of orchids in them. It was going to be simple and elegant, and relatively formal. And exactly what Maxine wanted. Charles wasn't interested in the wedding details and trusted Maxine with them.

At night, she and Charles went out to dinner, or they took the children to the movies. And in the daytime, the kids hung out with their friends on the beach. Everything was going fine until Blake arrived the second week that they were there. Charles turned into an iceberg the moment he did.

Blake dropped by the house to see her and the kids, and she introduced Charles to him. She had never seen Charles so stiff or so unpleasant. He bristled every time Blake spoke, although Blake was very relaxed about it, and as charming as ever. Blake invited him to a game of tennis at the club, which Charles frostily declined, much to Maxine's chagrin. Blake chatted with him good-humoredly and took no offense. Charles couldn't handle being anywhere near him, and picked a fight with Maxine for no reason that night. Blake had rented a house nearby, for the week, right on the beach, with a pool, which Charles felt was outrageous. He felt encroached on, and said so to Maxine.

'I don't know what you're so upset about,' Maxine commented. 'He was perfectly nice to you.' She thought Charles was being unreasonable. After all, he was the winner, and the groom.

'You act like you're still married to him,' he complained.

'I do not.' She looked shocked at what he had said. 'That's a ridiculous thing to say.'

'You were draped around his neck and hugging him. And he can't keep his hands off you.' Charles was furious, and so was she. His accusations just weren't fair. She and Blake were affectionate with each other, but there was nothing more to it than that, and hadn't been in years.

'That's a disgusting thing to say.' She was incensed. 'He treats me like a sister. And he made a huge effort to talk to you, and you hardly said two words to him. He's giving us the rehearsal

295

dinner, you could at least be polite to him, and make an effort. Shit, we just spent two weeks on his boat.'

'That wasn't my idea!' Charles stormed at her. 'You forced me to. And you know how I feel about the rehearsal dinner. I never wanted that either.'

'You had a great time on the boat,' she reminded him.

'Yes, I did,' he conceded, 'but I wonder if it occurs to you what it's like to make love to your fiancée in the bed she used to sleep in with her husband. Your life is a little racy for me, Maxine.'

'Oh for chrissake, don't be so uptight. It's just a bed. He's not sleeping in it with us.'

'He might as well!' Charles said, and stormed out of the room. He packed that night, and in the morning he left for Vermont. He said he'd be back in time for the wedding. It was a great start. He didn't even answer his cell phone for two days, which hurt Maxine's feelings, and he never apologized to her for storming off, when they finally talked. He sounded stiff and cold. Maxine hadn't liked his accusations, and Charles didn't like having Blake around, dropping in and out of the house. Charles said Blake acted like it was still his, and she was angry about that too and said it wasn't true.

'So where's the groom?' Blake asked, looking around when he dropped by the next day.

'He went to Vermont,' she said through clenched teeth.

'Uh-oh. Do I smell pre-wedding jitters?' he teased her, and she growled.

'No, what you smell is me pissed off at him for acting like a jerk.' She never pulled any punches with Blake. She could be honest with him, even if she had to put a good face on it for the children. She had told them that Charles needed a little peace and quiet before the wedding, and Daphne had rolled her eyes. She was delighted he had left.

'What are you so pissed off about, Max? He seems like a nice guy.'

'I don't know how you can say that. He hardly said two words to you yesterday. I thought he was very rude, and I told him that in fact. The least he could do is speak to you. And he snapped at you when you invited him to play tennis.'

'It probably makes him uncomfortable to have your ex-husband around. Not everybody is as cool as we are,' he said, laughing, 'or as crazy.'

'That's what he says.' She smiled at Blake. 'He thinks we're all nuts. And Zellie's baby gets on his nerves.' She wanted to say 'and so do our kids,' but she hesitated to tell him that. She didn't want Blake to worry about him. And she was still convinced that he and the children would get used to each other, and even like each other in time.

'I have to admit, Zellie's baby is a little loud.' He grinned at her. 'Do you suppose she'll ever find the volume button on that kid? His mother must have taken a hell of a lot of crack.'

'Don't let her hear you say that. And he's getting better. It takes time.'

'I can't really blame Charles for that,' Blake said fairly. 'What about you? Are you getting cold feet yet?' He was teasing her, and she shoved him, like two kids in the sandbox.

'Oh, shut up. I'm just pissed off. I don't have cold feet.'

'You should!' Daphne threw over her shoulder

as she walked by.

'You stop that!' Maxine called after her, and then shook her head. 'Bratty kid. Have you told them about your plans for the orphanage yet?' she asked Blake.

'I was planning to tonight. I hope they think it's cool and they don't get upset. They seem to have a lot of their own opinions these days. Jack just told me that my pants are too short, my hair is too long, and I'm out of shape. He could be right, but it's a little tough to hear.' He was smiling as Sam wandered in and looked him over.

'You look good to me, Dad,' he said with approval.

'Thanks, Sam.' Blake hugged him, and Sam beamed.

'Do you want to come out for pizza with us tonight?' he asked Maxine.

'Sure. I'd love it.' She had nothing else to do. She loved the way everyone came and went in the Southampton house and wandered around, and she liked Blake hanging out too. It was a shame that Charles couldn't relax and enjoy it. But he had said when he left that it was too much confusion for him. He called it the three-ring circus, and it didn't sound like a compliment when he did. There were times when she wanted to strangle him, like now, before the wedding. All the pre-wedding excitement and details were bringing out the worst in both of them. She wasn't as patient as usual, and she thought he was being a poor sport, stomping off to Vermont in a huff the moment Blake appeared. And Blake had been nothing but nice to him. It was obvious to Maxine that Charles had an inferiority complex about him. She hoped he'd get over it soon.

Blake picked her and the kids up for dinner that night, and as he had planned, he told them about his Moroccan orphanage as they ate. They looked a little stunned for a minute, and then realized what a wonderful thing he was organizing. They all told him how proud they were of him. And Maxine was proud of them for appreciating what their father was doing.

'Can we go to visit, Dad?' Sam asked with interest.

'Sure. Sometime we can all go to Marrakech together. The construction isn't finished yet, but when it is, I'll take all three of you over with me.' He thought that they should see it. It was a far cry from their safe, happy little world, and he felt it would do them good.

Blake told them then how terrific their mom had been when she came to Morocco to help him. He explained about what they did, and what they'd seen, and the children listened with interest. And then, out of the blue, Daphne asked him what had happened to Arabella.

'I fired her,' he said simply. They didn't need to know the rest.

'Just like that?' Jack asked, and Blake nodded and snapped his fingers.

'Just like that. I said, Out with you, Evil Spot! And off she went. Like magic. She disappeared.' He looked mysterious about it, and they all laughed, including Blake. Maxine could tell he was feeling better about it. He had recovered quickly. He always did. His feelings for the women in his life never ran too deep, although Maxine knew they had run deeper for Arabella than for most.

But it had been a pretty nasty ending, given the scene he had described in his bed. She knew he wouldn't tell the children about it, nor should he. She approved of how he had handled it with them.

'I'm glad,' Daphne said with conviction.

'I'll bet you are,' her father said. 'You were a little monster to her in Aspen.'

'No, I wasn't,' Daphne defended herself hotly.

'Yes, you were,' Sam, Jack, and Blake said in unison, and everyone at the table laughed, including Daphne.

'Maybe I was, but I didn't like her.'

'I don't know why,' Blake commented. 'She was nice to you.'

'It was fake. Just like when Charles is nice to us. He doesn't mean it.' Maxine looked shocked at her comment.

'How can you say a thing like that, Daffy? He's not fake, he's reserved,' she protested.

'He's fake. He hates us. He wants to be alone with you.'

'Well, that's reasonable,' Blake stepped in. 'He's in love with your mother. He doesn't always want you kids around.'

'He never wants us around,' Daphne said glumly. 'You can tell.' Maxine couldn't help thinking about his comments in praise of boarding school. It was amazing the instincts kids had, and she didn't comment further. 'Arabella didn't want us around either. I don't know why you and Mom don't just get married again. You're both nicer than anyone you go out with. You go out with such yick people, both of you.'

'Thank you, Daphne,' Blake answered for both of them with a grin. 'I happen to go out with some very nice people.'

'No, you don't. They're all bimbos,' Daphne announced, and they all laughed again. 'And Mom goes out with these boring, uptight, stuffy guys.'

'That's a reaction to me,' Blake volunteered with glee. 'She didn't think I was grown-up enough, so she goes out with very grown-up men, who are nothing like me. Right, Max?' She looked embarrassed by what he said, and didn't comment. 'Besides, your mom and I like it like this. We're good friends now. We don't fight. We can hang out with all of you. And I have my bimbos and she has her stuffed shirts. What could be better?'

'You two married again,' Daphne answered.

'That's not going to happen,' her mother said quietly. 'I'm marrying Charles next week.'

'And I'm giving the rehearsal dinner,' Blake added, to change the subject. The conversation was getting a little heavy for them, although Maxine knew it was normal for children to want their parents to get back together, and marrying someone else would end that hope forever. 'The rehearsal dinner should be a lot of fun,' Blake went on, to cover the awkward silence after Daphne's comments and Maxine's response. 'I have a surprise planned for that evening.'

'You're going to jump out of a cake naked?' Sam asked with delight, and everyone lightened up immediately as they squealed with laughter.

'Charles would *really* love that!' Maxine said, holding her stomach as she laughed.

'It really is a thought. I hadn't considered it,' Blake said with a grin, and then suggested they go over to his rented house and swim after dinner. It sounded like a great idea to all of them. They picked up their bathing suits at Maxine's, and then they went to swim at his. They had a great time, and the kids decided to spend the night with him. He invited Maxine to stay too.

'I would,' Maxine said honestly, 'but if Charles found out, he'd kill me. I'd better go home.' So she drove the short distance to her house, and left the children with Blake. It had been a lovely evening, and his announcement about his orphans had gone very well. Maxine was looking forward to meeting them, and checking them for the effects of the trauma they'd endured.

Blake came and went back and forth to her house for the rest of the week. And Maxine realized it was easier not having Charles there. He hardly called her all week from Vermont, and she didn't call him. She figured it was best to let him cool down, and he'd show up again sooner or later. The wedding was only days away.

The day of the rehearsal dinner, Charles returned. He just walked in, as though he'd gone to the store for a loaf of bread. He kissed Maxine, walked into their room, and put down his things. And when he saw Blake at the house that afternoon, he was actually civil, much to Maxine's surprise and relief. Charles was much more relaxed than when he left. As Daphne put it very elegantly to her father in a whispered aside, Charles looked like he'd gotten the broomstick out of his butt. Blake looked at her in astonishment and suggested she might not want to say that to her mother. Blake laughed to himself about it as he drove to the club to check on the details for the rehearsal dinner that night. What Daphne said was true. Charles did look a lot better. All Blake could hope

302

was that Maxine would be happy with Charles. He wished her well.

CHAPTER 23

Maxine had bought a new dress for the rehearsal dinner too, and when Charles saw her in it, he whistled. It was a pale gold filmy strapless evening gown that wrapped around her like a sarong. She looked like a young Grace Kelly. She was wearing it with high-heeled gold sandals. Blake had decided to make the rehearsal dinner black tie.

Charles looked very proper in a single-breasted black dinner jacket. And when they got to the party, Blake was wearing a double-breasted white one, with black tuxedo trousers, his proper black bow tie, and patent leather pumps. Maxine noticed immediately that Blake wasn't wearing socks. She knew him well, and it didn't surprise her. A lot of the men in Southampton did it. It was kind of a trendy preppy thing, although Charles made a comment about it and had worn his. Blake looked incredibly handsome with his black hair and deep tan, but so did Charles. They were both good-looking men. And with her long blond hair and pale gold dress, Maxine looked like an angel. Blake said all she needed was wings.

Blake had invited a hundred people from Max's list, and another dozen or so of his own. There was a ten-piece band playing everything from Motown to big band music to swing. And everyone was in great spirits. The champagne flowed like water, and Maxine saw Daphne take a glass, and signaled to her 'just one,' and Daphne nodded agreement. But Maxine was going to keep an eye on her anyway.

It was fun seeing all her friends, and introducing Charles to the ones he didn't know. Her parents were there, her mother in a pale blue evening dress with a jacket, and her father in a white dinner jacket like Blake's. They were a handsome group.

Maxine's father stopped to talk to Charles for a few minutes before dinner, and asked him how the boat trip had been. He hadn't seen him since. 'That's quite a boat, isn't it?' he said jovially, and Charles agreed that it was and said he'd had a very good time. It would have been hard not to.

Charles started the evening off by dancing with Maxine, and they looked happy and relaxed, and at ease in each other's arms. They made a very attractive couple. And it was a beautiful party. Blake had had the club decorated with thousands of white roses and delicate paper lanterns brushed with gold.

He made a witty speech before dinner, and told some very funny stories about Maxine that had everyone in hysterics, including Max. Charles looked a little pained, but he got through them. He didn't like the idea that Blake knew her better than he did, and had history with her. Blake wished them both well then, and said that he hoped Charles did a much better job of making her happy than he did. It was a moving moment, and brought tears to Max's eyes. And afterward, Charles stood up and toasted their very generous host, and promised to see to it that Maxine was blissful forever. Everyone was touched.

Blake asked Maxine to dance afterward,

between courses at dinner, and they whirled around the dance floor looking like Fred Astaire and Ginger Rogers. They had always danced well together.

'That was sweet of you to say,' she corrected him, 'but you made me happy. I was always happy with you, Blake. I just didn't see enough of you, and I never knew where you were. You outgrew me after you made all that money.'

'I didn't outgrow you, Max,' he said softly. 'I hadn't grown into you yet. I wasn't big enough to reach your boots in those days. I think I knew that, and it scared me. You were so much smarter than I was, and so much wiser about so many things. You always kept your eye on what mattered, like our kids.'

'So did you,' she said generously. 'We just wanted different things. I wanted to work, and you wanted to play.'

'I think there's a French fable about that. And look where it got me. According to Daphne, I'm surrounded by bimbos.' They were both laughing at the comment, when Charles cut in, and whirled Maxine away in his arms.

'What were you laughing about?' he asked suspiciously. 'You two looked like you were having an awfully good time.'

'Something Daphne said to him, about his bimbos.'

'That's quite a comment for her to make to her father,' he said with obvious disapproval.

'It's true, though,' Maxine said, laughing again. The dance ended, and they went back to their table. She had the feeling that Charles hadn't really wanted to dance with her, he just wanted to get her away from Blake.

Blake had seated the dinner perfectly. All her favorite people were at her table with Charles, and Blake's good friends were at his. He didn't have a date for the evening, and had seated Maxine's mother beside him, at his right, which was proper. Charles had noticed that too. He saw everything, and watched them both all night. He never took his eyes off Maxine or Blake. He looked like a worried man. The only time he relaxed was when Maxine danced with Jack or Sam.

Everyone continued dancing till midnight, after the dinner, and at the stroke of midnight, sparklers went off in the sky. Blake had organized a fireworks show for them, and Maxine clapped her hands like a child. She loved fireworks, and Blake knew it. It was a perfect evening, and the last guests straggled home around one A.M. Charles was staying at the hotel that night, as she had insisted he should. In the end, her parents had decided to stay there too instead of with her. She had one last dance with Blake and thanked him for the fireworks show. She had loved it. And she asked him if he'd mind driving the kids and Zellie home. She was going to drop Charles off at the hotel where he was staying so they wouldn't see each other till the wedding. Blake promised to have them home in half an hour.

And when the dance ended, she went back to Charles and they left.

The wedding was at noon the next day. But everyone agreed that the rehearsal dinner would be hard to top. She and Charles talked about it on the way to his hotel, which he had complained about. It seemed like a foolish tradition to him. He would have preferred to stay at the house, but Maxine had insisted. Charles kissed her good-night, which reminded her of why she was marrying him. She loved him, in spite of his being what Daphne called a 'stuffed shirt.' They were flying to Paris the following night, and they were going to take a driving trip through the valley of the Loire. It sounded like the perfect honeymoon to her.

'I'm going to miss you tonight,' he said huskily, and she kissed him again.

'I'll miss you too,' she whispered, giggling. She had had a reasonable amount of champagne at the party, but she wasn't drunk, and was sure that she was sober. 'The next time I see you, about ten minutes after that, I'll be Mrs. West,' she said, beaming at him. It had been a beautiful evening.

'I can't wait,' he said, kissed her for a last time, and he reluctantly got out of the car, waved, walked into the hotel, and she drove away.

When she got home, she walked into the living room and poured herself another glass of champagne. A few minutes later, she heard Blake's car drive in with Zellie and the children. Zellie had left Jimmy at the house with a sitter, who left as soon as they returned, and Zelda urged all the children upstairs to bed. They were exhausted and disappeared with mumbled goodnights to their parents, who were sitting on the couch, talking.

Blake was in good spirits, and Maxine seemed a little tipsy to him, more so than she had at the party. She had been sober then, but was less so now, after two more glasses of champagne. He helped himself to a glass of champagne too. They were having fun talking about the evening. Blake had had a lot to drink that night but was still sober.

And he looked like a movie star in his white dinner jacket. They both did, as they toasted each other with the champagne.

'That was a gorgeous party,' she said, twirling around the living room in her gold dress, and she twirled herself right into his arms. 'You give such good parties. It was very glamorous, don't you think?'

'I think you'd better sit down before you fall down, you lush,' he teased her.

'I am not drunk,' she insisted, which was a clear sign that she was. He had always liked Maxine when she was a little drunk. She was so funny and so sexy, and it happened so seldom, but this was a special night. 'Do you think I'll be happy with Charles?' she asked him with a serious expression. Suddenly, she had to work harder than usual to focus on him.

'I hope so, Max,' Blake said sincerely. He could have said otherwise, but he didn't.

'He's so grown up, isn't he? Kind of like my father,' she said, crossing her eyes a little as she looked at Blake, but she still looked prettier than ever, and he had to remind himself not to take advantage of the situation. That wouldn't have been fair. He wouldn't have done anything to harm her, and certainly not tonight. He had missed the boat, and he knew it. He switched from champagne to vodka, and poured her the last of the champagne she'd had in the house.

'Yes, he is kind of like your father,' Blake replied. 'They're both doctors.' He was starting to feel pleasantly drunk too, and he didn't mind it a bit. If he was ever going to get drunk, tonight was it.

'I'm a doctor too,' she informed him with a loud hiccup. 'A shrink. I do trauma. Didn't I meet you recently in Morocco?' She laughed uproariously at her own question, and he did too.

'You look different in combat boots. I think I like you better in heels.' She held up a shapely leg and looked at her delicate gold sandals and nodded agreement.

'Me too. The boots gave me blisters.'

'Wear heels next time,' he advised her, sipping his vodka.

'I will. I promise. You know,' she said, sipping the champagne, 'we have really nice children. I love them very much.'

'I do too.'

'I don't think Charles likes them,' she said, frowning.

'They don't like him either,' Blake said, and they both laughed hard at that too. And then Maxine squinted at him as though from a great distance.

'Why did we get divorced anyway? Do you remember? I don't. Did you do something bad to me?' She was definitely drunk by then, and so was Blake.

'I forgot to come home.' He smiled sadly.

'Oh, that was it. Now I remember. That's too bad. I really like you . . . actually, I love you,' she said, smiling benignly at him, and hiccuped again.

'I love you too,' Blake said gently, and then his conscience got the better of him. 'Maybe you should go to bed, Max. You're going to have a hell of a hangover tomorrow at your wedding.' Champagne was always a killer the next day.

'Are you asking me to go to bed with you?' she asked, looking a little startled.

309

'No, I'm not. If I did, Charles would be really pissed tomorrow, and you'd feel really guilty. But I think you should go to bed.' She finished the last of her champagne as she said it, and by then he could see she was really drunk. The final glass had made the difference, and he was feeling very drunk too. The vodka did him in after a long night of drinking, or maybe it was seeing her that way, in her gold dress. She was intoxicating. She always had been for him. He suddenly remembered, and wondered how he could have forgotten.

'Why do I have to go to bed so early?' she pouted at him.

'Because, Cinderella,' he said gently, scooping her up in his arms, and lifting her off the couch, 'you're going to turn into a pumpkin if you don't. And you're going to marry the handsome prince tomorrow.' He started walking her to her bedroom.

'No, I'm not. I'm marrying Charles. I remember that. He's not the handsome prince. You are. Why am I marrying him?' She looked suddenly annoyed, and Blake laughed as he staggered and nearly dropped her, and then got a better grip. She was light as a feather.

'I think you're marrying him because you love him,' he said as he walked into her bedroom, and put her gently on the bed, and then stood looking at her, weaving slightly. They were both as drunk as skunks.

'Oh, that's nice,' Maxine said pleasantly. 'I love him. And I really should marry him. He's a doctor.' And then she looked at Blake. 'I think you're too drunk to go home. And I'm too drunk to drive you.' It was a fairly accurate assessment of the

310

situation. 'You'd better stay here.' As she said it, the room was reeling around him.

'I'll just lie down for a minute and sober up, if that's okay with you. And then I'll drive home. You don't mind, do you?' he asked, as he lay down next to her in his dinner jacket and his shoes.

'I don't mind at all,' she said, as she turned toward him, and put her head on his shoulder. She was still wearing the gold dress and the gold shoes. 'Sweet dreams,' she whispered as she closed her eyes and drifted off to sleep.

'That's the name of our boat,' Blake said, with his eyes closed, and passed out cold.

CHAPTER 24

The phone rang interminably in Maxine's house the next morning. It was ten o'clock, and it rang and rang and no one answered. Everyone was still sleeping. Sam finally heard it, and got out of bed to go answer it. There wasn't a sound in the house.

'Hello?' Sam said, still wearing his pajamas, as he yawned. They had all been up late, and he was tired. He didn't know where anyone else was, except he knew Daphne had had too much champagne the night before, but he had promised not to tell when she threw up when they got home.

'Hi, Sam.' It was Charles. He sounded wide awake. 'Can I talk to your mom, please? I just want to say hello. I know she must be very busy before the wedding.' She had told him that she had someone coming to do her hair and makeup. And he was sure the house was a zoo. 'Can you go get her? I'll only take a minute.' Sam put down the phone, and padded in his bare feet to her bedroom. He looked through the open door, and saw both his parents sound asleep with their clothes on. His father was snoring. He didn't want to wake them up, so he went back to the phone and picked up the receiver.

'They're still sleeping,' he announced firmly.

'They?' Charles knew it couldn't be Sam, since he was talking to him. So who was she sleeping with at this hour, on their wedding day? It made no sense to him.

'My dad's in there too. He's snoring,' Sam explained. 'I'll tell her you called when she wakes up.' The phone clicked in Sam's ear before he hung up, and he went back upstairs to his room. Since no one else was awake, he didn't see why he had to get ready yet. He turned on the TV, and for once, he couldn't even hear Zellie's baby. It sounded like everyone was dead.

The hairdresser and makeup artist arrived promptly at ten-thirty. Zelda let them in, realized what time it was, and went to wake Maxine up. Zelda was surprised to see Blake sleeping beside her. But she could figure out what had happened. They both had their clothes on. They must have gotten drunk off their asses the night before. She poked Max gently on the shoulder, and after half a dozen attempts, she finally stirred, and looked up at Zelda with a moan. She closed her eyes immediately and clutched her head with both hands. Blake was still sound asleep beside her, and was snoring like a bulldog.

'Oh my God,' Maxine said, squeezing her eyes closed against the light. 'Oh my God . . . I have a

312

brain tumor and I'm dying.'

'I think it could be the champagne,' Zelda said quietly, trying not to laugh at her.

'Stop shouting!' Maxine said, with her eyes closed.

'You're in bad shape,' Zelda confirmed to her. 'Your hairdresser and makeup person are here. What should I tell them?'

'I don't need a hairdresser,' she said, trying to sit up. 'I need a brain surgeon . . . oh my God,' she said, looking down at Blake. 'What's he doing here?' And then she remembered. She looked at Zelda then in amazement.

'I think you're okay. You're both dressed.'

Maxine poked him then, and shook him awake. He stirred, and moaned just as she had.

'Maybe it's an epidemic of brain tumors,' Zelda suggested, as Blake opened his eyes and looked at both of them with a grin.

'I've been kidnapped. Hi, Zellie. How come your baby's not screaming?'

'I think he wore himself out. What can I get you both?'

'A doctor,' Maxine said. 'No . . . shit . . . don't even think it. If Charles saw us, he'd kill me.'

'He doesn't have to know,' Zelda said firmly. 'It's none of his business. You're not his wife yet.'

'And I never will be, if he hears about this,' Maxine moaned. Blake was beginning to think that wasn't such a bad idea. He stood up then, testing his sea legs, straightened his tie, and walked unsteadily toward the door.

'I'll go home,' he said, as though that was a revolutionary concept.

'Drink a lot of coffee when you do,' Zelda

suggested. They both still looked drunk to her, or had the worst hangovers she'd ever seen. 'How much did you two drink anyway?' Zelda asked Maxine as they heard the front door close behind Blake.

'A lot. Champagne always kills me,' Maxine said as she crawled off the bed, just as Sam came into the room to find her.

'Where's Daddy?' he asked, looking at his mom. She looked a lot worse than Daphne, who was hung over too.

'He went home.' Maxine tiptoed across the room as fireworks went off in her head. It was a repeat performance of last night, but not nearly as pretty.

'Charles called you,' Sam announced, and his mother stopped dead in her tracks and looked like she'd been shot.

'What did you tell him?' she said hoarsely.

'I said you were asleep.' She closed her eyes in relief. She didn't dare ask him if he'd mentioned his father. 'He said he was just calling to say hello and he'd see you at the wedding, or something like that.'

'I can't call him. I'm too sick. He'll know I got drunk last night, and then he'll worry.'

'You'll see him at the wedding,' Zelda said. 'You're a mess. We have to get you going. Take a shower, I'll get some coffee.'

'Good . . . yes . . . that's a very good idea.' She got in the shower, and it felt like knives on her skin.

While she was in the shower, Zelda ran upstairs to wake the kids. Daphne looked almost as bad as her mother, and Zelda scolded her and promised

314

not to tell. And Jack got out of bed, and ran downstairs for breakfast. He was fine. He had only had one glass of champagne, and soda the rest of the night, which saved him from a fate like his sister's.

Zelda poured two cups of coffee into Maxine, and scrambled eggs, under protest. She handed her two aspirin with the coffee, and the hairdresser went to work on her in the kitchen. Even having her makeup put on was painful, and having her hair done was worse. But she had to. She couldn't wear a ponytail and no makeup to her wedding.

Within half an hour, Maxine had her makeup on, and she looked better than ever. She felt awful, but it didn't show. The woman had done a good job, and Maxine's face was glowing. The hairdresser had swept her hair up in a simple French twist, and put a small row of pearls in it. Maxine could hardly move as she got up, and there were razor blades piercing her eyeballs every time she faced the sunlight.

'I swear, Zellie, I'm dying,' she said, closing her eyes for a minute.

'You're gonna be fine,' Zelda reassured her, as Daphne came downstairs, pale, but with her hair combed neatly and lip gloss on, which was all her mother would allow her. Maxine was too sick to notice that Daphne was also hung over, and Sam didn't say a word, nor did Zellie.

At twenty to twelve, all the children, including Daphne, were dressed. Zelda had made Daphne put the lavender dress on, with the threat that she'd tell she'd gotten drunk if she didn't. It worked. Then Zelda went to get Maxine's dress and shoes, while Maxine herself stood looking like

315

a lame horse in the kitchen, with her eyes closed.

Maxine slipped into the shoes and let Zelda help her with the dress. She zipped her up and tied the sash, and her children gasped when they saw her. She looked like a fairy princess.

'You look really pretty, Mom,' Daphne said, and meant it.

'Thank you. I feel like shit. I think I have the flu.'

'You and Daddy got drunk last night,' Sam said, giggling, as his mother gave him an evil look.

'Don't you tell anyone that. Especially not Charles.'

'I promise.' He didn't even remember that he had told Charles his father was snoring.

The cars were waiting for them outside, and a minute later Zelda came back in a red silk dress, black patent leather shoes, and she was carrying her baby. He was starting to stir, but he wasn't crying yet. Maxine knew that if he did, it would split her head in two, and she silently begged him not to. They were meeting her parents and Blake at the church. Charles would be waiting for her at the altar. Suddenly, mostly due to her extreme hangover, she assumed, the thought of a church service and a wedding made her feel slightly sick.

There was a car for Zellie and the children, and another one for her. She laid her head back against the seat and closed her eyes on the way to the church. It was the worst hangover she had ever had. She was convinced that God was punishing her because Blake had spent the night. That wasn't supposed to happen. But at least nothing else had.

The limousine she was in pulled up behind the church at five to twelve. And the one with the children was right behind her. They had made it. Maxine walked as steadily as she could into the rectory, and her parents were waiting for her there. Blake was supposed to come and get the children before the service, and he walked in right behind her. He looked worse than she did. They looked like a matched set. Two sorry drunks the next day. She smiled at him painfully, and he laughed at her, and kissed her on the forehead.

'You look gorgeous, Max. But you're a mess.'

'Yeah, you too.' She was happy to see him.

'I'm sorry about last night,' he whispered to her. 'I shouldn't have let you have the last of the champagne.'

'Don't worry, I did it to myself. I think I wanted to get drunk.' Her parents were listening with interest to the exchange, just as the rectory door flew wide, and Charles stormed in. He looked at all of them with wild eyes and then at Maxine in her wedding gown. He wasn't supposed to see her. He was supposed to be at the altar. As he glared at her, the florist handed her her bouquet and tried to pin a tiny orchid on Charles's lapel. He brushed him away.

'You were with him last night, weren't you?!' he shouted at Maxine, pointing at Blake. And at the sound of it, she clutched her head.

'Oh God, don't scream!'

Charles looked from her to Blake and realized how hung over she was. He had never seen her that way.

'I had too much to drink, and he fell asleep,' she explained. 'Nothing happened.'

'I don't believe a word of it!' he said, glaring at her. 'You're lunatics, all of you. You two act like

317

you're still married. Your children are brats. Crack babies, yachts, bimbos. You're sickos, all of you. And I'm not marrying you, Maxine. You couldn't pay me to marry into this family. And I'm sure you've been sleeping with him all along.' As he said it, Maxine burst into tears, and before she could answer him, Blake took a step forward and grabbed Charles by the lapels of his khaki suit and lifted him right off the ground.

'That's my wife you're talking to, you uptight son of a bitch. And those are my children you just called brats! And let me tell you something, asshole. She wouldn't marry you on a fucking bet. You're not good enough to shine her shoes, so get your sorry ass out of our sight.' He threw Charles toward the door then, and Charles turned around and left at a dead run, as Maxine stared at Blake.

'Shit, now what am I going to do?'

'Did you want to marry him?' Blake asked her with a worried look, and she shook her head, although it almost killed her to do so.

'No, I didn't. I figured that out last night.'

'Not a minute too soon,' Blake said as the children suddenly cheered. It was the first time they had ever seen their dad in action, and they loved the way he had made Charles run away. As far as they were concerned, it was about time.

'Well, that was an interesting start to the day,' Arthur Connors said, looking at his ex-son-in-law. 'What do you all suggest we do now?' He didn't look sorry, just concerned.

'Somebody has to tell everyone,' Maxine said, slowly sinking into an available chair, 'that the wedding's been called off.' The children cheered again, and Zelda smiled. The baby hadn't made a peep, and was sound asleep. Maybe he just hadn't liked Charles.

'It's a shame to waste a great dress like that,' Blake said, looking at her. 'And the flowers looked terrific when I peeked into the church. What do you say we put them to good use?' And then he looked at her seriously and lowered his voice as he spoke to her, so no one else could hear. 'I promise, this time I'll come home. I'm not as stupid as I was before. I'm bimbo'd out, Max.'

'Good,' she said quietly, looking him in the eye. She knew he was telling her the truth, and this time he would come home. He might even stay home. He was still a rogue, and she loved that about him, but he had grown up. They both had. She no longer expected him to be anyone but Blake. And she had discovered that she loved who she was with him. They brought out the best in each other.

'Max?' He shook as he asked her. It was twelve-thirty by then, and the wedding guests had been waiting for half an hour while the music played.

'Yes.' She breathed the word, and he kissed her. It was what they had both wanted to do the night before. It had taken Charles to get them back together again. Charles was everything she should have wanted, but all she wanted, and all she had ever wanted, was Blake.

'Let's go!' Blake said, springing into action, his hangover forgotten, and she was feeling better too. 'Jack, you take Grandma down the aisle to the front pew. Sam, you take Zellie. Daffy, you come with me. Dad'—he looked at his father-in-law, and they exchanged a smile—'is this okay with you, by the way?' Not that it mattered to either of them, but he didn't want him to feel left out.

'She would have died of boredom with the other guy,' Arthur said, smiling broadly at Blake, 'and so would I,' he added, and Maxine laughed.

'Give us five minutes, then you two come down the aisle.' The minister had already been out there, on the altar, for over half an hour, wondering what had happened.

They all ran out the door then, and the guests watched them come down the aisle. They all recognized Blake, and were a little puzzled when he and Daphne took their places at the altar, and were joined by Sam and Jack a minute later. This was obviously a very liberal modern wedding with the ex-husband helping to give the bride away. The guests were impressed and a little startled. Zellie and their grandmother were seated, and Blake and his children stood at the altar, waiting for Maxine and her father to come down the aisle. And suddenly the music changed, and she was walking toward Blake with eyes only for him, while her father beamed. She never took her eyes off Blake as they looked at each other and all the years they had shared with each other, the good and the bad, telescoped into this one shining moment.

The minister was watching them, and understood what had happened. Blake leaned over to talk to him and whispered that they didn't have a license.

'We'll wing it today,' he whispered back. 'Get a license on Monday, and we'll do it again privately. How does that sound to you?'

'Perfect. Thank you,' Blake said respectfully, and then turned to look at his bride again. They had finally reached the altar. He and Arthur shook hands, and Arthur gave him a little pat on the arm, and whispered, 'Welcome back.' Blake turned his full attention to Maxine then, and took his place beside her as their children watched. They could see that their mother had damp eyes, and their father did too.

The minister turned to everyone then and looked at them solemnly. 'Dearly beloved,' he began, 'we are gathered here together today to join this man and this woman, and as I understand it, or from what I can figure out, they have been joined before'—he glanced at the children with a smile—'with very handsome results. And what I want you all to know is that when I perform a wedding ceremony, it sticks. So you won't be coming back here for another round.' He looked pointedly at Maxine and Blake, who were beaming at each other. 'All right then, let's get on with it.

'We are gathered here today to join this man and this woman . . .' All Maxine could see was Blake, and all he could see was her, and all they could hear was each other and the buzzing of their hangovers until they both said 'I do,' kissed, and walked back down the aisle. And this time, not just the children and the minister, but everyone in the church cheered.

It wasn't the wedding any of them had come for or anticipated, not even Maxine or Blake, but it was the wedding that was meant to be, the one that was their destiny. It was the marriage of two people who had always loved each other, and each, in their own way, had grown up at last. It was the perfect union between a delightful, lovable rogue and his very happy bride.

Her father winked at them as they walked past

him, down the aisle. Blake winked back, and Maxine laughed out loud.

CHIVERS
LARGE
PRINT
−direct−

If you have enjoyed this Large Print book
and would like to build up your own
collection of Large Print books, please
contact

Chivers Large Print Direct

Chivers Large Print Direct offers you
a full service:

• Prompt mail order service

• Easy-to-read type

• The very best authors

• Special low prices

For further details either call
Customer Services on (01225) 336552
or write to us at Chivers Large Print Direct,
FREEPOST, Bath BA1 3ZZ

Telephone Orders:
FREEPHONE 08081 72 74 75